Blink of an Eye

OTHER BOOKS AND AUDIO BOOKS
BY GREGG LUKE:

Altered States

Do No Harm

The Survivors

Blink of an Eye

a novel

GREGG LUKE

Covenant Communications, Inc.

Cover image: *Man's Face Green Eyes Close Up* © Eric Hood, courtesy iStockphoto.

Cover design copyrighted 2010 by Covenant Communications, Inc.

Published by Covenant Communications, Inc.
American Fork, Utah

Printed in the United States of America
First Printing: July 2010

15 14 13 12 11 10   10 9 8 7 6 5 4 3 2 1

ISBN-13: 978-1-60861-026-6

To Marjorie Millar Luke (1928–2007)
mother, teacher, and a believer in the power of dreams

Acknowledgments

I am not aware of a single author who can claim total exclusivity in writing any novel. So many wonderful people help me with each new project, and my sincere gratitude goes out to each. In this novel, I particularly appreciated the technical input from clinical psychologist Brian M. Jensen, attorney Leslie Larsen, and pharmacy technicians Melissa Duce and Sarah Gudmundson.

Additionally, I would like to thank Covenant Communications for believing in me, and Kirk Shaw for his multifaceted skills as my editor.

CHAPTER 1

IT HAPPENED IN THE BLINK of an eye. When the light turned green, Joseph Ramirez edged forward to make a left-hand turn onto the county highway. The five o'clock traffic was exceptionally hectic, even for a small tourist town like Solvang, California. Five cars went before him—three of the drivers making the turn while talking on their cell phones.

As he followed the cars into the intersection, a blur of motion flashed in his peripheral vision. He heard a thick screeching of tires and turned his head just in time to see the grill of a large truck in his driver's side window. Before he could flinch, the sound of exploding safety glass and rending metal filled the air. Shards of glass flew into Joseph's soft flesh as the truck's grill entered his small Nissan Stanza. His vision narrowed as he felt a sudden weight press down on him. A moment later he was lying sideways across the passenger seat. The console between the front seats pressed painfully into his ribs. He thought he felt one crack—maybe two. He couldn't see anything other than the area below the dashboard and found it curious how he'd never noticed the airbag icon embossed in that section of the vinyl dashboard. He smelled diesel exhaust, burnt rubber, and the coppery scent of fresh blood. The ever-increasing weight compressed his left leg, snapped it.

The noises of destruction became a frenzied din. The extreme pressure against his skull felt like his head was in a vise. The crushing force limited his breathing and restricted all movement. Yet he was still moving—sliding sideways through a chaos of blurred images and brittle sounds.

Joseph knew exactly what was happening. He knew it would hurt at some point, too, but the adrenaline in his system was circumventing any immediate pain. The screeching, bending, sliding, shattering, and collapsing seemed to last forever.

Then he heard a deep, hollow pop and felt a shifting of bone just under his scalp. An instant later the tormented sounds vanished. The flashing lights darkened. He tried to stir but couldn't. Yet he still felt a languid motion, as if he were floating in some thick substance that prevented rapid movement or vision beyond a few inches. In fact, everything seemed to hover in a murky haze where each sense was distorted, slowed, confused. But the oppressive weight was still crushing, the odors still sharp and noxious, his breathing short and labored. His head felt particularly strange. It felt . . . *liquid.*

He knew pain was imminent.

Obviously, he had just been in a severe traffic accident. A large truck had broadsided him at full speed. His car had been totaled in a matter of seconds. The intense pressure in his skull told him he was seriously injured. Worse, he couldn't feel anything from the neck down. But he could still think. That *had* to be a good sign. Didn't it?

Slowly, the sounds began to fade into a muffled gloom. No light penetrated his closed eyelids. Even the taste of blood turned bland, flavorless.

Amidst a jumble of incongruous, amorphous thoughts, Joseph wondered, *Am I still alive? And if so, for how long?*

CHAPTER 2

A SOFT HUM VIED FOR identification in a hodgepodge of nonsensical dreams and external noises. Nothing seemed real. A gentle, fluttering light penetrated Joseph's eyelids, yet he could not bring himself to open his eyes. Essentially blind, he floated in the borderless void between sleep and consciousness. His throat ached with dryness—a rawness too real to be imagined. His head throbbed with a dull pain that sharpened just behind his temples. His skull felt heavy, as if it were a burden for his neck to support, even while lying on his back.

He tried to swallow—a big mistake. It was like gulping down a clump of razorblades. The surgically sharp burn caused tears to seep between his eyelids and trickle into his ears. His lips were swollen, blistered, his tongue stuck to the roof of his mouth. He took a calming breath and tried to focus. Obviously, he was still alive—the tactile clues proved that. He remembered being in an accident. He could list everything that identified him as Joseph Ramirez: a single, twenty-nine-year-old middle school science teacher from Solvang, California. Currently, his biggest concerns were his unbearable thirst and—

Something rustled off to one side. He heard someone—a woman's voice humming an older pop tune, slightly off key. Celine Dion.

He mouthed the word *water*, but no sound passed his lips. He tried again. "Water," he wheezed.

The woman gasped in surprise, and she touched his arm. "Well, hello there, Mr. Ramirez. You startled me. Are you back with us, then?"

Back with us? Whatever that meant, his impossible thirst was a more pressing concern. "Water," he wheezed again.

"I'm afraid you can't have water yet, Mr. Ramirez," the woman stated apologetically. "We're worried about you choking. Would you like some ice chips in the meantime?"

Joseph croaked a word meant to be *yes.*

A frigid, wet shock stung his lips as the woman pressed a shard of ice to them. It burned and soothed in the same instant. He let the sensation linger there a moment before opening his mouth. Like a thunderstorm replenishes the cracked soil of a desert, the chunk of ice instantly soaked into the arid dryness of his mouth and throat.

"Can you open your eyes?" the woman asked.

Joseph raised his eyebrows in an effort to comply, but his lids refused to yield. "No," he whispered hoarsely. "More ice."

The abrupt coolness was not as drastic the second time but just as refreshing.

"I'm Nurse Ginger Jameson, but folks call me Ginny."

"Hi, Ginny," he mumbled around a small shard of ice. "Am I . . . in a hospital?"

"St. Luke's in Goleta."

"The beloved physician," Joseph whispered, quoting the Bible.

"Excuse me?" Ginny asked as she wiped a cool cloth across Joseph's forehead.

"The . . . book of . . . Colossians," he mumbled. Joseph had to pause a moment before continuing. His thoughts had cleared enough to form complete sentences, but he had trouble making his mouth articulate the words. When he did, they came out slow and measured. "In . . . the New . . . Testament. Paul . . . calls Luke . . . 'the beloved physician.'"

"Oh yes, of course," she responded as if she'd known all along. "Are you a priest or something?"

"No." He paused again. Swallowed. "I teach science . . . Solvang Middle School."

"You just read the Bible a lot, then," Nurse Jameson guessed.

"Not as much . . . as I should . . ." he replied more to himself than the nurse.

"Can you quote a lot of scripture?"

Joseph hesitated, thinking. "No. It just sort of . . . came to me."

"Wow, good memory. I used to atten—Presbyt—little girl—ears ago . . ." Ginny's voice faded in and out as Joseph struggled to remain conscious.

It was a losing battle.

He was floating again. His mind filled with gut-wrenching sounds—not as memories but as real-time events: screeching tires, rending metal, exploding glass, cracking bones. Harsh, vivid images pushed all other thoughts aside.

He heard a man and woman who identified themselves as paramedics explain the procedure by which they fitted a neck brace to immobilize his head. Their forced composure and rote words of comfort did little to hide the anxiety in their voices. He tried opening his eyes, but his vision was somehow blocked. His eyelids felt heavy, swollen shut. A moment later, he felt a slow, undulating motion, as if riding on a boat. Then a strange, muffled thumping filled his ears, along with the whine of a powerful engine. EMTs were calling to him, encouraging him to hang tough, almost there. A weightless surge welled up past him as if he were falling, falling, and yet there was no abrupt landing.

The sounds common to a hospital came next. Voices requesting CT scans, MRIs, and a head-trauma specialist—a brain surgeon. And then the pain began to set in. He heard something about a morphine drip and flippant bets being made on the odds of his survival. He knew he was hooked to an IV, but the painkiller was only fogging his brain and doing little to quell the actual discomfort. His throat felt raw. A tube blocked his ability to swallow comfortably. Then temporary blackness came again until the bleep of medical equipment pierced the dark veil. The smell of alcohol and astringent and blood came next. The pain was now disorienting, blinding, agonizing. He wished for the blackness to come completely, permanently. *Please just let it end.*

He looked for a light at the end of a tunnel, even though he didn't believe such a thing actually happened to those passing on. He looked for loved ones in his mind, in the murky beyond, the other side. But there was nothing there—only the feeling of being in the present.

After another immeasurable span of emptiness, he felt a curious tingling on his scalp. No, not on—*in*. It scared him. His breathing turned to gasps. His heart pounded in concussive thumps. He tried opening his eyes—*fought* to open his eyes. A shocked voice said something about him being awake. Apparently, that wasn't a good thing. A request was made for more anesthetic. Then the blackness returned, much thicker this time.

Gently, gratefully, he drifted into a void without thought, emotion, or stimulus.

CHAPTER 3

FLASHING LIGHTS BORE INTO HIS eyes: intense blue, blinding white, blood red. He tried to shield them with his hand, but their intensity penetrated right through flesh and bone. Joseph forced his eyes shut, counted to ten, then opened them again.

His breath caught sharply. Suddenly, strangely, he was standing at the precipice of a great height. The wind buffeted him, jostling him. His balance faltered. Falling forward, he tried to scream but couldn't—

* * *

"Mr. Ramirez? Can you hear me?"

The voice was caring, gentle, familiar. *Nurse Ginny?*

"Mr. Ramirez. Come on, wake up now. Can you hear me?"

"Mmmm?" he mumbled incoherently.

"Ha! I thought you might be waking up. You've been talking in your sleep again and mumbling like crazy."

"Oh?"

"Stay with me, now. Come on. Try to stay awake this time."

"Sure. Okay," Joseph whispered.

"That's the ticket. I'm going to daub your eyelids with a moist cloth to remove some of the crusties, okay? Then maybe you can open your eyes."

"Super," he said in barely more than a breath. He was ascending very slowly. It felt like crawling up the face of a precipice made of cotton candy; very little substance yet sticky. The clear air was just within reach. *Almost there . . .*

He felt moist pressure on his eyelids. The action was firm yet tender. A couple of forceful tugs removed some eyelashes, but it didn't really hurt.

"There now, all done. Try to open your eyes for me."

Joseph blinked and stretched his face a few times before he was able to partially separate his eyelids. The fluorescent lighting was fuzzy and glaring, but not harsh. Perhaps the blur was *inside* his head rather than in goopy eyes. He wanted to shake his head to clear the inner fog, but couldn't. He blinked vigorously to clear the waxy feeling inside and out.

"Washcloth, please," he said, holding out his hand.

Ginny handed it to him. "Don't rub too hard."

With some persuasion Joseph was able to remove the remaining anchors of dried blood and mucus that cemented his eyelids. *There*—now he could focus a little.

He looked around slowly. The room was standard hospital design: two adjustable beds (both occupied), light earth-tone walls, white trim, pale gray-speckled linoleum floor, acoustic ceiling tiles. The artwork was imitation Spanish Impressionist, and the window dressing off-white vertical blinds. A mosaic of handmade cards and posters adorned the wall beyond the foot of his bed: *Get well soon, Mr. Ramirez. We miss you, Mr. Ramirez. You're the best teacher ever! Mr. Ramirez makes science fun!* He smiled, recognizing some of the handwriting, but most of it was still beyond his focus.

Joseph held the moist cloth to his eyes for a few moments. When he looked up again, things were clearer. To his left he saw his roommate: a man about twenty years older than Joseph, mercilessly connected to several tubes, wires, and monitors. Presently, his roommate was listening to the TV through a headset and seemed bored to tears.

Nurse Jameson stood off to his right, appraising Joseph's movements over half-lens reading glasses. She was in her late forties, with a failing perm, a pleasant smile, and about twenty extra pounds.

"Can you see okay?" she asked.

"Yeah. It's a bit blurry, but not bad. May I have some ice, please?" He smiled to himself, happy that he could articulate his thoughts better. When Ginny handed him a small cup of ice, he asked, "How about some water, too? I'm still terribly thirsty."

"I'll ask the doctor. We're still worried about your ability to swallow, and your empty stomach can't take too much of anything just yet, though I imagine you're pretty hungry."

His stomach *did* feel hollow, but not painfully so. "Yeah, I guess," he admitted.

Ginny chuckled. "You guess? My lands, after three weeks in a coma, *I'd* be starving."

Joseph blinked and swallowed hard. "Excuse me?"

The nurse smiled compassionately as she wiped his forehead with a fresh washcloth. "Sorry. Didn't mean to shock you, José. Your accident was twenty-three days ago. You were life-flighted from Santa Ynez Valley Cottage Hospital within a few hours of your accident. You arrived unconscious and didn't wake up until yesterday."

A thousand thoughts ricocheted through Joseph's mind, all of which combined to form a chilling conclusion: brain damage. Reflexively, his heart rate increased, his breathing grew shallow. He fixated on his immediate surroundings to get a grasp on reality. A sling supported his left leg a few inches from his bed with a bright blue cast encompassing his left shin. A catheter ran out from under the blanket, an IV drained into his left arm, and his ribcage was encircled with several layers of elastic gauze. Just how many serious injuries had occurred? "Am I . . . okay?" he asked nervously.

"You're doing great, Mr. Ramirez," Ginny said. "Your stats all look good: blood pressure normal, heart rate steady and strong, O-sat normal, good cholesterol and blood sugar levels, too. For a thirty-year-old man who's just been flattened by a cement truck, you're in surprisingly good shape."

"Twenty-nine. Don't push it."

Ginny chuckled. "A good sense of humor always helps. Keep it up."

Joseph took another mini gulp of ice melt before asking, "My leg?"

"One break in the tibia, two in the fibula, both just below the knee. It'll take some time to heal, no doubt, but there's no infection or blood vessel damage, so that's good."

"And my chest?"

"Three broken ribs, two completely and one hairline fracture."

"Punctured lungs?"

"Nope. Just bruised."

He took a quick breath. "And my head?"

The nurse took his hand and guided it to his skull. "This is undoubtedly why you were in a coma for three weeks."

Joseph felt a cast of sorts, a dry-plaster wrap that encircled his head from his hairline to the nape of his neck.

"Your skull was cracked along the sagittal crest. That's right here," she said, pointing along the top of her head from front to back. "And you had a depression fracture just off the midpoint. The doctor said he got most of the bone fragments out and that the cranial sack had a slight tear, but there was no significant loss of cerebral-spinal fluid. You now have a silver dollar–size piece of plastic to replace the lost bone, but it shouldn't cause any discomfort or impairment."

"He got out *most* of the fragments?"

"There might be a few microscopic slivers he couldn't find, but those will most likely dissolve in time. You'll have a scar, but it shouldn't be too bad either. We'll monitor you for headaches, vision loss, fainting, vomiting, seizures, and the like. If that happens when I'm not here, you let the nurse on duty know right away."

Joseph was silent, staring at Nurse Jameson in utter shock.

"Don't you worry, honey," she added cheerfully. "In a few weeks your hair will grow back, and no one will even see the scar. You'll be as cute as ever."

"Super," Joseph said softly as he focused on the middle-school artwork. "Who's covering my classes?"

"No idea, but the school calls every other day to check on you. They'll be very happy to hear you're back among the living."

"I'd like to talk to Principal Card as soon as I can," he requested.

"Fine. You just rest now and let that ice work its magic. I'll notify the doctor you're fully awake. Do you need any painkiller?"

"No, not yet," he said.

"How about something to help you sleep?"

"No way. I think I've gotten enough sleep to last me until the millennium," he said with unmasked acrimony.

"True, but I gotta wonder how restful it's been. You spend a lot of the time tossing and turning and even talking in your sleep."

"Seriously?"

"Oh, yeah. Mr. Richter, your roommate there," she said, pointing to the other man, "says you get pretty wigged-out sometimes. Must be nightmares resulting from your accident. You call out names and such."

Joseph frowned. "What names?"

"Emily, Antonio, Victoria, and a few others."

"My brothers and sisters." He paused and just then noticed a vase of assorted carnations on a counter next to the sink. Other than the artwork from his students and colleagues, there were no other cards he could see. "Has my family come by often?"

"Oh, yes. Your mother's been here the most. Your older sister brought the flowers the day before yesterday. Your younger sister has dropped by a couple of times too, but she's in school during the day, I believe," Ginny explained.

"Where is my mom now?"

"At work, I suppose. I'll give her a call if you like."

"Yes, please."

The nurse smiled softly and daubed the corners of his mouth and eyes once more before turning to leave.

"Ginny?"

"Yes?"

Joseph paused and felt his eyes burn with the forming of tears. "Is there any . . . any brain damage?"

She smiled again, this time with a large dose of remorse mixed with the compassion. "I'll get the doctor in here to answer all your questions. You just rest now, Mr. Ramirez."

Nurse Jameson left the room without further comment. Despite his best efforts to remain calm, Joseph felt a suffocating fear completely engulf him to the point that he almost wished he could slip back into a coma.

CHAPTER 4

JOSEPH KNEW HE WAS DREAMING and that he was reliving something from his childhood, but for some reason he couldn't recall any details—only snippets, vignettes. He was in his youth. He was hiding . . . from something dangerous, monstrous. He was incredibly scared. He had to remain motionless or it would find him. And that would mean the end of his life.

* * *

"Mr. Ramirez?" a male voice called from somewhere outside his head.

Joseph fought his way back to consciousness. No cotton candy this time. Instead, it was like trying to run through cold molasses.

"Mr. Ramirez?"

Joseph awoke to find a man in a long white smock standing at the foot of his bed. Clearing his throat, Joseph scratched out a thin, "Good morning."

"Morning. I'm Dr. Lindley, your neurologist. I stopped by last evening, but you were already asleep."

"Sorry about that."

"No problem. Now, I need to ask you some questions," the physician said in a dry monotone, getting right to the point while examining Joseph's chart.

Joseph swallowed painfully and croaked, "Fine."

"Good. First, how are you feeling?"

It sounded as if the doctor were asking out of habit instead of true concern, as if reciting a lengthy, uninteresting checklist mandated by the hospital.

"As good as can be expected," Joseph said, toggling the switch to raise the head of his bed.

Dr. Lindley nodded. He looked close to sixty, if not a bit older, with gray hair tufted around his head, no hair on top, a curiously thin nose, and a hollow concavity to his cheeks that reminded Joseph of an undertaker. His flat, straightforward recitation of Joseph's condition seemed more befitting a mortician. That seemed about right. After all, Joseph *had* come within inches of death.

The doctor continued as if reading from a script. "I did your skull reconstruction, a compression fracture laterally proximal to the sagital crest. I removed thirty-seven bone fragments and had to remove a significant section of compressed bone still connected to healthy skull. Your meningeal dura mater—that's the membrane that surrounds your brain—required some extensive repair, but what I couldn't fully close should grow back in time. Your case presented some remarkable challenges. It took a little over nine hours in the OR."

Joseph responded in an equally flat tone. "Thanks for the over-time."

The physician didn't look up or acknowledge Joseph's jesting gratitude. A lengthy silence stifled the air in the room as the neurologist turned from one page to the next in the chart.

Joseph watched Dr. Lindley, patiently waiting for his next question, but none came. Having just woken up, Joseph was having trouble not drifting back to sleep. He yawned and stretched as much as his confines would allow. He hated sleeping so much, but each time he awoke, he felt like he could use another week of rest. He yawned again and rubbed his eyes.

Toward the last page, a deep crease formed between Dr. Lindley's eyebrows. He turned back to the front of the chart and pulled out some reading glasses to help clarify the scrawl within. It seemed like everything this man did was in slow motion.

"Anything wrong, doc?"

"I think there's something missing here . . . or maybe it's just entered incorrectly. It says here upon admission your blood alcohol level was zero. After an accident involving someone of your—" The doctor stopped short as if suddenly realizing he'd said something he might later regret. "Well, someone of your demographic, one naturally expects to find an elevated O-H level."

Joseph drew a long breath. "'My demographic,' doctor?"

The physician cleared his throat. "Well, 'a young man' is what I meant," he hedged.

Joseph saw right through the weak clarification—and it had all the earmarkings of racial profiling. "You mean a young *Hispanic* man, right?"

Removing his glasses, Dr. Lindley tried to look shocked, but his voice remained flat. "I assure you I did not. A majority of today's traffic fatalities involving men and women in your age demographic usually include high blood alcohol levels. It's one of the first things we test for in severe accidents of this nature. I was not implying anything other than that."

Joseph knew the man was lying but decided to let it go. The insult to his heritage had lost its potency almost as quickly as it had come, dissipating in the lingering cobwebs of rough sleep. Perhaps the doctor *was* telling the truth. Perhaps he simply had lousy bedside manner. "If you say so, doctor. But you might want to check the alcohol level of the truck driver. He's the one who ran the red light and plowed over me. My level was zero because I don't drink."

Dr. Lindley cast a skeptical glance. "Never?"

"No, sir."

"Don't they still serve wine at Communion?"

"I suppose they do," Joseph said. "But I'm not Catholic."

The neurologist ran his finger down the first page of the chart. "It says here that you are," he stated with a hint of condescension.

Joseph frowned. "May I see that?"

Dr. Lindley moved to his side and showed him the scrawl on the admission form. Joseph instantly recognized his mother's writing. His jaw reflexively clenched as he tried to remain calm. His mother could be so frustrating. "So it does. Sorry about that, doc, but that's not correct. My mother still believes I will come back to her church, but I converted to Mormonism ten months ago, and I have no plans of going back."

The doctor nodded and made a notation in the chart, smirked, then shook his head as if in disbelief.

"Now what's wrong?" Joseph asked, trying not to let his temper get the best of him.

"Nothing really. But you might want to know your mother insisted on hanging a crucifix above your bed," he said, nodding toward the wall behind Joseph. "Is that okay with you?"

Joseph turned as much as he could and saw a wooden cross directly above his headboard. His mother's mulishness was a constant thorn in his side. But he couldn't blame her for loving her religion. He certainly loved his. "I'd rather not keep it up, if it's all the same to you."

Dr. Lindley reached over and removed the religious symbol, placing it on the counter next to the carnations. "So you're not Christian, then," the doctor stated.

Joseph bristled. He was wide awake now. "Quite the contrary—Mormons are very Christian, as our church's name attests."

The doctor's eyebrows inched over disbelieving eyes.

Joseph explained. "I belong to The Church of Jesus Christ of Latter-day Saints. We're called Mormons because of our belief in the Book of Mormon. We don't use crucifixes because we don't worship graven images and we prefer to remember Jesus as being alive, not dead."

The doctor held his silent gaze for a time, as if judging the information. "I see," was all he said.

"Super," Joseph said, still wondering what this had to do with his state of health. "Now, what's my prognosis?"

Dr. Lindley returned the chart to the bedstead and pulled out a penlight. Moving to Joseph's head, he checked his pupil response. "Actually, I am very impressed with how fast you are healing considering the severity of your head trauma. Do you have headaches?"

"There's a dull pressure, but no real pain."

"Vision disturbances or hearing loss?"

"None."

"Numbness or tingling anywhere?"

"Nowhere."

"Pain anywhere else?"

"Just a terribly sore throat, sore ribs, and I'm very thirsty."

"Do you have any trouble swallowing?"

"Not that I can tell," Joseph said.

The doctor moved to a sink and filled a plastic cup with water. "Try sipping this."

Joseph took a sip and swallowed. The pain was searing but healing. He sipped again, taking a bigger swallow. Less pain, more refreshing. He'd forgotten how wonderful water could not only taste but also feel. "Thanks," he said. "This is great."

"Just go slowly on it. We'll start you on some soup and maybe some half-strength Ensure or something this afternoon. But nothing solid for a couple days at least."

"Okay. So . . . my prognosis?" Joseph asked again, suspecting the doctor was avoiding the question.

The man's didactic lecture voice was anything but comforting. "Head trauma is a difficult one to predict, especially with damage as extensive as yours. You could have no ill effects whatsoever. On the other hand, you could go along just fine for weeks, even months or years, before any repercussions exhibit. What we're mostly concerned with is elevated pressure in your skull. That can result from inflammation and blood seepage. So far, neither of those seem to be a problem. Let me know if you experience any vision, hearing, or tactile aberrations, as well as any motor-skill dysfunction, or anything that comes across as bizarre or not quite right."

"In other words, you don't know."

The surgeon checked Joseph's pupil response a second time with his penlight. "It's too early to make any promises."

"Okay, then, how long do you think I'll be in St. Luke's?"

"Again, we're not sure. At least another couple of weeks, maybe more. I'm going to schedule physical therapy as soon as possible. Plus, I'd like you to have a psych evaluation. Is that okay with you?"

Joseph cringed. "No, thank you. I'd rather not."

"How come? After severe head trauma it's highly recommended—if only to establish a baseline."

"Had a bad experience with that in my childhood. I'd rather not revisit it."

Dr. Lindley held a lopsided smile for a second or two before making a notation in the chart. "I'm still going to recommend it in your chart. Whether you take advantage of it or not is up to you. In the meantime, just try to relax, Mr. Ramirez," he said as he slipped his glasses and penlight into his breast pocket.

Currently, *relaxing* was the furthest thing from Joseph's mind. Most of his unease stemmed from his inability to sleep without experiencing terrible dreams, but he figured that was accident-induced and would pass with time. He'd only been "awake" for two days, and the times he had drifted off were fitful and confusing—he couldn't remember what he had dreamed, only that it had been terrifying. Undoubtedly he needed something to help him sleep, but he didn't want to get addicted to sleeping pills and planned on turning them down when the nurse offered them.

Aside from the sharp dryness in his throat and difficulty taking a deep breath, his pain was minimal. His broken leg and head throbbed dully, but it was tolerable. He guessed he'd be on crutches once he was no longer bedridden, and he looked forward to the time he could get a little movement back in his limbs.

All told, his ailments were negligible. For someone whose skull had been crushed, he could easily have been completely paralyzed, a vegetable . . . or dead.

He examined the IV bag draining into his arm. It said something about lactated Ringer's and TPN solutions. He saw nothing that said painkiller or antibiotic, or even any recognizable chemical name, except maybe phenytoin sodium, whatever that was. That didn't mean there weren't any. He wasn't familiar with much pharmacy-related chemistry, but as a science teacher, he felt he could recognize a drug name when he saw one.

"If you need anything, don't hesitate to ask," said Dr. Lindley, again without emotion, as though he knew what was required and was merely going through the motions. "You can press the nurse-call anytime, day or night." He gave another curt nod and left the room without saying good-bye.

As soon as he was gone, Ginny poked her head in the room. "How're you doing, José?"

"Hungry, thirsty, frustrated, and anxious to get back into life."

"We're doing all we can for you, hon. You just hang tight."

"Do I have a choice?"

"Nope—not for a couple of days. But don't be discouraged, José. You're our little miracle man here. We're all rootin' for you."

"Thanks. And I'd really rather you called me Joseph."

She smiled. "Okay . . . but your chart says José."

"Please have Dr. Lindley change that for me. I've never liked that name. I'd rather be called Joseph."

"Sure thing, Joseph. I'll personally make the switch and make sure the hospital records the change, too."

"Thanks."

Nurse Ginny Jameson reminded Joseph of his fifth grade teacher, Mrs. Cuthbert. She was about the same height and weight, the same mousy hair color. Ginny's eyes were a bit lighter—as was her temperament—but the rest could pass the two as sisters. Melba Cuthbert had been a good teacher—very caring, very nurturing. Joseph recalled that she constantly wore her hair in a bun. Her husband's name was Bud. They had two kids: a boy named Aaron and a girl named Kathi. Oh, and a yellow Labrador named Happy. She drove a blue Corolla with California plates reading GRL 1159—

Joseph blinked and frowned. How in the world did he remember all that? There was no way he could have retained that information from the fifth grade . . . and yet, the images were crystal clear in his mind. Not as a memory, but as an actual image. It struck him as miraculous, because, for some reason, he'd lost all memory of his early childhood a long time ago. He figured it was simply part of growing older. And yet, rather than being delightfully surprised at the strange recollection, he felt disturbingly anxious.

CHAPTER 5

THE MONSTER WAS CLOSE. YOUNG Joseph cowered under his bedsheets. It wasn't much of a hiding place, and he knew it. He was frozen with fear and couldn't bring himself to look for another place to hide. It was too late anyway. The monster was right *there*!

He had awoken with a start, hearing the monster rage just down the hallway. His parents had told him time and again that the monster wasn't real. But even at nine years old, Joseph knew better.

"Get under the bed, quickly," Antonio whispered urgently from the next bed.

Joseph followed his older brother's suggestion without hesitation, squirming into the blackness under the narrow bed. The room was very dark, heavy bedroom curtains preventing the moon from casting anything more than ill-defined shafts of light. Under the bed was darker still.

"Don't move. Don't make a sound. Pretend to be asleep, and you'll be okay," Antonio promised in a forced whisper.

Antonio was four years older than Joseph. He was a good-looking boy with deep brown eyes and a ready smile. He was Joseph's best friend and his hero. He had saved Joseph from the monster many times.

Young Joseph screwed his eyes shut. He tried not to tremble, tried to think of happy things to mask the danger outside their small bedroom. The monster sounded very angry and extra mean tonight.

Joseph's oldest brother, Xavier, with whom they shared the room, was at work and wouldn't be home until after midnight. The family dog, a medium-sized mutt named Zip, stood just beyond the bed with his head lowered, hackles raised.

A loud *thump* landed just outside the bedroom. A low, fearful groan followed, sounding like something from a scary movie, like something that had clawed its way from the hell Joseph had learned about in catechism. He opened his eyes enough to see that a shadow now blocked the thin strip of light at the base of the door. The monster was right there! Looking up, Joseph saw the green glow of Xavier's digital clock, reading 11:40 PM. Twenty more minutes until Xavier came home.

The shadow twisted as the monster slammed against the door, causing young Joseph to flinch. Zip recoiled and let out a less than confident, one-note yelp. *The dog heard it!* That *proved* that the monster was real.

Joseph's parents didn't believe him about the monster, but it *was* real. He had heard its angry cry, had seen the evil in its eyes, had smelled its sour breath. Even Antonio said monsters weren't always what they seemed to be. Joseph knew Antonio believed in *this* monster. And when it raged like this, he knew Antonio was just as frightened as he was. He heard it in his voice.

With renewed courage, the dog began to growl low and deep in his throat. His head drooped even lower, and the hair on his shoulders stood up like porcupine quills.

"Easy, Zip," Antonio whispered.

The dog did not move, did not break his focus from the thing on the other side of the bedroom door. He took a hesitant step forward. His growl intensified. When the shadow shifted again, his courage withered as fast as it had grown, and his deep growl turned into a high-pitched, frail whine. Even in the dark, Joseph could see Zip's legs quivering to the point that they could no longer support his body. With a yip—half bark and half whine—the dog dropped to his belly and placed his head between his paws. The dog was a coward at heart, but Joseph couldn't blame him.

Slowly, the shadow grew, filling the narrow gap with darkness. A slithering noise scraped against the door. It sounded reptilian, like a snake dragging its scaly, raspy skin along the thin wood veneer. Soon a muffled scratching joined in—as if the beast were raking its claws against the flimsy, hollow partition.

Zip's whimpering became a whine, thin and sorrowful. The doorknob began to turn but did not unlatch. Perhaps the monster's claws were too big to allow for a good grip on the polished knob. Joseph swore he could hear its gurgling breaths—it was *that* close. He could almost smell the death-stink of its mouth.

Whimper, yelp, whine, growl—Zip was a trembling lump of fur and bones. It was as if he wanted to turn tail and run, but he didn't dare take his eyes from the door.

The monster issued a low, anguished moan that sounded needful, hungry. The throaty, wet noise grew in volume until it reached a roar filled with pain and anger. Then—

Wham! The monster beat a fist—or paw—or tentacle—against the door, causing the thin veneer to bend with a splintery *crack.* Joseph cringed and scrunched tighter against the wall under the bed. Antonio lay motionless, pretending to be asleep. Zip yelped and began to urinate. The monster's wet, gooey voice turned semi-human. It tried to speak but somehow couldn't find the words. Perhaps it couldn't remember *how* to speak. Finally, it managed to form one word in a thin, wheezing tone. "Joooossssséééé . . ."

Joseph clapped his fists to his ears and refused to answer, refused to even listen. Perhaps Antonio had the right idea. If he kept very quiet, very still, the monster would go away.

Zip had retreated to a far corner of the small room. The stench of his urine filled the air.

The clock read 11:55.

Just five more minutes—unless Xavier had decided to go out with friends. *Oh, not tonight. Please, Xavier, not tonight.*

The doorknob rattled sharply. The wood frame creaked and groaned.

Blessed Virgin Mary, please don't let the monster get—

The door burst open with a deafening crash.

* * *

Joseph awoke with a start. His hospital room was shrouded in darkness. A few monitors hummed peacefully and offered scant pinpoints of light here and there. Vague traffic sounds filtered through the windows. He swore the thumping of his heart echoed off the walls.

He glanced over at his roommate. The man appeared to be sound asleep. Or dead. Joseph couldn't be sure. And he certainly did not want to guess. Not after the nightmare he'd just had. It had involved a dark night, a monster, his old dog Zip, and . . . and what? He wasn't sure. The details had vanished the moment he awoke. It was a dream he'd never had before, but it had conveyed an event he *knew* he had experienced once. Maybe more. It'd been more than a nightmare. *What was the term? Oh yeah, a 'night terror.'* That was what he'd had. Possibly. One thing he did know for sure, he didn't want to experience one again.

CHAPTER 6

"José, dis never happen if ju don' leave da Church," Consuela Ramirez scolded her son, her heavy Hispanic accent twisting her English.

"Mama, you know that's not true. It was an accident, nothing more," Joseph replied wearily, hating that she continued to treat him like a preteen.

"Well, I e'still light a candle for ju at Our Lady of e'Sorrows," she said defiantly.

Joseph sighed and smiled. "Thanks, Mama. I'm sure that'll help."

Consuela Guadalupe Ramirez was a short, solid woman with long salt-and-pepper hair, dark and weary eyes, and a generous girth. Sitting at her son's bedside, she wore a plain cotton dress, old multi-colored tennis shoes, and knee-high nylons that slumped around her ankles. In her lap sat a large canvas carryall that promoted shopping at La Cumbre Plaza.

Consuela was the proud mother of five children. The oldest two, Xavier and Emily, were married and producing lots of grandchildren. Antonio, her third child, had died when he was fourteen, supposedly from gang violence. Joseph, her fourth child, was still unmarried and childless—something she reminded him of during every conversation. Consuela's last daughter, Victoria, was now nineteen and still lived at home.

Consuela's husband, Estefan, had left shortly after the birth of Victoria and was never heard from since. Mrs. Ramirez had supported her children by cleaning houses during the day and cooking at a Mexican restaurant in the evening. She was a hard-working, no-nonsense kind of woman who had an indomitable faith in her religion. And because she was completely obedient to her church, she expected total obedience from her children.

"A' course a candle will help, *mi'jo*. I also e'said prayers to da Virgin Mary for ju, but it help more if ju pray too."

"I do, Mama, all the time. I pray every morning and night that you'll start calling me Joseph instead of José."

Consuela gasped and crossed herself. "Don' ju make fun of praying to God."

"Sorry, Mama. You're right. But I do pray all the time, I promise."

"*Sí*, José, but ju pray to a gold man blowing a horn," she countered, ignoring his request.

Joseph choked back the comment he wanted to make about the Catholic's veneration of saints and the millions of prayers offered to statues of them each day. "I pray to Heavenly Father in the name of Jesus, Mama. I've explained that to you many times before. The 'gold man' is the Angel Moroni—an *angel*, Mama—a messenger from God. We don't pray to him or to Joseph Smith."

"That not what Margarita Ximena Corona de-Alquien say," she replied as if quoting the world's foremost authority. "She say ju believe in a gold man an' a gold bible, an' . . . an' many wives at da same time! *Santa Maria*, dat's so wrong, José!"

Joseph was already beyond tired, both from his lack of restful sleep and from having the same old arguments with his mother. Ever since his conversion to Mormonism, he'd waged this battle innumerable times. Half the time he simply let her ramble away while his mind drifted to other topics. "Mama, Señora de-Alquien is ninety-two years old. She doesn't know what day of the week it is, let alone anything about my beliefs."

"*Mi'jo*, dat's no way to talk about jur elders!"

Joseph rubbed his eyes again and bit his lower lip. Changing the subject, he asked, "How's Victoria?"

"Oh! She heading for trouble, I promise ju. She going to a dance wid a boy I don' even know." Mrs. Ramirez drew her voluminous purse against her frame and held a hand over her heart. "*Mi corazon!* I tell ju e'someting, it not good for my blood pressure to have my children go against der fader's wishes all da time."

Not taking the bait to talk about a father he barely remembered, Joseph said, "I'm sure the boy she's seeing is very nice. Victoria is a smart girl. She won't make any dumb choices."

"I don' know. She wan' to go to college now. Es not too good for girls to be too e'smart."

"She's always wanted to go to a culinary college, you know that."

"*Sí*, but why go to e'school to learn how to cook? I can teach her dat."

Joseph had had this argument with his mother before, too, as had Victoria. Once Mama's mind was set on something, it took a miracle to change it—like getting a goose to lay a golden egg. It was never going to happen. Besides, arguing with his mother always made him feel unbalanced. It was never a discussion—just contention.

This was not to say Joseph didn't enjoy a thoughtful exchange of opinion. The debate of ideas—weighing pros and cons—was a crucial foundation of science. *Discussing* issues and topics was constructive and progressive. *Arguing* was the antithesis of progress, and he hated it.

His soul wanted nothing but serenity and the joy of enlightenment. Joseph had always had an inquisitive mind. He always sought for answers to the unknown, sought to make sense of the illogical or confusing. That's one of the reasons the LDS faith appealed to him. In addition to the overwhelming spirit he felt, the doctrine just made sense. It was also why he became a science teacher. Sharing knowledge, discussing theories, bantering concepts, and asking questions enlivened him. His curiosity was insatiable. It was a trait he'd had as long as he could remember. If he could instill that love of learning into even a few of the next generation, he would consider life a success.

But with Mama, sharing, discussing, and bantering ideas was something better left alone. The effort always left him very worn out, even depressed. Like now.

"Mama, I'm getting tired again." He yawned. It was not a total lie.

"*Sí*, es okay. Ju take a nap. I'll see ju later."

Consuela leaned over and kissed Joseph on the forehead. He smiled and thanked her.

Closing his eyes, he let his mind drift wherever it chose. It was good to see Mama again, to hear her voice—even to hear the same old arguments. It was like being home again.

Sleep came easily, but it didn't remain that way.

CHAPTER 7

THE IMAGES WERE FUZZY AT first, then everything came into focus with astounding clarity. An old photo of Joseph's father stood on the curio cabinet in his mother's living room. The photo was nestled between a small statue of St. Peter and one of John the Baptist, as if Estefan Salvador Arango Ramirez were holy enough to complete a trio of venerated persons.

The picture was taken a few months after the birth of Xavier Salvador Ramirez. In it, Papa looked no different than any other Hispanic man Joseph knew while growing up in the Santa Barbara barrio: dark hair and eyes, a thin mustache, a wardrobe consisting solely of white T-shirts and chinos. In the photo, Papa was grinning from ear to ear—an expression Joseph had rarely seen his father wear in person . . . maybe. He couldn't remember. His early childhood had always been somewhat of a blur . . .

Without warning, the scene began to change. Morphing from one vignette to another, Joseph was assaulted with a random flurry of recollections about his home, his childhood. Most were mere bits and pieces, like a rapidly edited movie where no one scene was on screen long enough to make sense. Then quite suddenly, one stuck.

Papa was shirtless, working on his 1959 Cadillac Eldorado—a car just smaller than a tuna boat, equally attractive, and with similar handling. It was a hot, sticky summer afternoon. The humidity was near eighty. Young Joseph stood behind his father, nervously holding a socket wrench, awaiting the command to hand it to him. An elaborate tattoo was inked across the breadth of his father's back. The body art depicted Jesus' face gazing up to heaven, with tears streaming from his eyes and a bloody crown of thorns encircling his head. Joseph marveled at how the sweat dripping from his father's back looked like Jesus was actually crying. Every now and then his father would lean forward and move just so, and Jesus would look directly at Joseph and weep. It frightened him to death.

"Give it to me now!" Estefan bellowed in Spanish.

Joseph held out the wrench, handle first as he had been taught.

"*Quiero una cerveza.*"

Little Joseph sprinted into the house to get a beer from the fridge. He knew if he did not return before his father needed another tool, he'd be punished. If he didn't get a beer from the back of the fridge where they were coldest, he'd be punished. If he took too long with anything, he'd be punished. His father had a stout, rattlesnake-hide *bastinado* or bludgeon that he brandished liberally. At the tender age of seven, Joseph had already received countless bruises for various "disobediences." Upon returning with a frosty Dos Equis, Joseph misjudged the last step on the porch, stumbled, and almost dropped the bottle of beer. Papa's eyes immediately flared with anger and disgust. Tears sprang to Joseph's eyes. He knew what was coming. There was nothing he—

* * *

"José?" It was a woman's voice—not his father's. "José!"

Joseph snapped from his dream at the sound of his mother's sharp tone. "*Sí*, Mama?"

"Are ju okay? Jur e'skin es so pale. And ju are e'sweating like crazy."

"*Sí.*" He opened his eyes and wiped his brow with his sleeve. Not surprisingly, his hands were trembling. He glanced at the clock on his bed stand then to his mother. "It's almost supper time, Mama. What are you still doing here?"

"I'm lookin' after ju, *mi'jo.*"

Joseph took a couple of deep breaths and willed his pulse to steady. "I'm fine, Mama. You have your job at the restaurant. You really don't have to stay here."

"No, I callin' *el doctor*."

"No, Mama, really," Joseph insisted. "I was just dreaming of . . . I was remembering when . . ." Joseph closed his eyes and concentrated. Why couldn't he remember? He just woke up, for heaven's sake. And yet . . . it was gone. *That's strange.* "Oh, never mind," he said. "It was just a bad dream."

His mother moved to his side and daubed his forehead with a hankie she'd pulled from her purse. "It mus' have been a *muy* e'scary dream."

Joseph swallowed deeply. "Yeah. I think it was."

CHAPTER 8

JOSEPH SPENT A GOOD PORTION of each day asleep. He could only focus for a few hours at a time. Each day was better then the previous, but his body seemed to demand the chance to rest and recover from the accident. Exactly how much rest he got was up for debate. His nights were plagued with fever, chills, sweats, and terrors; his naps were fraught with disturbing visions. And what struck him as most bizarre was that he remembered so little of each dream upon awakening. He mentioned the problem to Nurse Ginny. She put it in his chart.

* * *

Two days later, Joseph sat in his bed fighting intense boredom. He tried in vain to focus on a *Sports Illustrated.* It seemed that every other picture reminded him of something he'd seen or heard somewhere in his past. A few memories were fun and exciting; others brought melancholy; still others, remorse. Most were remembrances of things he was certain he'd never experienced. But then, why was he *remembering* them? They were not fantasies; they were intimately personal, horrific events he had somehow forgotten.

"You about done with that?" his roommate asked, interrupting his thoughts.

"Yeah, sure," Joseph said, closing the magazine and tossing it to Clyde Richter.

The older man deftly caught the monthly, even with a restrictive plastic tube draining into his arm. "Thanks, Joe."

Clyde was fifty-nine and was shaped like a block. He had a stocky upper body, no neck, and way too much excess around his midsection. His beady eyes and loose jowls would shame a bulldog. In his younger days Clyde would have made a great football lineman. Or a sumo wrestler. Or a ship's anchor. Joseph couldn't decide which.

Residing in San Luis Obispo, California, just north of Santa Barbara, Clyde was a public sanitation engineer. That really meant he drove a waste management truck to pick up trash in the early hours of the morning. He claimed it was the perfect job. He got to drive a huge truck with lots of cool gizmos and switches, worked only a few hours each morning, got great government insurance, and got every possible holiday off. He had four ex-wives and four kids—three boys, one girl. His enlarged liver was from too much beer, not enough water or green vegetables or exercise, and possible familial hepatitis. He was headstrong, imposing, and of the opinion he could still take on the world.

"Anything interesting in it?" Clyde asked, leafing through the periodical.

"There's a lineup of college kids destined for the NBA draft."

"Any names you recognize?"

Joseph pushed against his skull cast in an effort to quell an itch. "Not really. I only saw a list of six-figure sign-on bonuses for a bunch of guys barely old enough to buy beer."

Clyde snorted in derision. "What—you got a problem with that?"

"Yes, I do. Something's wrong with a society that pays a guy who can toss a ball through a hoop more than a fireman saving lives or a teacher trying to educate the next generation."

His roommate scowled at him for a time before speaking. His look was harsh and penetrating. "My son played minor league baseball for three years. You saying he didn't earn his keep?"

"No, Clyde, that's not what I'm saying."

The older man huffed. "Good."

Earlier, Joseph had tried to strike up a friendly conversation with Clyde Richter, but that one ended in a bitter tone, too. The man figured because he had already lived over half a century, his opinion counted three times that of a guy half his age. The arithmetic didn't make sense, but Joseph figured such a calculation topped the extent of the man's mathematical abilities anyway, so he didn't push the issue. It wasn't that Clyde was a mean person. He was probably just grumpy from being confined in the hospital.

A knock sounded at the door. A man in a well-tailored suit stood with his hand still poised in mid-rap. He had slick, motionless hair and a plastic smile. "Mr. Ramirez, I hope?"

The man was almost too polished to be trustworthy. Joseph was instantly leery. "Yes?"

The man's smile widened into a perfect crescent, filled with movie star veneers. He entered with his hand extended. Joseph shook it but found it hard to return the man's smile. "We heard you regained consciousness last week, but they wouldn't let me in here until today. We are extremely relieved to hear you're recovering so well."

"So far, so good," Joseph replied, thinking of the less-than-enthusiastic reports Dr. Lindley had given him.

"Excellent. Well done." The man beamed. "My name is Brick Wiseman. I'm with Stansbury, Vail, and Jenkins. We represent Sierra West Construction."

"Ah," Joseph said.

"Now don't jump to any conclusions, Mr. Ramirez. I'm really a nice guy representing a very respectable company."

"You a lawyer?" Clyde asked from his side of the room.

Wiseman flashed him a cautious look. "Yes, sir, I am."

"Don't say a word, Joe," Clyde hissed between clenched teeth. "I can pick out a lawyer in a crowd of suits a mile away. They all act like they're Mother Teresa, but they're all slick and shtick and a crock of—"

"I get the idea," Joseph interrupted.

"I'm tellin' you, Joe, they'd just as soon strip you naked to find a nickel in your pocket as offer any real help."

Wiseman chuckled good-naturedly. "Well, I'm sorry you feel that way, my friend."

"I ain't your friend, pal."

Another conciliatory chuckle. "Fine, fine, have it your way. Now, Mr. Ramirez, we need to discuss the matter of your accident. As it turns out, there's some question as to whether the light was green before you entered the intersection. Do you recall much about the incident?"

Joseph hesitated. "Shouldn't I have my lawyer present before I answer any questions?"

"Why, sure, sure. Would you like me to call him for you?" Brick Wiseman offered as he pulled a sleek cell phone from his pocket.

Knowing his bluff was called, Joseph said, "I don't have one yet. But I still don't feel comfortable discussing the accident until I know I'm protected."

"Protected?" the lawyer asked, flashing another blinding smile. "Protected from what? I'm here to offer you a very generous remuneration for your inconveniences and discomfort."

"Inconveniences and dis—" Joseph stopped, unable to finish the sentence. "You're calling a broken leg, cracked ribs, a crushed skull, and three weeks in a coma a 'discomfort'?"

"You tell him, Joe," Clyde cheered, as if he were suddenly Joseph's best friend.

The lawyer laughed out loud as if the two roommates had cracked a collaborative joke. "Yes, I see your point about the terminology. But I still can't believe you're saying you want 'protection' from free money!"

"Nothing in life is free, Mr. Wiseman," Joseph said.

An altruistic smile graced the lawyer's face. "So true. You are a very bright young man, Mr. Ramirez. That's why I'm sure you understand the importance of getting everything on paper as soon as possible."

"I agree with that. But I won't sign anything without personal legal representation, Mr. Wiseman."

"Of course, of course. No trouble there. In fact, if you like, I can personally suggest someone I know quite well to make everything pass on through smooth and easy, without any stress or strain."

"Now you sound like a laxative," Clyde called from across the room. "Put that with a name like Brick and it paints up a pretty bad picture."

Joseph pretended to cough to cover his laughter.

Wiseman acted like he hadn't even heard Clyde's crude remark.

"Isn't that a conflict of interest?" Joseph asked. "Having input on both sides of the issue, I mean?"

"Perhaps in some instances. My company and I simply want to help you recover without any stress or fear of what the future may hold."

"Super. Why don't you leave me your offer and your card, and I'll get back to you when I can."

Wiseman balked. "I'm afraid that's not possible, Mr. Ramirez. I was instructed to bring back a signed offer today. I'm sure you appreciate that time is of the essence; the offer probably will not be as sweet tomorrow, and even less the next day. Trust me, you'll want to grab the iron while it's hot, sir."

"Trust *you?*" Clyde shot from behind his magazine. "That's rich."

Wiseman pushed on. "If negligence is established, we'll cover all hospital costs as well as six months of rehab, plus buy you a new car of your choice."

"Ask for a Ferrari and see what happens," Clyde chuckled.

"Six months of rehab? My doctor said it could take six months for any symptoms to even show. What happens after that?"

"We have a team of medical specialists who have reviewed your file and believe you'll make a 100 percent full recovery. We're confident there's nothing you need to worry about."

"Really? You've already reviewed my file? I believe that's a privacy violation," Joseph said, feeling his temper rise. "The HIPAA law or something."

"Actually, we have your mother's signature allowing access to all your records, Mr. Ramirez. I can show you a copy, if you like."

What? When did she—? Oh yeah. "That was undoubtedly done while I was in a coma. Since my mother does not speak English very well—and if you used the same pressure you're pushing on me—I'm sure she did so without complete understanding. Irrespective of that, I am now awake and fully alert, and anything she may have signed now has to be approved by me. I forbid you or anyone outside of this hospital access to any of my medical files from this point on."

"I got your back on that, Joe," Clyde affirmed. "I'm a witness."

"Thanks." Joseph depressed the call-nurse button on his bed frame. "Rescinding my mother's signature is the only piece of paper I'll sign right now."

Wiseman frowned but maintained a carefree air. "Whatever you deem best, Mr. Ramirez. Honestly, we are here to help you in any way we can."

Joseph nodded. "Thank you. If you'll leave your card and any paperwork you want me to look over, I'll get back with you as soon as I can."

"But the time constraint—"

"Will have to wait," Joseph nearly shouted. "I'm sure when all the facts are in, Sierra West Construction will be more than amenable."

"Mr. Ramirez," Wiseman said with an air of censure, "if you're just fishing for a bigger offer, I should warn you that my company will *not* be as amenable as you may think."

"Is that a threat, Mr. Wiseman?" Joseph asked without malice.

"No, sir. Of course not."

"Speakin' of fishing," Clyde chimed in. "Hey, Joe, what's the difference between a lawyer and a catfish?"

Joseph didn't answer. Wiseman just closed his eyes.

"One's a slimy, bottom-feeding scavenger and the other one's a fish." Clyde followed up his joke with laughter so intense that he ended up in a fit of coughing.

This time Joseph didn't hide his smile.

Brick Wiseman slid the papers back into his briefcase and smoothed out his lapels and tie. "We'll be in touch, Mr. Ramirez."

"Whatever you say, Mr. Wiseman," Joseph said to the lawyer's exiting form.

CHAPTER 9

JOSÉ! EL FALLA!

Joseph's eyes opened instantly. He was hyperventilating, and his heart felt like it was about to burst from his chest. Fractured morning sunlight angled into the room. The window was open a crack, allowing an occasional breeze to stir the dust motes into a frenzied aerial dance.

Joseph sat up and took a sip of water. He wiped the cold sweat from his brow and willed himself to calm down. He'd just awakened from another nightmare, but for the life of him he couldn't remember what this one was about either.

Next to his bed stood a telescoping tray on which sat a small can of Ensure, a slice of dry toast, a shot glass of low-acid orange juice, and one hard-boiled egg. It had been his standard fare for five days, yet he'd tired of it after just two. Glancing to his left, he found that his roommate was missing. The man was probably having a *real* breakfast in the hospital cafeteria. It just didn't seem right.

Just after he'd downed the juice, Ginny entered the room pushing a wheelchair. "Oh good, you're finally awake. Ready for a ride?"

"A ride? Are you taking me to IHOP or Carrow's for an honest breakfast?" he asked, already knowing the answer.

She sniggered. "You wish! No, it's PT time." Her malevolent glee did not fill Joseph with much comfort.

"Super," he groaned, pushing his unfinished breakfast to the side.

In addition to a bland diet, Joseph was rarely allowed out of bed, and he was anxious to burn off the physical and emotional blah that came from extended inactivity—and lack of sleep. Ginny helped him swing his legs off the bed then allowed him to grab her shoulders as he pivoted into the wheelchair. She raised the left footrest to elevate his cast and then pushed him out into the hallway.

"PT's on the first floor," she said, heading toward an elevator.

"Are you sure I'm up to it?" he asked.

"A strapping young man like you?" she quipped. "Piece of cake. Oh, I mentioned your dreams to the doctors, and they said they'd discuss it."

"That's it?"

"For now. But don't fret. We're taking one step at a time, remember?"

Joseph shrugged. One day at a time was about all he could handle. For now he relished being out of his bed. The muscles required for moving to the wheelchair tingled with renewed use, and his head already felt a bit clearer. But that was just what he expected. As a science teacher, he understood the need for physical and mental exercise, proper nutrition, and the like, and consequently kept his frame in tiptop condition. Perhaps that was partly why he was recovering so well.

They exited the elevator and turned down a long hallway flanked by large picture windows. Joseph asked Ginny to slow down so he could take in the view. The morning mists that prevailed along the Santa Barbara coastline muted the Santa Ynez Mountains in varying hues of purple. But Joseph knew it wouldn't last. When the mists evaporated, the sage-gray of the scrub oak and the burgundy-colored bark of the Manzanita would stand out, as would the brilliant orange patches of California poppies and purple-blue splotches of bush lupine.

"So what science courses do you teach?" Ginny asked as she continued to wheel him down the hallway.

"General science and biology, and some chemistry and health science," he said.

"That's great. Where'd you go to school?"

"I'm pretty much a home-state boy. I got my bachelor's and teaching certificate at UCSB and my master's at Cal State, Camarillo."

"Camarillo, huh? So how did you end up in Solvang?"

"I prefer smaller communities to big cities, and I have an incurable addiction to Danish pastries," he said, smiling.

Solvang, California, was a quaint tourist town settled by Danish immigrants back in 1911. They'd moved there to escape the harsh Midwest winters. The town boasted numerous souvenir shops, an equal number of authentic Delft fine china shops, and several excellent bakeries, including one owned by Joseph's next-door neighbors.

Like many of Solvang's residents, Joseph loved the small-town ambiance, the rich Scandinavian history, and the green, rolling countryside that made up the popular community and surrounding area. He had accepted a position at the newly opened Solvang Middle School right out of college and had never regretted the decision.

Leaving the picture windows, they maneuvered down another hallway until they came to a room marked Physical Therapy.

"Here we go," Ginny said. "Welcome to Connie Olsen's House of Pain."

A tall, svelte blonde with vivid blue eyes, square shoulders, and well-toned arms met Joseph and Ginny with a granite expression. "You know I've never liked that title," she told the nurse in a hard yet mischievous tone. "I'm as gentle as a feather on a summer breeze."

Ginny whispered in Joseph's ear, "Don't you believe her. She puts the *hell* in *healthy.*"

Therapist Connie looked like a seasoned decathlete from the old Soviet Union. Still sitting in his wheelchair, Joseph could tell she was a good two inches taller than his five ten.

"So then, Ginny, what have you brought me today?" the PT asked while appraising Joseph with a critical eye.

"Joseph Ramirez. A science teacher who likes to play chicken with cement trucks," Ginny announced.

"Ah. I heard about you, Mr. Ramirez. You're somewhat of a miracle man, they say," she commented as she accepted Joseph's chart and nodded good-bye to Ginny.

"It's Joseph, and I was just lucky."

"That's a matter of perspective, Joseph. You'll find everything we do here a matter of perspective. See, everyone has their own perspective on things, but they're not always correct. For example, in the 1400s most everyone perceived the world to be flat. A broader, more enlightened perspective proved that to be incorrect. As far as physical therapy goes, after we're well into your exercises, you may *perceive* that you've reached your max, but *my* perspective will always be the final determinant."

"Broader, more enlightened," Joseph said with mild mockery.

She fixed him with a steely gaze. "I'm here to push you to health, Joseph. My theory is that the body responds to demand, not denial. If you just kick back and relax in a misguided effort to give your body 'time to heal,' it'll take forever, and you'll likely never heal completely. Force your body in precise, regimented exercises, and you'll cut your recovery time in half. It all has to do with the stimulation of growth factor and anti-inflammatory response from c-reactive protein release during prolonged, focused micro-trauma—which is another term for exercise. It's never easy, but it's always worth it. See, you have to *push through* the pain before the healing can begin."

Joseph just stared, frankly afraid to bring words to his mouth.

"First off, let's get on an even playing field. I'm Dr. Olsen, but you can call me Connie," she said as she pushed him into a large room filled with all kinds of exercise equipment. A few people were dutifully working out, one was on a treadmill, but most did not seem to notice their entrance. "No pretenses here. You can regard me as your physical therapist, your drill sergeant, your task master, or your friend . . . I don't really care—as long as you understand I'm here to help you recover. Now, let's take a look at your chart, shall we?"

Joseph gave a weak smile. *Like I'm going to say no,* he thought. He tried not to look nervous but wasn't sure how successful he was. Dr. Connie Olsen was one of the most intimidating women he'd ever met. In more ways than one!

After a few seconds of uncomfortable silence, Connie gave a low whistle. "A crushed skull, huh?"

Joseph lightly tapped his cranial plaster cast. "It's okay. There wasn't much inside to damage."

Connie's eyebrow raised a fraction. She turned back to the chart, read some more, then started to laugh. "Who filled out your demographics?"

"My mother. I was in a coma when I came in."

"English her second language?"

"Yeah."

"Ah. That makes sense. Have you read it?" she asked, still snickering.

"No. Why?"

"Under marital status she marked single, then wrote, 'Please find him a wife.'"

Joseph felt his face redden. "Great," he mumbled.

"Wow. Under education, I think she meant to say you graduated magna cum laude from UCSB; only, she wrote 'magma come loud'—like you're a volcano or something," she said through a grin so wide it was difficult to articulate. Then, seeing Joseph was not laughing, she sobered quickly. "I apologize, Joseph. I shouldn't laugh at your mother's writing. I was just going to say that your comment about not having much brain to damage is obviously false modesty."

Joseph smiled. "My mom tends to exaggerate everything. But thanks."

Therapist Connie then got down to business. "So, we know how well your brain works. Let's see how well the rest of you does." She hugged Joseph under his shoulders. "On three: one, two, three." With the ease of an Olympian weight lifter, she hoisted him out of the wheelchair. Joseph couldn't believe how firm her shoulders and arms felt. "You let me know of any issues with balance or undue pain."

She had Joseph latch onto a handrail resembling a ballet bar as she kicked his wheelchair out of reach. "Now, I've already told you I'm here to push you, and I plan on doing just that. But with a head trauma as extensive as yours, in addition to a broken leg and busted ribs, I don't want to put too much stress on your system. Not right away, at least."

Joseph nodded. Because of Connie's tight embrace, he couldn't draw enough breath to answer vocally.

"Okay. I'm going to let go now. Can you stand by yourself?"

"Won't know until I try," he wheezed.

"That's the spirit, Joe. Get things into perspective right away. I like it."

As Connie stepped away, Joseph held onto the bar with one hand and extended the other. The cast on his broken leg was fitted with a rubber nub on the bottom that allowed him to walk. He applied light pressure to it and was pleased at the lack of pain. He held his head up and released his grip on the bar. His head still felt uncomfortably heavy because of the skull cast, but overall his balance was unhindered.

"We're off to a great start," Connie announced. "A couple weeks under my care and you'll be able to chase down any woman you want for a wife."

Joseph closed his eyes and failed to suppress a humorless grimace. "Super."

"Oh yeah," Connie said, "I'm gonna make your mama proud."

CHAPTER 10

THE SANTA BARBARA BIRD REFUGE was located at the south end of Cabrillo Boulevard, just before the scenic beachfront road merged with Highway 101. It was a large, placid lagoon-like estuary surrounded by reeds, grass, and cypress trees. In the center of the sizable lagoon stood three small islands, each no more than twenty feet in diameter, and so overgrown with trees and vegetation you couldn't see any soil. They were the roosting sites for pelicans, terns, seagulls, sandpipers, and probably a dozen other bird species. From the west side of the lagoon, the estuary drained into the ocean via a narrow slough. On hot, windless days, the stink of decay, stagnation, and guano kept most visitors away from the protected area. But on cooler days, and on days with steady on- or offshore breezes, the secluded spot was quite pleasant and beautiful. And it was only two miles from the Ramirez home.

Estefan used to take his kids there to feed the assorted waterfowl bread crumbs and popcorn. It was a favorite place for all the children, especially young Joseph. Even though he had a fear of the dark, murky water, and of the more aggressive birds, he loved and envied the ducks, and the love they received from those who came to feed them. He didn't know where his fear of most birds came from, but he suspected it had something to do with their cold, inexpressive eyes, their sharp beaks, and their noisy cries and unpredictable nature. Perhaps it was nightmares he'd suffered after being forced to watch Hitchcock's *The Birds* one Halloween. But ducks were different; they loved him while other birds were always mean to him.

Young Joseph asked his father about the little islands every time they visited the bird refuge. What was on them? How big were they? Did the water ever wash over them? Was it possible to go out to them? Joseph's young, adventurous mind envisioned campouts and secret meetings held within the entangled branches, where no one could see his boyish plotting and scheming. The tiny island would be bird-free, of course, except for a few ducks. It would be *his* hideaway, his private fortress. He'd have unlimited resources, too. A rubber Zodiac landing boat, the kind Jacques Cousteau used on his TV specials; a complete set of boy-sized scuba gear, the kind Jonny Quest used on Saturday-morning cartoons; unlimited Hostess snack products; a soda pop dispenser; a comfortable bed; and, heck, why not a mini submarine, too?

Joseph and Antonio had planned to take a couple of inner tubes to one of the islands on numerous occasions. But they rarely made it further than stepping onto the banks of the lagoon at night. Joseph was too afraid of the many strange sounds and creepy shadows moving around the edge of the lagoon—and in and under the water. His older brother never forced the issue, but Joseph suspected he was a bit scared too.

When Joseph asked Papa the "island questions" on their next family outing, he seemed to hit a raw nerve. The fire that constantly smoldered in Papa's eyes suddenly ignited like a flamethrower. He growled and grabbed both sides of his head as if expecting his head to suddenly explode. "Not again! Why must you ask the same stupid questions over and over? There is nothing but trees, bushes, and bird crap out there!"

"He knows that, Papa," Emily said in her soft way. "He just likes to be sure."

Thirteen-year-old Emily flashed a warning look at her younger brother, but his curiosity was extra strong that day. As always, his thirst for understanding was unquenchable. Besides, Papa said never to doubt him because he was *always* right. So who better to ask? "But how do you know, Papa? Have you ever been out there?"

"Don't be a fool. Of course not."

"Are there many nests out there?"

"Probably."

"But Papa, what if the tide rises? How do you know all the baby birds won't drown?"

Estefan closed his eyes and pulled at his hair while letting out a second growl. He took several deep breaths with his fists balled on either side of his head. After a minute, he relaxed his grip, pulled out a comb, and raked his greasy hair back in place. "I'll tell you what I know, José. I know of other fathers who have taken their sons out there when they misbehave and ask too many questions. Then they leave them overnight with the birds and snakes and all that black water." There was a hateful gleam in his eyes as he spoke to his son. "I'm beginning to think that's not a bad idea."

"Papa, you shouldn't tease him like that," Emily said with her fists on her hips.

"I have to, little princess," Estefan said, looking down at his daughter. "José is not like other boys his age. He's not very bright, you see? He keeps asking many, many questions. So I have to make things easy for him to understand."

He spoke loudly, obviously not caring that Joseph was standing right beside him.

"José is too bright," she shot back. "He's just very curious about things. That's why he asks so many questions."

"Yes, about stupid things that have no importance!" Estefan snapped.

"About *everything,* Papa!" she hollered right back.

Joseph cringed at the way his older sister talked back to their father. He wouldn't dare speak to him that way. It would earn him a punishment. But Emily seemed to get away with it, though she was wise enough not to do it too often.

Luckily, Papa did not lash out at Emily. Instead, he tenderly cupped her cheek and winked. "You're a good girl, Emilita. You take after your mama so much. Now, let's feed the ducks, okay?"

"Okay, Papa. Come on, José."

"No," Estefan said harshly. "José, you stay here and watch those little islands you keep asking about, and think about living there for the rest of your life if you can't be good."

The thought of banishment to one of those overgrown islands presented a mix of images completely opposite from his previous adventure-rich daydreams. The dank, twisted tree roots now looked menacing, dangerous, even hungry. And then there were the birds, too.

"Okay, Papa," was Joseph's small reply. "I'll be good."

Emily was about to say something, but her father grabbed her hand and quickly led her away. Joseph watched his father and Emily walk hand in hand toward a group of children feeding a large gathering of waterbirds. When they got ten yards away, Emily turned to look back at Joseph. When she did, Estefan yanked her arm to spin her back around. The two kept walking away, leaving Joseph by himself. After a few paces, Emily reached her free hand behind her back and crooked her index finger to entice her brother to follow.

Joseph hesitated. Papa would be furious if he disobeyed. But what if a bird approached him wanting food, and he had none to give it? It would get mad. It might attack. Tears balanced on Joseph's lashes as he watched his father and sister move farther away. He took a tentative step toward them then stopped. No. As much as he wanted to join them, it was better to stay right where Papa told him to stay.

He turned his attention back to the islands and forced his mind to re-create the images of adventure and happiness. It took some doing, but after a while he could imagine a Swiss Family Robinson home on the small island. Xavier and Antonio were there. So was Emily. They looked very happy. They beckoned for Joseph to join them. Slowly, his tears dried. He took a step toward the water. Just as he was about to smile, an enormous brown pelican passed just inches above his head. Reflexively, he flinched, tripped, and fell hard—

* * *

Joseph jerked and opened his eyes. It was dark—darker than normal. It was also stuffy, smothering. He gasped for breath and flung his arms about. Twisted bedsheets flew off him, exposing his hospital room, which was cast in a monochromatic, nocturnal glow. Forcing his breathing and heart rate to steady, he sat up and looked around.

All was as it should be. Clyde lay softly snoring in the next bed. Soft light filtered in from the hallway. His clock read 3:13 AM.

As he lay back and dropped his chin, a tear trickled down his cheek. He wiped it away, surprised to realize he'd been crying. He tried to recall why but couldn't. It was his dream—some event from his childhood, an experience that had bothered him then and apparently still did. But try as he might, he could not recall what the dream had been about.

He adjusted his bedsheets, fluffed his pillow, and lay back down. He closed his eyes and tried to think of pleasant things. He was only partially successful. If his dream had been about his childhood, then it would all be new to him. He didn't know why he couldn't remember anything from his early years—he'd never been able to. As a science teacher, Joseph acknowledged that there might well be a medical—or psychological—reason he couldn't. It was a fact he'd lived with for a long time. And up until now, it had never really bothered him. But it did now. Deeply.

Perhaps it was time to finally resolve the issue once and for all—a prospect that, strangely, sat in his stomach like a tangle of barbed wire.

CHAPTER 11

The following day, Principal Samuel Card entered the room with a small bouquet of gladiolas. He was smiling, but Joseph thought it looked forced. His mannerisms were out of sorts, as if he was unsure how to act around a man who'd been in a coma for almost a month.

"Flowers? You *know* I prefer chocolates," Joseph said in mock censure.

"I tried, but the staff here says you're on a restricted diet," the principal explained.

"Ah, don't worry about it," Joseph chuckled. "It's great to see you, Sam."

"Yeah, you too. I thought you'd never come out of that coma. You scared the heck out of me, Joseph."

"Is that why you look so . . . uncomfortable?" he asked his boss. "Or are you here to tell me I'm fired?"

Samuel guffawed. "Hardly."

"Excommunicated, then?"

"Not yet," he said with a wink.

In addition to being the principal of the new Solvang Middle School, Samuel Card was also bishop of the Solvang Ward of the LDS Church. Because of that, Joseph had to constantly remember when to call him bishop or principal and often ended up just calling him Sam. His friend didn't seem to mind.

Samuel was an affable man with an easy manner that hid a deeply compassionate, very intelligent individual. He was of medium height and build but carried himself with the confidence of a giant. That's why his current awkward smile and hesitant movements seemed so out of place.

"Not yet, huh?" Joseph mused. "Good, then I still have a chance to repent."

The bishop/principal winked again. "Better make it quick."

Joseph liked this man immensely. He had been instrumental in Joseph's conversion and, perhaps more importantly, his retention in the Church. Like many new members, Joseph had been tracted out by the missionaries then converted soon after. At first, Joseph struggled with fitting in with his new affiliations. He had no problem believing the principles of the gospel or following the commandments, but he was somewhat intimidated by the overwhelming expectations of the members. It was as if they assumed he would come out of the baptismal water fully versed in the Mormon way of life. Quite frankly, the culture hit him like a tidal wave.

He quickly learned that the Mormons had their own mannerisms, class distinctions, and worst of all, language. Words with alternate meanings like *beehives, sunbeams, laurels, ward, stake, temple, fast Sunday,* and others were volleyed like tennis balls launched from an automated server. It was suggested that Joseph attend the Los Olivos Spanish Branch in Santa Barbara to begin with, but he declined the invitation. He wanted to become part of his local LDS family. He had visited the Mesa Oaks Ward in Lompoc once and the Solvang Ward several times during his conversion, and they'd each welcomed the new schoolteacher with open arms.

"We love new members," Bishop Card had explained, "but membership, at first, can be daunting. Just take one thing at a time and don't worry if you don't understand everything or feel like you're measuring up. Mormons, as a people, have a knack for perfection complexes. We're all human, Brother Ramirez. Accept that fact and you're halfway to perfection already."

Joseph smiled as he watched Samuel place the flowers on the counter adjacent to his bed and then stuff his hands in his pockets.

"So is this a school district visit or a Church assignment?" Joseph joked.

"How about a friendship call?" Sam suggested.

"Even better," Joseph said happily. "How're things back home? Wife and kids good, I assume? Everything at the school okay?"

Sam nodded the affirmative to each question.

"So . . . why the long face?"

His friend chuckled and waved off the question as inconsequential. "Oh . . . you know. Pressures of life, I guess. I'm getting phone calls and hate notes about the increase in property taxes to fund the new school—like it was solely my decision to do that. In spite of that, we're already over budget, and we're only halfway through the term." He grimaced and rubbed the back of his neck. "I shouldn't admit this, but sometimes I get tired of all the stupid things I have to endure as principal . . . and as bishop."

"Stupid things?"

"Well, perhaps *stupid* isn't the best word. Petty? Trifling? Banal? Basically things that are minor in significance but are blown into national crises because people are too myopic to see the big picture and figure things out for themselves."

Joseph smiled. "Like . . . ?"

"I wish I could unload some of this on you, but I can't." Sam shook his head.

"Probably do you some good, you know."

"Well . . ." His friend leaned closer. "Without revealing names, there's a certain teacher at a certain middle school who says he's not going to teach anymore unless we move the drinking fountain to the other side of the hall, because listening to the constant trickle of water makes him have to run to the restroom every thirty minutes."

Joseph rolled his eyes. "Mr. Thompson."

Samuel blinked. "Okay, then there's a certain sister in a certain ward who is sending letters to the First Presidency asking them to allow her Bichon Frise lapdog to be sealed to her in the temple, because she can't stand the thought of spending eternity without him."

"Sister Anders?"

"Dang it! See, I can't tell you anything," Samuel complained with a grin. "Sometimes I envy that coma you've been in."

"Wouldn't work, Sam. When you woke up, the challenging people would still be there—only more desperate and harried because you'd been unavailable for so long."

Both men laughed knowingly. It felt good to open up and purge frustrations through laughter. Usually, Sam was the sounding board on which everyone would vent their grievances, but today the roles were reversed. Joseph was glad his friend felt comfortable enough to open up like he had, even if it was just a little.

"Too true, Joseph." Sam continued to chuckle.

"So, Mr. Principal, *is* everything okay at school?"

"Don't even worry about it, *Mr. Ramirez*. We've got your classes covered, although the kids keep telling me the subs are boring compared to you."

Joseph warmed inside thinking of his students and the connection he had with them. He loved how their eyes lit up when they grasped the concepts he was sharing. Joseph instilled in his kids his infectious enthusiasm for learning. He constantly encouraged questions, pushed for enlightenment, and rewarded curiosity. He loved teaching science more than anything in the world and couldn't understand how teachers could ever make the subject boring.

"Tell my kids I'm sorry and that I'll be back as soon as I can." Despite his best effort to sound jovial and optimistic, Joseph's words came out with an edge of trepidation.

"Sure, Joseph." Sam nodded. He paused and searched Joseph's face with kindly eyes. "Now . . . how about we be totally honest with each other, and you tell me how you're *really* feeling."

"I'm doing fine, *Bishop*. I know I look like I've been run over by a truck—literally—but I feel okay. The leg's not throbbing, ribs are still sore but not really painful, head's coming along . . . okay."

Samuel Card slowly folded his arms and asked, "Just okay?"

Joseph sighed and glanced over at Clyde. His roommate was into a hockey game via TV and headset.

"I'm having these . . . these weird dreams," Joseph told his bishop. "Scary stuff that wakes me up in the middle of the night. Only, I can't remember what they're about."

"You asked the doctors about it?"

"Yeah. They're not sure. Gonna run a bunch of tests, so we'll see."

Bishop Card stood silently as if pondering Joseph's statement. "You're thinking it's from your accident? Or something else?"

"I don't know," he sighed. "I never used to have bad dreams *before* I got hit."

"Anything I can do?"

Joseph nodded. "How about a blessing?"

Bishop Samuel Card smiled warmly. "I'd be honored." He rounded the bed, closed the curtain separating Joseph's side of the room from Clyde's, then pulled out a small vial from a pocket. Joseph's full cranial plaster prevented the bishop from daubing the crown of Joseph's head. Instead he placed a small drop on Joseph's forehead just below the cast then placed his hands on Joseph's head and took a steadying breath.

After the blessing, Joseph felt better. He knew he'd heal just fine . . . physically. But he still had concerns about the strange recollections he was having. Somehow he knew something life-changing was about to happen, something that had to do with the childhood he couldn't remember. Strangely, regrettably, he knew it wouldn't be a pleasant journey.

CHAPTER 12

Joseph felt himself falling headfirst. He wasn't sure from where, but he could see a sidewalk approaching fast. He flailed his arms in a futile attempt to slow his descent. Wind pummeled his face and tore at his clothes. He tried to scream but could not draw enough breath to make the sound; a plaintive, raspy wheeze was all he could manage. Broad squares of concrete raced toward him. There were no decorative trees or shrubs in his path—nothing to arrest his fall or soften his landing.

Mustering all his willpower, he finally sucked in enough air to let out a sustained, panicked cry. The speckled white-gray cement continued to rush upward. He curled into a ball, still falling. His wheezing turned into a fervent whimper, increasing in pitch with each exhalation. He tried to draw one last huge breath to brace for impact but only got in a quick gasp before—

* * *

Joseph bolted upright and gagged on a scream. His bed was rocking, swaying as if it had just stopped a rapidly moving object. He was struggling for breath with abrupt, staccato gasps. Sweat poured from his body and face. His heart felt ready to burst from his chest, his lungs burning, aching. His hands shook uncontrollably. The wound on his scalp crawled, as if the sutures were maggots squirming in and out of the hot, swollen flesh.

Outside, the moon cast a cadaverous glow through the open blinds. The light from the hospital hallway was musty and flat.

His bedside clock read 1:21 AM. Joseph tried to sit up but found his muscles would not comply. He was totally exhausted.

He toggled the controller on his bed frame to rise into a sitting position. Thankfully, the new position helped him breathe somewhat easier. After wiping his face and neck with his bedsheet, he cast a glance toward his roommate.

Clyde was lying on his side, facing Joseph. The older man's eyes were wide with alarm. He stared at Joseph, shrinking from him as if he were a hideous beast.

"You okay, Clyde?" Joseph asked softly, his voice still shaky and raw.

The older man nodded.

"Did I wake you?"

Another nod. "You could say that."

"Sorry about that. Guess I was having a bad dream."

Clyde swallowed hard. "They're getting worse."

"Getting worse?" Joseph knew he was having nightmares, but he had no idea they were being manifested outside his head. And even if they were, he couldn't fathom *what* was being manifested. Almost fearing the answer, he asked, "What makes you say that?"

Clyde stared in silence for a moment. "First, tell me if *you're* okay," he said, easing out from under his blanket.

Joseph rubbed his eyes and took a deep breath. "Yeah, I'm fine. Just a little spent. Why?"

Clyde adjusted his bed to a sitting position that matched Joseph's. "You scare the crap out of me, kid, I don't mind telling you. The first couple of times you were just fussing and groaning a lot. I figured you was just reliving your car wreck. But lately you've been saying things out loud, calling out names, even cursing and screaming. It happens almost every night—sometimes two or three times a night."

"You serious? What in the world do I say?" Joseph asked with a forced chuckle, trying to lighten the mood in the dark room.

A look of distrust crossed Clyde's face and settled in his eyes. He scowled. "You tellin' me you don't remember?"

"Only bits and pieces. Like the one I just had: I was falling from somewhere in a city toward a cement sidewalk. When I hit, I woke up."

"And you don't remember what was going on before that?"

Joseph concentrated a moment but came up blank. "Uh-uh."

Clyde locked a critical gaze on Joseph for nearly a minute. His expression was a mix of skeptical judgment and guarded accusation. "Well, perhaps it's better to keep it that way."

"Why? What have I been revealing about my sordid past?" Joseph asked flippantly. "Exposing some of my darkest, most appalling secrets?"

Clyde's gaze intensified. A few times it looked like he was going to speak, but he didn't. He then glanced at his bedside clock and stretched. "It's pretty late, Joe. Let's take this up tomorrow," he said, lowering his bed and turning his back to his roommate.

"Wait. Clyde?"

The older man did not answer.

"Hey," he whispered loudly.

Clyde still did not respond.

Joseph lowered his bed and stared at the acoustic ceiling tiles. His heart rate had stabilized, and his breathing had steadied. But because of Clyde, he was even more anxious than before—not so much at what the man had said as *how* he'd said it.

To distract himself from that issue, Joseph tried to place the location of the dream he'd just experienced. Downtown Santa Barbara? Maybe. But most of the sidewalks there had traditional Spanish tile insets and other decorative features that gave the downtown area a distinctive flavor. He didn't remember that detail in the dream, but he couldn't be sure. Cautiously, he tried to replay the dream in his head, but the only thing he could recall was plummeting toward off-white concrete—

Wait a minute . . . On second thought, he wasn't even sure if *he* was the one falling. It almost seemed as if he were experiencing the tragedy vicariously.

For as long as he could remember, Joseph had only two fears: one of birds and one of heights. The first one seemed silly, especially for a science teacher. The second fear was a debilitating—at times nausea-inducing—fear that predicated a lot of his daily life. If he was walking on a balcony, he hugged the wall opposite the railing. If he was in a building higher than two stories, he avoided the windows. And he never flew anywhere. Once again, something from his childhood had frightened him so badly he could not shake the lingering, residual fear. It was his acrophobia that had made his latest dream a virtual nightmare.

After a minute's hesitation, he depressed the call-nurse button. He had to have *something* to help him sleep—even if that meant an addictive pill. A night nurse Joseph didn't recognize answered the call and asked what he needed. When he expressed his concerns, she said, "How about a Benadryl? They're OTC and nonaddictive."

"Thanks," Joseph said, liking the idea.

A moment later the nurse returned with a pill in a small paper cup. With a sip of water, Joseph swallowed it and thanked her again. The nurse nodded and left.

Before settling into bed, Joseph clasped his hands and bowed his head. He asked God to help him cope with the trials he was going through. He asked that his family be comforted and assured that he would recover fully. Then he ended his prayer as he always did with, "Nevertheless, Thy will be done."

CHAPTER 13

THREE DAYS LATER, JOSEPH FELT stronger, more alert, but still very much in need of rest. His trail of sleeping pills lasted only two nights. When Joseph took the first one, he ended up sleeping through most of the following day. The hospital pharmacist explained that medications have a greater effect on people who are not used to taking them, especially drugs that affect the CNS. At the pharmacist's suggestion, Joseph tried one more, hoping the prolonged effect was a first-dose quirk. No such luck. He awoke the following day at the crack of noon. He opted not to repeat the dosing. He'd simply try to relax on his own, yet it did little good. *Just my dumb luck,* he said to himself. He was in particular need of coherency that afternoon.

Presently, two lawyers stood at his bedside. Only one of them was smiling.

Attorney Michelle Haas, Joseph's lawyer designate, was there at the suggestion of the Santa Barbara School District main office. Although she did mostly freelance contract law for the school board, she occasionally offered pro bono and contingent fee work for schoolteachers in need of legal assistance.

She had told Joseph his case appealed to her for three reasons: First, she had grown up spending her summers in Solvang with her grandmother, and she still had a soft spot in her heart for the Danish community. Second, she hated the law firm of Stansbury, Vail, and Jenkins—a big-money office rumored to specialize in covering up billion-dollar corporate dirty laundry. And third, she absolutely loathed the sleazy legal representative SVJ had assigned to this case.

Michelle took her time reading every word of the document Attorney Brick Wiseman had brought with him.

"As you'll readily surmise, it's a standard reduced-fault acknowledgment," Brick said smoothly to his female opponent.

"Um-hm," Michelle mumbled in reply.

Turning to Joseph, Brick continued. "You've hired a great attorney, Mr. Ramirez. I've known Ms. Haas since law school down at UCLA. She was in the class just behind mine—a stand-out student, always at the top of her class. We even dated a few times. Believe you me, we were quite the item. I mean, look at her: tall, slender, very pretty. Yes, sir, she turned more than a few heads, I can bear witness. Still does, I'm sure. As I recall, her specialty was real estate law. Now she's in business or contract law or some-such, but I'm sure she'll do fine with a small personal injury case such as yours."

"Once," Michelle voiced flatly.

Both men stared at Ms. Haas, waiting for more, but nothing came.

"Excuse me?" Joseph finally said.

She flipped a page and read a bit before speaking. "We dated *once*. We were never an item."

An awkward silence followed as the men in the room watched her finish the legal brief. She then adjusted the stack, aligning the edges by tapping them lightly on the adjustable table next to Joseph's bed.

"Well? What do you think?" Joseph asked.

Michelle smiled at him. "Well, this is no 'small injury case,'" she said calmly, moving her gaze to Brick.

"Of course that's always subject to debate," Brick replied with equal composure. "You are welcome to draft a reply which we will gladly exami—"

"Great," she interrupted, holding up the legal brief and tearing it in half.

The sound of shredded paper seemed to ricochet off the walls and hang in the air.

"Ms. Haas. That was totally uncalled for," Brick Wiseman blustered.

"Oh, yes it was," she replied. "A. You accuse my client of entering the intersection before the traffic light turned green. Caltrans video clearly shows five cars making the turn *before* him, verifying that the light *was* green and that he had the right-of-way. I've already seen the clip.

"B. You state his initial drug screen was questioned by the attending physician, implying that my client may have been under the influence. However, in reviewing the follow-up, my client's drug panels came back crystal clear with no indication of *any* drug in his system—not even any caffeine or nicotine. This undoubtedly stems from his religious convictions, and, being a teacher, certain conduct codes enforced by the California Board of Education.

"C. Missing from your brief is the fact that the driver of the Sierra West Construction truck *was* under the influence. He was in a state of euphoria brought on by drinking numerous cans of Tribe energy drink—Dingo's Dance, in particular."

"It's a perfectly legal beverage with no restrictions on driving after drinking," Brick replied, as if he were stating the obvious to an obstinate child.

"That's a matter of debate—one I'd gladly contest in court, Mr. Wiseman," she said in a steady, metered tone. "And D. There's the fact that the driver—a Mr. Eddie Foy—was operating heavy machinery with an expired CDL. In all, Mr. Wiseman, you don't have much of *anything* substantial with which to argue who caused the accident. And by implying in your inane brief that my client was even partially to blame is not only laughable, it's morally reprehensible."

Wiseman's slimy smile widened another inch. Jerking his head toward Clyde, he said, "I believe you just violated your attorney-client privilege with those details, counselor."

Michelle scoffed. "Those same facts are in yesterday's newspaper. I'm just pointing out how sophomoric your brief is."

"A lot of highly paid time and consideration went into the preparation of that brief, Ms. Haas. It's anything but sophomoric."

"Listen. Brick," Michelle said with a slight crinkle forming at the corner of her eyes. "Let's not banter fact with fallacy. You and I both know you're grabbing at straws. My client was almost killed by your client's negligence. My client may have as-yet-to-be-manifest brain damage. He's lost over a hundred hours of work time, not to mention the physical and emotional stress he continues to endure."

"Each of those points can be argued," Brick huffed. "We have an excellent staff of physicians and specialists who have dealt with this kind of accident hundreds of times. We're awaiting their evaluation, but I assure you their findings regarding your client's inconveniences won't be as gratuitous as you imply they are. I'm equally sure a judge will agree with our assessments."

"So you're saying you *want* this to go to court?" Michelle asked with raised eyebrows.

"Not necessarily. I'm saying that to tear up our treatise was childish and meant solely to impress your client with Hollywood theatrics."

Michelle was wide-eyed and slack-jawed as she picked up the halves of legal brief. She looked more than baffled—she looked appalled.

"Mr. Wiseman. Please take this joke back to your office and have your highly paid staff try to draft something less offensive and much closer to the truth." She shoved the paperwork into Brick's hands. "If you come back with a sugarcoating of the same manure, please print it on something soft, absorbent, and two-ply so my client can put it to a beneficial use."

Across the room, Clyde Richter burst out in a loud guffaw. Joseph smiled broadly at the flush-faced lawyer as he gathered up the papers and exited the room.

With eyes closed, Michelle let out a slow, steady expulsion of air. Joseph thought he saw a slight tremor in her hands. He had only met Michelle that afternoon, but he already knew he had someone who truly cared about helping him.

"You think they will come back with something better?" Joseph asked.

Michelle nodded. "Oh yeah. They don't have a leg to stand on, Mr. Ramirez. Once they realize they can't bamboozle you, you'll be set for life."

"Please, it's Joseph. And I don't care about being set for life. I like the idea of working for my living. Believe it or not, I love teaching. No offense, ma'am, but I believe there's not a more noble or life-influencing profession on earth."

She smiled. "I agree with you, Joseph. But nobility doesn't always pay the bills, now does it?"

"That depends on your lifestyle. I'm perfectly happy keeping things simple."

The impressed look in Michelle's eyes showed a good mix of surprise, respect, and . . . and what? *Admiration? Delight?*

"Joe, don't be a fool," Clyde cried. "If you don't want the money, give it to charity. Heck, give it to me. But you gotta make 'em pay!"

Joseph pinched the bridge between his eyes and took in a prolonged, deep breath. "I'll consider it. What do you have in mind, Ms. Haas?"

"Sierra West Construction is definitely responsible for all medical expenses, lost salary, and your car. It's the things beyond that where it gets tricky—and potentially very lucrative."

Joseph shrugged. "Like I said, if my medical needs are covered for the next few months, I'll be content."

Michelle stared at him long and hard, the stunned look still shining in her eyes. She nodded. "Whatever you say, Mr. Ramirez."

"Joseph," he corrected.

"Okay. Joseph. You have my card. I'll go draw up a proposal for SVJ and Sierra West Construction. You don't worry about a thing. If Mr. Wiseman calls, tell him you have nothing to say without my being present. And don't you dare sign anything unless I'm here."

"Yes, Ms. Haas."

"Michelle," she corrected in turn.

"Michelle, then."

"Good. Do you have any questions before I go?"

Joseph grinned. "Yeah. Did you really date that snake?"

"'Snake' is being too kind, but I'm afraid it's true. Once. He paraded me around a frat party. Every time he'd place his hand where it didn't belong, I'd punch him in the shoulder. But it kept happening. So I finally told him the next time I'd aim for his face. He ended up with a sore shoulder, a black eye, and a very bruised ego." Her shoulders shook as if trying to shed cold water. "Anything else, Joseph?"

"No," Joseph chuckled. "But thanks."

Michelle Haas left quickly in a confident stride. Joseph thought he could detect a hint of a perfume lingering behind—a soft yet asser-tive fragrance.

"Holy cow, I think I'm in love," Clyde announced.

"What—with a lawyer?" Joseph asked with a wide grin.

"Yeah, but one with real spunk. Boy, if I was ten years younger, she'd be a potential new Mrs. Richter. I tell you what, Joe: you know I don't care much for lawyers, but that one's a firecracker with teeth and claws and brains—and a figure to boot."

"Easy there, Clyde. Think of your blood pressure."

"I am."

"But . . . she's half your age."

"So? That makes me twice the man for her."

Joseph laughed in spite of himself. "So you think that means you could catch her?"

"Chasing women's what keeps me alive, boy. You should try it."

"It's probably also what keeps you in divorce court," Joseph said.

Clyde laughed heartily. "Yeah. Maybe so, Joe. Maybe so."

CHAPTER 14

A YOUNG NURSE NAMED MISTY wheeled Joseph into a room with what looked like a dental chair positioned in the center. The nurse helped him settle in the chair and tipped it back about forty-five degrees. "The doctor will be here shortly," she announced with a radiant smile.

"Thank you," was Joseph's listless reply. He had not slept well again, waking up after another bad dream had scared him to death and put him in a cold sweat. He still had no recollection of its content.

Twenty minutes later, Dr. Lindley entered and, without acknowledging Joseph's presence, began washing his hands.

"Am I getting my teeth cleaned today, doc?" Joseph jested.

The doctor answered in his usual droll voice. "Your last set of X-rays looked great, so I'm going to remove a crown."

Confused, Joseph said, "But—I don't have any crowns."

The doctor walked over and tapped the hard plaster on Joseph's head. "This one."

It was the closest thing to humor Joseph had heard from the physician.

Joseph chuckled. "Oh good, the itching is driving me batty."

"That'd be the nerves reestablishing themselves in your scalp and your hair growing back," the doctor explained as he switched on a palm-sized saw with a narrow circular blade attached. It looked and sounded very much like a dentist's drill. Though he had no cavities, the high-pitched whir made Joseph's teeth crawl.

In a matter of minutes, the doctor had made two complete breaks in the thin plaster and gently tugged until the gauze separated from

Joseph's head. Sudden, burning pain flashed across his scalp as the dressing took with it stubs of hair, clotted scabs, and a little skin. But once it was off, Joseph couldn't believe how light his head felt. He instantly forgot the pain. The pressure inside his skull even felt less debilitating.

He raised his hand to feel his head, but Dr. Lindley stopped him. "Don't touch it just yet, Mr. Ramirez. I have to debride it a bit and dress the suture."

"Can I see it?"

The doctor handed him a small vanity mirror. "Don't be too shocked."

Even with the doctor's warning, Joseph flinched. An angry, swollen scar ran from his hairline to somewhere near the base of his skull. Crisscrossing the scar was a lacing of stout sutures crusted with blood. The taut stitches blanched the skin and created irregular bumps and creases along the surgical site. The pale, bunched tissue stood a good eighth of an inch above the rest of his scalp. It looked like something out of a Dean Koontz novel.

"The swelling will go down eventually, but I'm afraid you'll always have a scar," the neurologist explained. "If we keep it moist and tight, it won't be much more than a narrow line. Luckily, the scalp doesn't move much, so there won't be any undue stress on the sutures, which will reduce the incidence of scar tissue buildup. Besides, with your thick head of hair, no one will ever notice."

Joseph fought the urge to touch the hideous disfigurement on his head. It itched like the dickens! He stared at it from as many angles as he could and determined that the doctor was right: already his hair was growing back and would soon overgrow the incision.

"I hope my hair grows fast," he mumbled while still frowning at the appalling wound.

"That's a wish I've had for a long time," Dr. Lindley replied. *Joke number two? Both in the same day? Impossible.*

The doctor then applied an antibiotic ointment and covered the area with light gauze that wrapped around Joseph's head to hold the ointment in place. "Any more issues with bad dreams or memory flashes?"

"Yes. They seem to be getting worse, too. But I don't know what can be done about it."

Dr. Lindley made a note in Joseph's chart. "Looks like this has been happening ever since you regained consciousness," he mumbled to himself. "How about your physical issues?"

"No problem there. I'm not bothered with headaches, nausea, vision changes, bowel issues, or real pain," he said, highlighting the areas he knew the neurologist was going to pinpoint.

The physician nodded. "Excellent. Your recovery is quite astounding."

"Comes from clean living," Joseph replied.

Dr. Lindley smirked and left the room. A moment later, Nurse Misty entered and helped Joseph into his wheelchair. As she pushed him toward his room, Joseph asked, "Hey, do I have to go right back?"

The nurse paused. "No, I don't think so. Why?"

"Could you wheel me someplace outside? I've been cooped inside this hospital for days—and that doesn't include my coma."

"There are windows everywhere, including in your room," she argued.

"It's not the same and you know it," Joseph said flatly.

The nurse bit her lower lip and looked behind her as if expecting to be followed. "I . . . I'm not sure I'm allowed to . . ."

Joseph turned as much as possible and looked up at her. She was in her early twenties, with big cheerful brown eyes and short streaked hair. Her golden-brown skin identified her as a sun-worshiper. "Is that a spray-on tan?" he asked with a grin.

"No way," she huffed. "That stuff's a joke."

"Then you understand where I'm coming from. Come on, Misty. Please?"

The young nurse smiled. Her brown eyes twinkled with mischief. "Well . . . okay. But only for a minute."

Heading down a side hallway, the two escapees went down an elevator to the first floor and exited through a side door near the outpatient pharmacy.

The warmth of the sun caressed Joseph's face with featherlike tenderness. His naturally olive-brown skin glowed bronze in the solar rays. His jet black hair, even as nubs, shimmered with deep purple-blue highlights. Joseph tipped his head back and reveled in the sunlight and fresh air. He had grown up outdoors, and the sensation of no walls and no artificial lighting brought back feelings of comfort and happiness to his soul. Having lived only a couple miles from the beach, most of his later memories involved sand between his toes, the smell of brine and seaweed, and the cries of gulls and sandpipers. Memories before that remained locked away, but Joseph was certain they were similar to what he was currently feeling.

Outside of St. Luke's, the temperature was about seventy-eight degrees, he guessed. He closed his eyes and stretched out his arms, soaking in the delicious warmth. A soft breeze caused the leaves in the ficus trees to tap and flutter, and the fronds in the palms to scrape noisily. Breathing deeply, he caught the salty tang of the ocean only three miles away. Light clouds heading inland offered scant shade from the sun, but Joseph didn't mind. Being outside was rejuvenating, almost intoxicating, and astoundingly healing.

The young nurse chose a cement bench on which to sit and leaned back with her eyes closed, her chin pointed toward the sun, and her legs stretched out in front of her. Joseph was certain she too acknowledged the day as glorious.

After a moment, Joseph quietly coaxed his wheelchair down the walkway toward the front of the hospital. Passing a small parking section, he paused at the hissing sound of two-way radio static. Easing around a massive cluster of Mediterranean fan palms, he happened on a police cruiser parked in a handicap stall. An officer sat inside reading something while the car's engine purred deeply.

A sudden, unbidden memory transported Joseph back in time: flashing lights—red and blue; the blinding whiteness of high-beams; the static crackle of numerous two-way radios; the mumble of low conversation; an occasional swear word; flashlights sweeping his family's house and yard; gloomy shapes; silhouettes of cops moving about in the harsh, angular lights; inquisitive neighbors peering over low chain-link fences.

It was past midnight. The air was dark and chilled.

Standing on his porch in briefs and a tank tee, ten-year-old Joseph was shaking from fright and cold and pain. With arms folded across his frail chest, he trembled uncontrollably. The right side of his face was scratched, his wrists were red and raw, and his left elbow was swollen to about twice its normal size. Spent tears stained his cheeks.

A few yards away, clutching his little sister to her chest, Mama was also in tears. A large bruise had formed under her left eye, her lips still seeping blood from a fresh split. Baby Victoria had her face buried in Mama's shoulder and was crying. A police officer was trying to communicate with Joseph's mother in a mix of English and Spanish. In a state of near hysteria, Mama seemed to have forgotten most of her English.

A large officer approached young Joseph. The bright lights behind the man amplified his size and increased his sense of foreboding. Joseph backed flat against the door frame. His trembling increased, causing his knees to knock together.

"Take it easy, son," the officer said in a soft voice. "I just need to ask you a couple of questions. *Hablas ingles?*"

Joseph nodded slowly.

The officer sat heavily on the porch step with his back to Joseph and looked out at the flashing lights. "They're kinda pretty in a way, aren't they? The lights, I mean."

Joseph nodded again.

Turning, the man smiled. It was a natural, unforced expression. "Just a guess, but I bet you're not used to being up at one in the morning, are you? You must be freezing too. Would you like a blanket?"

A slight hesitation, then a third nod came.

Speaking into a microphone clipped to his shoulder, the officer made the request. Tapping his badge, he said, "My name is Officer Bird. Can you believe that? Do I look like a bird to you?"

Joseph shook his head.

"I mean, look at me," the cop continued, "I'm as big as a rhino, for heaven's sake. Kinda silly to be named after some tiny little thing that hops around the yard looking for bugs and worms, don't you think? Especially because I hate the taste of worms."

A small smile flashed across Joseph's face. "That's gross," he whispered.

"Tell me about it!" The man laughed and resumed watching the ordered chaos in the front yard. He leaned forward and rested his elbows on his knees. "Man, I could sure use a Hershey bar about now, how about you?"

"*Sí.*"

"Okay. Tell you what: you answer me a couple of questions, and I'll make sure you get a big one. Deal?"

Joseph stood his ground, still unsure if he could trust this guy. So many of his neighbors always said such terrible things about cops. But this one seemed nice enough. And he had a friendly voice and a warm smile.

"Listen, you know my name is Officer Bird. Your mom says yours is José, right?"

"*Sí,*" he said softy. "José Ramirez."

Just then, a second policeman walked up with a gray wool blanket in hand. His face was anything but friendly. He extended the blanket toward Joseph with an expression that revealed his distaste for the menial task. The man frightened Joseph enough that he pressed tightly against the doorjamb once more.

"Look, do you want this or not?" the officer snapped.

"I got it," Officer Bird said, reaching for the blanket. Shaking it out and holding it open, he said, "Come on, José. Let's get you warm first."

Joseph waited for the second cop to go before he inched forward. Officer Bird draped the blanket around Joseph's shoulders and let it hang. He then patted the empty porch next to him before resting his elbows on his knees again. Joseph sat on the porch but as far away from the big policeman as possible.

Still not making eye contact, Officer Bird asked, "How'd you hurt your arm?"

Joseph didn't answer. He was too scared to.

"It looks pretty sore to me," the officer said. "We'll get that looked at right away. So, José, do you know where your dad is?"

Joseph hesitated before answering. He was afraid he'd get in trouble if he said *anything*. Yet he felt he could trust this man enough to answer his questions—as long as they didn't involve too much about his father. "No, *señor.*"

"That's okay. You getting warmer yet?"

Joseph nodded.

"Has he been gone long—your dad, I mean?"

"About an hour."

"Do you have other brothers or sisters?"

"*Sí.*"

"Where are they right now?"

Joseph shrugged. When his father had burst into the house yelling incoherently, they had all bolted for the backdoor. Having awakened from a deep sleep in his room, Joseph wasn't quick enough to make his exit. His father had grabbed him by the wrist, smacked him on the side of his head for struggling, and dragged him around the house until they found his mother asleep in the girls' bedroom. When Estefan reached for her, Joseph tried to wrench free but couldn't break from Papa's grasp. When Papa yanked him back, his elbow popped, and he felt a sharp pain shoot up his arm. Mama had awakened and immediately tried to loosen her husband's grip on their son. A struggle ensued with Joseph in the middle. Yanked, pulled, and smashed, Joseph finally broke free and, cradling his hurt arm, ran for the backdoor. Just outside, he frantically scanned the small backyard. There was no way he could scale the fence. He'd have to run around front or . . . what? He paused, unsure what to do. When Papa yelled for him to come back, Joseph bolted.

Hiding under the overgrown shrubbery bordering the house, he had curled into a ball and covered his ears to block out the terrible sounds he knew were coming.

"Are your brothers and sisters hiding near the house?" Officer Bird asked.

"No, *señor*. They ran away."

"To where?"

"I don't know. Friends maybe. Maybe to the ravine. We sometimes play down there."

"Do you think they are safe?" The officer sounded truly concerned.

"I think so. *Sí.*"

"That's good," Officer Bird sighed. "My first concern is always for the children in situations like this. Does you elbow still hur—"

* * *

A woman's voice snapped at Joseph—not in his memory, but just behind where he sat. "There you are, Mr. Ramirez! I close my eyes for one second, and you run off to do who knows what. You trying to get me fired while you sit here daydreaming?"

Joseph opened his eyes to see a concerned look accompanying a wide smile on Nurse Misty's face. It took a few seconds to get a bearing on reality. Remembering where he was, he smiled back at the nurse. "Heaven forbid. No, I was just imagining how I might get a different perspective on things."

"Well, we'd better get back inside before we get in trouble. Come on," she said, grabbing the handles of his wheelchair and turning him toward the hospital doors.

"Yeah. It's just as well," he said softly as he cast one last glance toward the police cruiser. "It wasn't a very pleasant perspective."

CHAPTER 15

Consuela Ramirez opened her purse and pulled out a sandwich-sized package wrapped in several layers of paper towel. "I brought ju a gift," she said in a forced whisper.

"Illegal contraband, Mama?" Joseph asked, grinning.

"No! I brought ju empanadas," she said, as if offended at her son's jesting accusation. She lifted a couple layers of paper towel to reveal two golden-brown, cinnamon-crusted half circles, each about the size and shape of a taco. Hard sugar glistened in caramelized perfection across their surfaces, darker along the fluted crescent edges. They were still warm, and the smell of baked pastry, warm cream cheese, cinnamon, and sugar quickly filled the room.

"Dis much better dan dat German e'strudel ju get in e'Solvang."

"I'm sure they're delicious, Mama, but I don't know that I'm allowed to eat something this rich just yet."

"I'll help you with 'em," Clyde stated from his bed, as if offering a magnanimous service. The man was salivating like a dog.

"I don't know that you're allowed to eat them either," Joseph said with a raised eyebrow. "You're supposed to be watching your blood sugar and cholesterol and—"

"Blah, blah, blah," Clyde interrupted with a wave of his beefy hand. "Why miss out on the good things in life? Eat well, stay fit, die anyway, I always say. So what's it really matter? Beside, I can smell those clean over here, and man, do they smell good."

Consuela shot a scowl in Clyde's direction and quickly folded the paper towel over the Mexican dessert. He returned the woman's expression with his best lost-puppy smile.

Joseph enjoyed the silent exchange immensely. Plus, it gave him a bargaining chip. "Okay, Mama. I'll take them, but only if I can share one with my friend."

An expression of genuine disappointment filled her formerly hopeful eyes. She looked from Clyde to the empanadas then to Joseph several times before speaking. "Ju have to try one right now," she insisted.

Joseph hesitated. "I don't know. My doctor—"

"*Mi'jo*! Why ju always argue wid me? I only try to help, but no one let me do *nada* for ju. Da nurses, dey won' let me bring ju herbs or *medicinas,* dey won' let me give ju—my own son—a bath or a—"

"Because I'm almost thirty, Mama," Joseph said, a bit red-faced.

"I can only visit certain hours," she rattled on, her voice becoming more strained by the second. "I work e'so hard for ju, *mi'jo,* I light candles in da church, I ask Padre Constantaré to say e'special pray for ju, and now ju don' even take a bite of dis *delicioso* gif' I bring."

"Okay, okay," Joseph said, holding up his hands in a truce. "I'll try a piece. But you have to give one to Mr. Richter, too. I insist."

Another caustic scowl shot in Clyde's direction, but he remained smiling in spite of it. "Atta boy, Joe," he cheered softly.

Consuela sighed in resignation and carried an empanada to Clyde. She handed it over without a word.

"Thank you, ma'am," Clyde said. He looked manifestly elated for the reprieve from the hospital's lack of yummy desserts.

Clyde peeled away the napkin with reverence then took a generous bite from the corner of the pastry. Even before chewing, he closed his eyes and leaned back into his pillow while issuing a prolonged moan of pure epicurean bliss.

"Good?" Joseph asked.

His roommate held up an index finger while his jaw slowly worked at the bite of empanada. Joseph didn't really need an answer—Clyde's actions said it all.

Joseph gave a chuckle and took a small bite of his treat. The pastry was airy, smooth, and sweet. Absolute heaven. "*Está buenísima,* Mama. These are wonderful."

Consuela's face lit up. "Hones'? Ju really thin' so, Joseph?"

"I sure do. Perhaps the best you've ever made," he said just before a second bite.

"Good. 'cuz I didn' make dem. Yolanda Vasquez did. Ju 'member her from e'school, *si*? She live down da block from us. She still not married—can ju belief it? She a very e'sweet girl, Joseph. An' I know she e'still really like ju!"

Joseph guessed he was heading for trouble when his mother called him Joseph instead of José. But that trouble doubled, solidified, and fermented when she mentioned Yolanda's name. He remembered the lovesick, truly homely girl all too well, and he couldn't be less interested.

"Mama," he began.

"But ju like her cooking, *si*?"

"Yes, Mama, her empanadas are very good, but—"

"Den ju can tell her juself," his mother said, scooting quickly to the door.

"Mama," Joseph cried.

"Yolanda," Consuela hollered out the door. "He wan' ju to come in now."

"Mama!" Joseph hissed.

"Ah, Joe, any gal who bakes like this can't be all bad," Clyde said while using the paper towel to wipe the corners of his mouth.

Consuela Ramirez smiled and stood back from the doorway. A young woman about the same height and weight as Joseph's mother entered with her head bowed in shyness. She wore a pink blouse that strained against her considerable bosom and green slacks that appeared to have been sprayed on her generous backside. Her coarse black hair was block cut at the shoulders, and her makeup was applied with the free-form panache of a graffiti artist.

"Whoa. I was wrong," Clyde mumbled.

"*Hola,* José," Yolanda said demurely.

"Hi, Yolanda," Joseph said flatly.

"I so sorry to hear about your accident."

"Thank you."

"Your mother said I should visit to cheer you up."

"That's Mama for you."

"So . . . you like my cooking?"

"Your empanadas are very good."

A blush fought its way through her pancake foundation. "*Gracias,* José."

"Joseph."

Yolanda blinked in confusion then glanced at Joseph's mother. Consuela shrugged.

"Jo-seef," she overemphasized.

A two-ton silence fell on the room, stifling the possibility for any light conversation. Consuela scowled at her son for not saying anything more. Joseph kept his eyes fixed on the remaining portion of pastry in his hand. Yolanda gazed at Joseph with doe-like eyes filled with hopeful expectancy. Clyde sat back, watching the scene with arms folded and an enormous grin on his face.

Eyes begging for help, Joseph stole a glance at his roommate. Clyde just snorted.

Time stood still.

Finally, the older man blatantly forced a yawn and stretched. "Well, it's about time for my afternoon nap, so if you ladies will excuse me."

Yolanda nodded and shuffled close to Joseph. With jerky, hesitant movements, she reached out and gave his shoulder a quick pat. "*Adios*, Jo-seef. Call me." She then turned and fled the room.

Joseph let out a burst of air that sounded more like a tire going flat than a sigh of relief.

"She *es una muchacha bonita, sí*, Joseph?" Consuela asked hopefully. "An' such a good cook."

"She's very sweet," Joseph said, desperate to avoid incrimination.

"Twice the gal I was expecting to see," Clyde mumbled just above a laugh.

"Mama, thank Yolanda for bringing the empanadas. They were delicious."

"Ju thank her," Consuela said. "I have 'er e'cell number."

"No, Mama. She would read more into it than there really is," Joseph said. "And so would you. Now—before you bring up any of your usual arguments or lectures, I think Clyde does need some rest, and I'm feeling a little tired myself. So if you'll excuse us . . ."

Consuela Ramirez gathered up her purse, stood on her toes to kiss Joseph on the forehead, and left with a frown of disappointment tugging at her face.

CHAPTER 16

EMILY RAMIREZ ORTEGA HAD ONE of those smiles that lit up a room, and her youthful, bouncing laugh was downright contagious. "Joseph, you always crack me up," she giggled after he told her his blood work had been switched with a patient in OB, and the hospital was now trying to figure out how he could be thirty-two weeks pregnant.

"It is so good to see you, Em," Joseph said with a broad grin, holding her hand as she sat next to his bed. "How're Miguel and the kids?"

"They are all fine. Little Estella keeps asking about you. You're her favorite uncle, you know."

"Since Xavier moved to Florida, I'm probably the *only* uncle she knows."

"So? You're still her favorite."

Joseph shook his head. "She is so dang cute. Those big, chocolate-brown eyes of hers are going to break a lot of hearts when she's sixteen."

"What do you mean 'when she's sixteen'? She could get away with murder and the only thing the judge would say is how adorable she must have looked while pulling the trigger."

Joseph laughed. He loved his older sister and her family. Miguel was a good husband and a great father. He was foreman for a landscape contractor, which brought in a surprisingly comfortable income. They weren't rich, but because the denizens of Montecito, Hope Ranch, and other high-end communities in Santa Barbara prided themselves on immaculate yards, Bonita Vista Landscapes was kept busy year-round.

Emily had brought Joseph a small vase of plumeria blossoms, his favorite. Their fragrance was perhaps the most intoxicating of any flower he'd ever smelled. And the five perfectly symmetrical, white-and-yellow petals of each flower reminded him that even the simplest things can have breathtaking beauty.

Joseph and Emily talked about many things for over an hour, comfortably skipping from one topic to another, trying to catch up on the lost weeks, lost months. Both commented on the irony of needing a disaster to bring family closer together. Their conversation was healing and nurturing in many ways. Yet each time Joseph tried to steer the dialogue to his forgotten childhood, Emily skirted the issue and changed the topic to something entirely different. It frustrated Joseph. He desperately wanted to discuss the past but wasn't completely sure he should open himself—and his sister—to potential heartache.

"Emily, not to put a damper on things, but I need to ask . . ." Joseph stretched out the sentence, as if he weren't sure how to phrase his request.

"Need to ask what?"

Joseph hesitated, feeling suddenly uncomfortable, leery. Was his past really that awful? He remembered so little of it, which was why he found it so strange that his dreams seemed to be focusing on that part of his life. And not in a good way. One would think that a rotten childhood would be a sore spot, like a scar that reminded you of an injury each time you saw it. But he remembered nothing like that. To the best of his knowledge, his childhood was pretty normal: the handful of vignettes he recalled comprised a day at the beach, a walk downtown, a birthday party, and a couple of Christmases. So why were his recent dreams so alarming?

"Joseph?"

He looked up at his sister. "I—I'm not sure. I haven't been sleeping well."

"Are you in pain?"

"No, not so much that. I've been having these dreams . . ."

"What dreams? About your accident?"

He shook his head. "No. About . . . about my past . . . I think . . ."

Unaware he had done so, Joseph had gone silent again and stared off to one side with vacant eyes. He knew that man's greatest phobia was a fear of the unknown. Perhaps he'd forgotten his past because it was too horrible to relive the memories. Did they have something to do with Papa's leaving? With Antonio's death? *Why can't I remember?*

Joseph scowled in frustration at his open palms, as if angry the answer wasn't readily within his grasp. A tear trickled down his cheek, causing him to flinch and angrily wipe it away.

"Joseph, what's wrong?" Emily asked, her concern sullied with trepidation. "Are you sure you're not in pain? You can tell me."

Joseph looked over at his roommate's empty bed. Clyde was having another battery of MRIs that afternoon and wouldn't return until supper time. He was glad the man was gone. It would be easier to confide in his sister now. But he couldn't seem to bring himself to do so. Joseph hated to admit it, but he was . . . *terrified*—which seemed strange . . . and kind of silly at the same time. Why should he be afraid of a few memories—especially ones that occurred almost two decades ago? Sequestering away a random event or two might make sense, but to lose the entire first ten years of his life seemed . . . impossible. Yet it *had* happened. The question remained: why? And why was it coming back out of its own volition? Like a thick fog slowly dissipating to reveal an evil better left unseen, Joseph's dreams seemed to be revealing a heretofore hidden monstrosity.

"Joseph?"

Joseph wiped at his eyes again and drew a deep breath between clenched teeth. *Just do it!* "Emily, did I . . . did *we* have a good childhood?"

The look in her eyes revealed the answer. It was a look of sadness and regret. She shook her head and wouldn't—or couldn't—maintain eye contact with her brother. "No, Joseph. It was not very good."

"Why? What happened?"

Emily pulled a tissue from her purse and daubed her eyes. "You still don't remember?"

"I never have, you know that."

"I know we've discussed it in the past, but I assumed you just didn't *want* to remember. You're saying you can't recall anything?"

He shrugged. "Only bits and pieces. The parts after Papa left are pretty clear, but everything before that is a blur."

Emily stared long and hard at the tissue in her hand. Her look was a confusing mix of anger, sorrow, and indecision. She then stood and kissed Joseph on the forehead. "Perhaps it's better that way."

Joseph balked. "Isn't that for me to decide?"

His tone was much harsher than he had intended, but he didn't apologize for it. If this was information that would help him resolve his sleep-robbing dreams, then it would be worth hearing.

Emily nodded but took a moment before she answered. "Papa was not a good husband. He drank too much. He wasn't a good father either."

In a much softer voice, Joseph admitted, "I sort of remember being afraid of him when he got mad, but the few memories I have are of happy times."

"Then let's leave it that way."

"I can't, Em. My dreams . . . they're . . . they're terrifying. But I don't know why."

Tears misted in Emily's eyes and traced down her cheeks. She sat on the edge of his bed and placed a hand on his knee. "Oh, Joseph, he was so mean to you. Anything you did seemed to make him mad."

"Was he that way with you?"

"Oh no. Xavier got him riled now and then, but that's only because he was the oldest and the most headstrong. He was the only one who ever really stood up to Papa. Antonio had a nice bond with him; they got along most of the time." She paused and looked at trees just outside the window. "He seemed to like me the most, but I still tried to avoid him when I could. As soon as I . . . became a woman, Mama thought it best if I stayed away from him as much as possible. As I recall, Xavier avoided Papa by having two jobs."

"I think I remember that," Joseph remarked. He took a deep breath and held it. He hated asking the next question, but he was grabbing at straws, trying to find anything that might help him recover his past. "Did Papa molest you?"

Deciding her tissue could hold no more, Emily grabbed a few more from a dispenser on an adjacent counter. "No, not really. But he started staring at me a lot when he thought I wouldn't notice—if you know what I mean. That's when I started hanging out with friends to stay away. I hated that because . . ."

"Because why?" Joseph prompted.

She choked on a sob and held the tissue to her nose. "Because I couldn't watch out for you."

"Did he . . . molest me?" Joseph asked, unbelieving.

Emily shook her head forcefully. "No. At least not that I know of. He was just mean to you. All the time. I hated what he called you: *el falla.*"

"The failure?"

"Yes. But from where he came from it also means 'the mistake.'"

"The mistake? Why'd he call me that?"

"Please, Joseph, let's leave it at that," she urged him. "Papa was a terrible father most of the time. It is better you remember him as a nice man."

"Emily," Joseph pleaded. "You have to tell me. Please!"

She shook her head, stood, and kissed him on the forehead. "Maybe when you're feeling better. I have to go now."

"Emily, please."

She smiled tenderly and ran the back of her fingers along his cheek. "You became such a handsome, generous, and happy man. I'd rather you stayed that way."

And with that, she turned and walked briskly from the room.

CHAPTER 17

JOSEPH PONDERED THE HIDDEN TRUTHS of Emily's information the rest of that day. He wished she would have opened up completely, but he realized it had been hard on her—perhaps harder on her than it had been on him. *Perhaps.*

After a standard meal, Joseph was allowed an assisted walk around his floor, then returned to bed totally exhausted. He hated that, but he knew it was part of healing. His psychological limitations were a different matter. Lamenting his frustrations, he drifted off . . .

* * *

Seven-year-old Joseph carried a bag of stale popcorn that bumped against his leg as he ran toward the bird refuge. Mr. Castignola, the manager of El Centro, a small corner market a few blocks from the Ramirez home, always saved a bag of the day-old stuff for Joseph. He knew young Joseph loved feeding the ducks and seagulls at the bird refuge.

Joseph arrived at the refuge just after noon. The place was crowded with adults and kids feeding the birds. To get a place on the shore where most of the birds gathered would be very difficult, especially for someone as small as he was. He moved to the shoreline and slowly edged in next to a mom and dad and a little girl about Joseph's age.

"Hey, this is my spot," snapped the girl. She had long, light brown hair and strange greenish eyes, much like Joseph's own.

"Sorry," Joseph replied in a soft voice.

"Back away. You're scaring the ducks!"

Joseph couldn't see how he was influencing the ducks one way or another, but he took a couple of steps back anyway. He tossed a few of kernels of popcorn into the water, hoping a duck or two might see them. Instead, a huge, ugly catfish came up from under the murky water and sucked the fluffy kernels below the surface.

The unexpected appearance of the disgusting, flat face made Joseph stagger and lose his footing. He landed on his backside and let out a sharp cry of pain. Popcorn flew everywhere. The ducks and birds went crazy with the sudden abundance of food. They swarmed toward Joseph, squawking and flapping, clambering over each other to get at the corn. Because the bag landed directly on Joseph's belly, the popcorn scattered all over his T-shirt. Before he could blink, three very aggressive seagulls and a couple of blackbirds were on him, fighting and screeching at the ducks. Joseph panicked. He cried out and flailed his arms and kicked his legs to get away. One forceful kick to the ground launched a small stone that struck the little girl's shin. She screamed and fell to the ground, spilling her popcorn, causing a second free-for-all amongst the birds. Joseph was wide-eyed, gasping for breath, expelling each intake with a shrill, panicked cry.

The girl's father stepped to her and shooed the birds away while her mother helped Joseph to his feet and brushed off his shirt.

"You okay, honey?" The woman was a very pretty brunette with dark blue eyes and a generous, white smile. Although Joseph hadn't ever seen any movie stars in person, he was certain this lady must be one. Yet despite the woman's friendliness, the bird attack had left him in shock and trembling with fright.

"Mommy, he threw a rock at me," the girl cried. "I think my leg is broken."

The man glanced at his daughter with a hard look. "Your leg's not broken, Dawna. I saw the whole thing; it was an accident." He then winked at her. "I think you'll be fine, sweetheart, but if you need one, I'll call an ambulance."

"Stop kidding, Daddy. My leg really, really hurts!"

Still smiling, the mother said, "Come here. Let me see."

The girl hobbled over with an amplified limp and pointed to the injured leg. The woman rolled up her daughter's jeans and looked it over. There wasn't a scratch or a bruise or anything Joseph could see wrong. "I don't know how to tell you this, but I think you're going to live," her mother teased.

The girl slapped her pant leg down and stormed to the water's edge with her arms folded tightly in anger.

The woman snickered and turned to Joseph. "So are you okay? Did the birds peck you or scratch you?"

Joseph was slowly regaining his composure but was still too shaken up to speak.

"Hey, it's okay, hon," she soothed, using her light jacket sleeve to wipe the dirty tears from his face. "My name is Crystal. I'm a doctor. I can help you if you're hurt."

After a pause, Joseph softly said, "I'm okay, but is she . . ." He nodded and pointed at the little girl.

"Oh, don't worry about her," the man said with a chuckle in his tone. "She's a bit headstrong and unfortunately gets upset when she doesn't get her way. But she's not hurt."

Joseph looked up at the man's face. He was very tall. Normally Joseph was afraid of strange men, especially one this big. But this dad seemed different. He had been firm with his daughter but then winked at her and joked with her. That confused Joseph. When his papa got mad, it usually lasted for a long time and included a punishment. Instead, this man's face was gentle, and even though Joseph had just made his daughter cry, his eyes still twinkled with friendliness. Joseph had never seen that kind of friendliness on his dad's face— well, at least not when he was looking at Joseph. What he wouldn't give to have Papa smile at him like the little girl's father had.

Joseph picked up his empty bag and began putting in the few kernels of popcorn he could find on the ground. He then held it out to the woman.

"No, no. That's okay. We still have plenty of our own. In fact, why don't you take some of ours?"

"Mother!" the girl cried. "Then I won't have enough!"

"Dawna, we have more than enough," her father said.

Joseph couldn't accept their duck food. He had already ruined the little girl's adventure with the ducks. And he'd spoiled her time with her mom and dad. Joseph's papa would have been furious with him. But these parents were just as concerned about a clumsy little boy as they were about their own daughter. They were probably the kind of parents who would never yell at their kids. They might be firm, but they would never scream, hit them, or raise welts on their backs and arms and legs.

"You sure you're not hurt?" the woman asked again.

"*Sí,*" he replied.

"Well, I think you are a very brave boy."

Joseph shrugged. He knew she was stretching the truth, but he kind of liked the sound of it. He walked over to where the girl was pouting and handed her his nearly empty bag. "I'm sorry for scaring the ducks," he said barely above a whisper. "You can have my popcorn."

With arms still folded tightly across her chest, the girl turned away from him and stared off in the opposite direction.

"Dawna Grimes! That's no way to act toward someone who's trying to apologize," her father said firmly.

The girl cast a bitter glance over her shoulder at her dad. His look was hard but not angry. "Fine," the girl said, whipping around and grabbing the bag.

Joseph turned and said to the parents, "I'm sorry I hurt her."

The woman knelt on one knee. "The only thing you hurt was her pride. And she's got way too much of that." She smiled again. "So what is your name, young man?"

"José. No—Joseph."

The woman chuckled lightly. "Well which do you prefer?"

Joseph shrugged, embarrassed for stumbling over his answer.

"Well, I've always liked Joseph," she said, offering her hand. "It's a pleasure to meet you, Joseph."

"Same here, Joseph," the man said.

Joseph's face reddened. He stuffed his hands deep into his pockets. "Okay," was all he could think to say. He wasn't about to shake her hand after his hand had gotten so filthy in the dirt.

He turned and began to walk briskly away. The woman called to him, but he just kept on walking. He had already made a mess of everything. He wasn't going to make things worse by sticking around. He began to walk faster. If Papa found out he had hurt a little *gringa* girl, he'd be in real trouble. *Punishment* kind of trouble. He hoped the kind family would forget the whole thing. He shouldn't have told them his name.

Joseph glanced back. The man and woman smiled and waved. The little girl looked up at her mom, saw she was distracted, and stuck out her tongue at Joseph. He ducked his head and sprinted for home.

* * *

When Joseph awoke, he had tears in his eyes. His heart swelled with nostalgia. The remembrance was one of the few terrors that had turned to happiness. He wiped his eyes and then paused in surprise. For some reason, he fully remembered the dream he'd just had. He could still see the faces of the pretty mom and kindly dad. He knew it was the reason he preferred Joseph to José. Well, one of the reasons. More importantly, he remembered how quickly the shock from the bird assault faded when the mom and dad showed true emotion, true concern for his well-being. And although it was a short episode, he recognized the one emotion he'd never felt from his father. *Love.*

CHAPTER 18

PHYSICAL THERAPY WAS EXTRA INTENSE the following day. Therapist Connie had lined up a course of strength training that taxed Joseph to his limit. But that was *his* perspective because she kept pushing him to do one or two more reps. He tried to explain that his nights were not very restful. She said he needed to work harder so he *could* sleep more restfully. She then went on to cite studies from six different universities that proved so. He gave up trying to argue.

The cast on his leg had come off a couple of days earlier, and recent X-rays showed wonderful alignment and knitting of the bones. The orthopedist said he shouldn't have any problems with his leg in the future. Just to make sure, Connie had Joseph building his calf, thigh, and hamstring muscles, as well as stretching the tendons more than he thought possible.

"Did you know the best way to strengthen bones is *not* by taking calcium supplements or biphosphonates like Actonel and Fosamax?" she asked. Before Joseph could reply, she rambled on: "That's the trouble with people today. They want a pill to do it all, but our bodies just don't run that way. Bones respond to the demand put on them. You subject them to stress on a regular basis, they will grow thicker and stronger. No demand, no growth. In fact, without exercise, they actually become porous and brittle."

"Good to know," Joseph groaned while doing a set of eighty-pound leg extensions.

"Perspective, Joseph. If you want osteoporosis when you're old, don't do anything about it when you're young. Of course, *your* bone density scan looked great. You obviously try to keep fit."

Joseph watched Connie's arm muscles ripple with movement as she helped him complete a final two reps. "I wish I was in the shape you're in," he said.

"No, you don't."

Joseph blinked. "Excuse me?"

"You don't." She poked an index finger in the palm of her opposite hand, as if pointing to a study embedded in her skin. "Look, the way I see it, if you truly wish for good health, a good body, or pretty much anything in life, you'll work hard to obtain it. If you don't put forth the effort—and then stick with it—you must not want it that bad."

"What if I want to go to the moon?" Joseph tested her.

"Then become an astronaut and go. If you're just dreaming about going, it's doubtful you ever will. But if you *really* want to go, you'll find a way. I get sick and tired of people saying they want to be skinny or lose weight and then don't do what is necessary to get there. To me, they really don't want it. Or they should instead say, 'I wish it were *easier* to lose weight.' That'd be closer to the truth."

"Oh."

"There's always room for improvement when it comes to our bodies, Joseph—and I'm not just talking about looks. The truest saying in the world is 'when you got your health, you got everything.' That goes for physical *and* mental health."

"How about spiritual health?"

She cocked her head to one side. "Say, that's some good insight, Joseph. I like it."

"Perspective," Joseph said with another push against the weights.

She laughed. "Now you're getting it. So—how about giving me three more reps?"

Joseph strained against the weights but was finally able to give the PT the reps she wanted.

"Speaking of wishes," Joseph said, wiping his brow. "Tell me how I can get my stamina back. I used to be able to go for hours because—"

"Dude, you were run over by a cement truck. It'll take time to get back to 100 percent."

"No, it's not so much that. You didn't give me a chance to explain why. I just don't get any rest when I sleep anymore."

Connie appraised him thoughtfully. "Okay—why?"

"It has to do with my dreams."

"About your accident?"

"I don't think so."

"You don't *think* so?" she echoed.

Joseph paused and took a fortifying breath. "It's more complicated than that. The docs here want me to have a psych evaluation."

Connie shrugged. "So?"

Joseph frowned. "So I don't like the idea of someone probing into my past, only to come up with some hogwash about having narcissistic proclivities or an overbearing mother with gender confusion. I've had some experience with that before. It wasn't pretty."

The PT laughed. "Well apparently you've done *some* reading on the subject."

"A bit," he said.

Joseph used his cane to move to the next piece of equipment, the leg curl machine. Lying on his stomach, he said, "Look, I'm not saying I disagree with the practice of psychology. I just wonder how much they can determine from dreams I barely remember myself. What I really need is a Daniel or Joseph to tell me the dreams then interpret them for me too."

"Who?"

"Old Testament prophets known for interpreting dreams."

"Oh yeah, the Technicolor coat guy," Connie said as she adjusted the weights to six pounds, and had Joseph begin his reps. "So you don't remember *anything* about them?" she asked.

"Some. Mostly snippets of events. Nothing that ties one thing to the next. But I know there's *something* there."

"How's that?"

Joseph finished the first set of curls and rocked onto his elbows. "Promise not to laugh?"

Connie smiled. "No. But I'll keep an open mind."

Joseph lowered his gaze. "Because the parts I do remember scare me to death."

"Meaning you get zero rest; I got it." The look on Connie's face showed her true concern. "Look, sleep is just as important to your health as exercise, Joseph. But like I said, so is mental health. I'd see that psychiatrist right away."

Joseph sighed in acknowledgment. "I suppose you're right."

"Of course I am. I've got a better perspective on it than you. In fact, I insist on it. I'll put in your chart a suggestion to see Dr. Wilder."

"Wilder? That doesn't inspire much confidence."

"Nonsense. He's one of the best."

"I . . . I don't know. I think I'd rather try to work it out on my own."

"Look. It's ridiculous to try physical therapy on your own. I certainly wouldn't recommend you tackle mental issues solo."

Joseph closed his eyes in resignation, thinking of the countless hours of lost sleep he'd already suffered through. "Perhaps you're right."

"I'm glad you see it from my perspective. Now—let's have another set of reps, okay? Only this time, add two more."

CHAPTER 19

JOSEPH HOPED THAT HIS INTENSE physical therapy session would get him so fatigued that he'd sleep better. Unfortunately, almost as soon as he closed his eyes, he was thrown into a terrifying past.

* * *

Two people stood on the edge of a building. Joseph knew it was a tall building because all he could see beyond the edge was blue sky and the tops of some trees in the distance. One was a man, maybe thirty-something, the other was a boy about thirteen. Joseph rubbed his eyes and looked again. He immediately recognized the two people: his father and his brother, Antonio, both looking just as he remembered them when he was younger. They were arguing. At this young age, Antonio was half the size of his father, and less than half his age.

Familiar pangs of anxiety fluttered in Joseph's gut. He didn't recognize the scene as one he had experienced, but watching it unfold, he felt certain it was an authentic replay. He saw Antonio yelling at his father. That was not a wise thing to do. Joseph wanted to call out to his brother, wanted to make him stop before it was too late.

Papa was known for sudden violent acts. When he was in a rage, he lost all sense of reason. When he was in a rage *while drunk,* he lost all sense of humanity. From this distance, Joseph couldn't tell if his father was drunk. But he recognized the volume and harshness of his voice and knew he was close to losing control.

Joseph tried to move toward the two on the far side of the rooftop but couldn't. His feet were planted, stuck to the rooftop by some unseen power. He waved his hands and tried to shout. His mouth moved, but no sound came out. The two individuals on the precipice were oblivious to his presence.

Joseph watched helplessly as his brother grabbed Papa's shirt and tried to pull him away from the edge. Papa cursed him and slapped him away with the back of his hand. In doing so he lost footing and staggered to one side. It was then that Joseph saw that his father was holding another boy by the shirttail—a younger boy—holding him facedown over the edge of the building!

It was madness! What was Papa doing? How could he be so cruel? What was he trying to accomplish with an act so dangerous—so insane? Joseph could hear fierce, high-pitched whimpers coming from the poor young boy hanging over the edge. The youth was trembling, his mouth gaping wide as if his next breath might be his last. Papa yelled at the boy to be quiet. With the pasty sheen of abject horror, the youth looked plaintively across the roof at Joseph. The expression in his eyes caused Joseph's stomach to twist. It cried wordlessly for mercy, for rescue.

Joseph's breath caught short—his heart stuttered and felt like it lumbered to a stop. Joseph instantly recognized the endangered youth. It was himself! But—but Joseph still couldn't remember this incident *ever* occurring. Still, the detail and emotion of what was happening was simply too real to be the random machinations of a dream.

Papa shuffled a bit to regain his footing. Young Joseph notched an inch farther over the ledge. Was Papa *preventing* him from falling over the edge . . . or *delaying* it? Antonio seemed to find some inner courage and reached up to pull on his father's pant leg. Papa cursed again and started pounding on his son's back. But Antonio refused to let go, causing his father further unsteadiness.

From across the rooftop, Joseph repeatedly grappled with a blank memory to recall this event, yet he came up empty again and again. Why? Surely something this traumatic would stick with him. Joseph cried out for Estefan to stop, but his mouth refused to make a sound. Angry tears came to his eyes as he continued to silently scream at his father.

Pivoting on powerless legs, the young Joseph continued to stare at the older Joseph. He was pleading with him, mutely crying out for him to intervene, to stop this madness from happening. But Joseph was immobile, inexplicably paralyzed in his dream.

Then, when Papa gave one last effort to shake Antonio from his leg, his grip on his younger son's shirt faltered and—

* * *

Joseph found himself sitting upright in bed with a scream stuck in his throat. It was late, well, early, really: 3:13 AM. He took several long, deep breaths to calm himself. His throat was raw and dry, as if he'd been yelling for a long time. On his nightstand were a couple bottles of water. He drained one in a half-dozen huge gulps. Sweat poured from his face and neck. His hands quivered with pent-up anxiety.

Just like the incident at the bird refuge, for some reason Joseph remembered a large portion of the dream he'd just had. And it disturbed him—made him sick to the core.

To his right, Clyde lay with his back to Joseph. He hoped he hadn't awakened the man again. He opened a second bottle of water and took a long drink. He forced himself to be calm, said a quick prayer, and tried to return to sleep. It was a long time coming.

CHAPTER 20

JOSEPH SAT IN A COMFORTABLE armchair in an office rich with dark earth tones, lots of polished cherry millwork, plush burgundy carpet, and an enormous picture window that faced west. Being on the fifth floor of the hospital, the window afforded an unobstructed view of the UCSB campus and the blue Pacific beyond. Joseph was infinitely glad his armchair was not next to the window. His fear of falling from a great height had a lot to do with it. A modest desk, two additional armchairs, and one suede couch occupied the center of the room. An ego wall behind the desk was barely big enough to hold all the diplomas, awards, fellowships, and accolades the psychiatrist had earned. The wall opposite the window was lined with shelves so meticulously organized that adding a single additional knickknack would have upset the cosmic balance of the universe. The remaining wall was the bulwark for two treadmills and two recumbent exercise bikes.

Joseph waited nearly twenty minutes before the psychiatrist showed up. When he did, Joseph was mildly surprised. Expecting someone who matched the self-aggrandizing trappings of the office—either an überprofessional with a micro-trimmed beard and a three-piece Armani suit, or a throwback from the sixties in rumpled tie-dyed attire, long unkempt hair and a goatee—the twenty-something black man who entered looked more like one of Clyde Richter's overpaid NBA draftees. He stood about six foot six, was clean cut, trim and fit, and had amazingly perfect teeth. He wore pleated Dockers, a button-down shirt, a bold tie, and wingtips.

"I apologize for being late, Mr. Ramirez. Please, don't get up," the young man said, extending his hand to Joseph. He had a voice so deep and resonant, Joseph felt it as much as he heard it. "I'm Dr. Alexander Wilder."

Joseph shook the firm hand. "Don't worry about it, doctor."

"Oh, but I do," he said. Dr. Wilder forced a smile through a mask of frustration as he sat casually on the edge of his desk. "I'm usually a stickler for punctuality. You see, every time the ER has a suspected or confirmed attempted suicide, they call me in for a quick eval. The sad thing is how often that happens."

"The call or the attempt?" Joseph asked.

"More the latter than the former," he sighed. The psychiatrist seemed sincerely troubled over the number of patients who would consider such desperate action.

"I feel the same way," Joseph admitted. "Especially when it involves young kids with a lot of life ahead of them and no clue what they're giving up."

Dr. Wilder favored Joseph with a brilliant smile. "I like you already, Mr. Ramirez," he said, rounding his desk and taking a seat.

"Thank you," Joseph replied. "But I'd rather you called me Joseph."

Dr. Wilder was already scanning Joseph's hospital chart and didn't respond right away. After a moment, he asked, "So you don't go by José?"

"No, sir."

"And why is that?"

Joseph shrugged. "A stranger called me Joseph once, and it just stuck. It's a long story. I guess I've always just preferred Joseph."

"An attempt to hide your Hispanic roots?"

"No, not at all. Honestly, I've just always liked the name."

"Growing up, what did your parents call you?"

"Mom still calls me José. As far as I can recall, my dad usually called me José. My brothers and sisters have always been cool with Joseph."

"And how long have you been using this name?"

"Since I was about seven or eight, I think."

The psychiatrist absently scratched his cheek. "Well, they *are* derivations of the same name; one's English, the other Hispanic. Are both your parents Hispanic?"

"Yeah."

"What do they think about your decision?"

"Like I said, Mom still calls me José, except when she's trying to schmooze me. Dad left just before I turned eleven, so I have no idea what he thinks."

"Do you ever hear from him?"

Joseph scoffed. "Not even a whisper. He hasn't shown up for family events—or Christmases or baptisms or weddings or anything."

"Is he a religious man?"

"Not to the extent my mother is."

Dr. Wilder made a notation on a legal pad and then read some more of Joseph's chart. "Joseph, I want to ask you some questions in a somewhat unusual way, and I want you to be as honest as possible. Can you do that?"

Joseph nodded. "I believe so. Should I move to the couch?"

Dr. Wilder looked up. "Would you prefer that?"

Joseph shrugged. "Nah. This chair's relaxing enough."

"I know, and that's why we're moving to the recumbent bikes. Can I help you up?"

Joseph was baffled. "The bikes?"

"Yes. Current research shows that the brain functions better when blood flow is increased. And the best way to do that is with aerobic exercise. I normally prefer the treadmills, but with your leg still healing and the severity of your head trauma, I'm worried about your equilibrium."

Joseph slowly rocked to his feet and positioned his cane for balance. "You've been kibitzing with Connie Olsen, haven't you?"

The psychiatrist chuckled. "The physical therapist and I share notes, of course, but mostly about research, not much about patients."

"Did she tell you about my bad dreams?"

"She said you're having trouble sleeping, that's all. Rest assured, Joseph, whatever you say in *this* office stays in this office."

"I have nothing to hide," Joseph said in a voice more defensive than he had intended.

"Excellent," Dr. Wilder said, moving to the bikes. "Then let's talk about these bad dreams you're having."

"Okay. But I've got to warn you, I don't remember much about them—except for one, maybe two."

The psychiatrist nodded. The two men each reclined on a bike and began pedaling.

"This isn't a race," Dr. Wilder said as he reached up and switched on a digital voice recorder. "Just go slow and steady. The longer we ride, the more the capillaries in your brain will respond. It's usually not noticeable on a physical level, but you'll be surprised at how clearly you can think and, hopefully, remember."

Joseph went at a very easy pace. He felt better almost instantly.

"Okay, so tell me about the dream you remember the most."

Joseph recounted the experience at the bird refuge in generous detail. He even remembered the woman's name and her daughter's as well. He mentioned that it was the only time he had met them, and yet he remembered them clearly. The doctor of psychiatry just watched the meter on his bike but didn't otherwise respond until Joseph was finished. "Touching story. I can see why you prefer Joseph to José."

"Me too. So why am I just *now* recalling it?"

"Could be any number of reasons, actually. Dreams are still an area of science that has no substantiated facts. *Why* they occur is still hotly debated. What they *contain* can sometimes be reasoned out, but it never follows a set pattern. Some dreams are primed from past experiences, others come from more recent events. Freud said all dreams are representations of sexual frustrations. A pair of researchers named Hobson and McCarley theorized that dreams are simply the cerebral cortex trying to impose order on the static caused by the random firing of neural networks during REM sleep. Why we *forget* things is equally enigmatic. It is thought that our subconscious stores *everything* we experience. So why is it we can't remember everything? Your case is particularly interesting. Apparently you've forgotten some momentous events from your childhood, and then suddenly—in the blink of an eye, as it were—they're resurfacing, creating significant emotional difficulties. Physical difficulties too, if you take into account the body's need for sleep."

"You can say that again! But why now? Why not back then, when the events happened?"

Dr. Wilder smiled. "That's what I'm here to find out. But, before we jump right into the mysteries behind Joseph Ramirez and his dreams, let's discuss other aspects of your life to help establish a background and baseline before we come to any conclusions, okay?"

Joseph nodded, still unsure what to think of this psychiatrist's approach.

The two men talked about random stuff—schooling, teaching, exercises, favorite foods, favorite movies, literature, etc.—for almost thirty minutes before Joseph began to get frustrated. He wanted help, not chitchat. "So when do we start my psychotherapy?" he asked during a pause.

"About a half hour ago."

Joseph scoffed. "Really? Somehow it doesn't seem like standard psychotherapy."

"Oh? Based on what?"

Joseph opened his mouth but couldn't think of a response.

"It's going very well, too," Dr. Wilder continued.

"Super," Joseph said unenthusiastically. He was silent for a minute then asked, "So should I be concerned about my dreams?"

"Of course. If they're robbing you of needful rest, then they should be addressed. But there's no need to rush right into it."

"I'm not so sure about that," he countered. "They seem to be getting more detailed, and some of the details aren't pleasant. I had one last night that scared me to death."

"Okay. Tell me about that one."

"I wish I could. I only remember bits and pieces."

Dr. Wilder nodded and placed his hands behind his head. "Tell you what. Next time you dream, doesn't matter if it's horribly scary or one filled with complete happiness, just go with it. Don't try to make it end or find any moral conclusion in it. Just let it ride. The minute you wake up, write down as much as you remember. Then go back to sleep. Don't analyze it. Just say to yourself, it was only a dream, and let it go." The psychiatrist stopped pedaling and stood, then offered his hand to help Joseph stand up. "You okay?"

"Yeah, fine," Joseph answered, a little out of breath. He grabbed his cane and followed the doctor to the door.

"Good. I'll see you again in three days. If anything serious comes up, you let me know. Until then," he winked, "sweet dreams."

CHAPTER 21

THE FOLLOWING DAY, GERN AND Helga Vandenlundervaldt entered Joseph's room with broad, cherubic grins. Gern carried a basket covered with a white and blue–checkered cloth; Helga carried a light blue canvas satchel. The couple was large-boned and generously dimensioned. To Joseph, their physical size was in perfect proportion to their personalities, as well as to their giving nature.

"Zo! Dis is vhere you've been hidink all dis time," Helga said in a voice that could be mistaken for a shout.

"Ach, Yoseph, you look zo 'tin!" Gern exclaimed.

Joseph smiled warmly at his two friends. He wasn't expecting a visit from them but was very glad they'd stopped by. When Joseph had learned he got the job at Solvang Middle School, he immediately went house hunting. The very next day he signed the papers on a small, single-level, 1930s bungalow in the old historic district of town. Two days after that, he began to move in. As he lifted the first box out of his trunk, a large figure suddenly loomed behind him. It was Gern Vandenlundervaldt. Wearing a disarming smile and eyes that danced with friendliness, Gern took the box from Joseph's arms, nodded, and carried it into the bungalow. Helga was right behind Gern carrying a large basket filled with hot rolls and cookies. "Goede morgen. Velcome to ze neighborhoed," she said with a smile that matched her husband's. "Ve live next door." She nodded in the direction of their home, a delightful little Tudor surrounded by multicolored tulips and lupine. "Zo, you are ze new teacher, no?"

"No—I mean, yes, I'm the new teacher," Joseph stammered, marveling at their thick accent.

"Ach, zo. Education is zo important. You are goede man to teach. Ve like you already."

Joseph felt the same. The three become fast friends.

The Vandenlundervaldts were from Aalborg, Jutland, a midsized city on the northern shores of the Cimbria Peninsula, Denmark. They had immigrated to California as newlyweds some fifty years earlier and had settled in Solvang at the suggestion of cousins. Gern had hired on as a farmhand for one of the huge dairies in the Santa Ynez valley and worked long, hard hours until he and Helga had saved enough money to purchase a local pastry shop just off Hans Christian Anderson Square. They immediately dropped the fast food menu to offer nothing but Danish pastries and assorted baked goods, of which Helga had countless recipes from the old country. Because of his association with the local dairies, Gern was able to get the freshest ingredients, and their fare quickly became recognized as some of the finest and most authentic in the little hamlet.

"How's everything at the Dansk Sødtbrød?" Joseph asked.

"Goede. But ve sure miss you. Are you feelink all right?" Helga asked, eyeing his lengthy scar.

Joseph patted his stubby scalp. "It'll be a while before I can enter any beauty contests, but I'm coming along okay."

Gern bent forward for a better look. "Auch, zat looks zo terrible. And your skin is hangink from your face. Here, you must eat," he said, handing Joseph the basket.

Joseph pulled back the tablecloth to reveal various pastries, cheeses, and sliced meats. "Thank you very much," he said. "The food in this hospital is not very tasty, but I probably shouldn't eat any without checking with my doctor first—which breaks my heart because this sure looks good."

"Are you on a *forbundten* diet? How you say—*restricted*?"

"Not really, but they still like to monitor everything I eat," Joseph explained.

"Hey, whatcha got there, Joe?" Clyde asked, scooting upright in his bed.

Joseph aimlessly poked around inside the basket. "Oh, nothing much. Nothing you'd be interested in, anyway. Some butter cookies, some aged cheeses, smoked sausage, hickory-cured ham, a few yeast rolls, a couple of chocolaty-looking things. But none of this is very good for the condition you're in, Clyde," Joseph declared, shaking his head. "No, I think I'd better eat it all myself."

In silent shock, Clyde stared with vacant eyes for a full half-minute. Then, slowly, the stunned expression morphed into a hateful, acid glare. "You are the spawn of Satan, Joseph Ramirez," he said through clenched teeth.

The Vandenlundervaldts watched the exchange with worried expressions. "Vat do you mean is no good for him?" Helga asked Joseph evenly.

He laughed. "I didn't mean it, Helga. I'm just teasing him."

"Oh, a yoke. I see." Holding out the satchel, she said, "I brought your mail, too. Ven da school learn of your accident, dey ask us to vatch your house. Of course, ve do dat anyway. I have Gern vater your lawn and do ze movink."

"Thank you very much. You didn't need to go to so much trouble."

"Ach, 'tis no trouble, Yoseph," Gern said. "Now, you eat and ve vill brink more next veek."

Clyde cleared his throat and gave Joseph's visitors his best lost-puppy pout.

"You won't mind if I share a little with my roommate, will you?" Joseph asked.

"Of course not," Helga said. "If he is your friend, he is our friend."

"Joe's my best friend in the world!" Clyde nearly cried.

Helga placed a concerned hand on Joseph's shoulder. "Yoseph, is der anyting else you need? Any kind of trouble you need help vith?"

The look in her pale blue eyes belied a disturbance she was hesitant to reveal. Gern held the same expression.

"No. Why—is something wrong?"

She cast a quick glance at Clyde Richter then lowered her voice. "Der haf been police around your house. Many time, at all hours of ze day, too. Dey taken ze photograph and look in ze vindows and such. Dey even haf dogs sniff around your yard."

Being hospital-bound, Joseph was actually grateful the police had checked out his place. But why would they treat his home as a crime scene?

"Really? Dogs too?"

"Jah. Many times."

"Have they gone inside my house?"

Gern shook his head. "I don't know. But ve cannot vatch your house all ze time. I don't tink so, but you never know vit ze *polizei*."

Joseph scratched his prickly hair. "Yeah. Okay. I, uh . . . I'm sure it's just a precaution they offer because I'm stuck here in the hospital."

"Vat should ve do?" Helga asked.

"Nothing," he said. "I'll call the Santa Ynez county offices and ask what's going on. But thanks for telling me. And thanks for these wonderful treats. The hospital has nothing like this, I promise you."

"Zuch hospital food cannot be goede for you," Gern grumbled. "Just look at you! You lose zo much veight."

Joseph balked. "Geez, you make it sound like I was huge before the accident."

"Der is difference between huge and husky," Gern said patting his generous belly.

Clyde barked a short laugh. "Amen, brother."

"Come," Helga snapped at her husband. "Ve go now. Yoseph, you get better. Ve be back real soon. *Tot ziens*."

Joseph said good-bye in Dutch as well. "*Tot ziens*."

A moment after the Scandinavian couple left the room, Clyde said, "Those are good people, Joe. The kind of neighbors everyone should have. You're a lucky man."

Joseph didn't respond. His mind was focused on the police interest around his house. Why would they be taking pictures and be snooping in the windows? Had they actually gone inside and looked around? And if they had, what were they looking for? What kind of dogs had they used—drug-sniffing, bomb-sniffing? Or was this an action mandated by Stansburg, Vail, and Jenkins? Something inside his gut convinced Joseph that whatever the police were doing, it wasn't for his protection. Not sure why he felt that way, Joseph had a sickening premonition it was inevitably something that would lead to more trouble than good.

In spite of what Clyde just said, Joseph felt anything but lucky.

CHAPTER 22

"Do you really need the cane, Joseph?" Connie Olsen asked the following morning.

Joseph was proud of his improvement in gait, but he still had a bit of a limp, and his injured leg tired quickly. "I'm doing my best, ma'am."

The PT smiled skeptically. "We'll see about that."

She ran Joseph through a series of balance tasks and more weight lifting. After an hour of grueling exercise, she led him to a small room in which sat a narrow, padded exam table.

She handed him a towel and asked to him remove his sweats and wrap the towel around his waist. "Lie faceup here when you've changed clothes," she said, patting the table.

Joseph made the change in a couple of minutes. Connie returned to the room with a squeeze bottle in her hand. She dribbled some warm, balsam-scented oil on his leg and began to massage his left thigh. The heated oil penetrated Joseph's skin and relaxed his muscles.

"Okay—why in the name of all that's holy haven't you done this before?" he asked in a languid voice.

"It wasn't necessary before," was her blunt answer.

He closed his eyes and let the therapist's strong hands work magic. Before long, she moved to the other thigh and did the same thing. She then had Joseph roll over, and she repeated the massage on his calves and hamstrings.

"Not that I'm complaining, but is this medically necessary, or are you just being nice?" he asked.

"Massage increases circulation, particularly in injured tissues. It helps prevent the formation of scar tissue, and it helps properly break down muscle tissue so it can rebuild even stronger. I know of a couple studies that show massage releases catecholamines, endorphins, and oxytocin that not only make you feel better but that stimulate healing of damaged tissue and organs."

Joseph groaned appreciatively. "Seriously? And I thought it just felt good—ouch!" He stopped short, and his moans became pain-filled. "That one hurts. Ow, okay, I give, I give!"

Instead of lightly manipulating the tissues, Connie was now bearing into his muscles as if deciding they needed to be moved to another location in his body. She used her elbows and forearms to exert as much pressure as possible, ignoring Joseph's cries for a truce.

"Come on, Connie. Lighten up. That kills. It can't be good for me."

"Perspective, Joseph. Everything is a matter of perspective. Speaking of which, how's it going with Dr. Wilder?"

Joseph found it difficult to talk through clenched teeth. "Fine. He says I'm likely to make progress."

"That's his perspective. What's yours?"

Joseph took a deep breath as Connie moved from his leg to his lower back. "I've only had the one visit. We talked mostly about standard stuff: my family, my job, my lifestyle. You know."

"How about your dreams? They getting any better?"

Joseph sighed. "They're getting clearer, but I wouldn't say that's better. If anything, I'm getting even less sleep than before."

"How come?"

"Apparently I have a past I'm not aware of. And it ain't pretty."

"Really? Like what?"

Although Joseph felt comfortable with his PT, the details of the dreams he'd written down were not something he wanted to share. Not right now, anyway. "Oh, nothing much. Just some family stuff."

"Um-hum," she mumbled. "Just remember, they're dreams, Joseph. You never know what's going to happen in one. I once had an incredibly real dream that action hero Arnold Schwarzenegger became governor of California."

"Um . . . I don't know how to break this to you, but . . ."

"His running mate was Chewbacca the Wookiee."

"Oh."

"He had to have an interpreter, but he actually had some sound political ideas," she said in a serious tone.

"Yeah? Which one?"

Connie laughed. It was high-pitched and giggly. It surprised Joseph so much he started laughing too—at least until she bore into the small of his back with bone-cracking force.

"You keep doing exactly what Dr. Wilder tells you to do, Joseph. He's a brilliant man and can help you get through this, I promise."

"How about we make a deal?" Joseph asked between gasps.

"What deal?"

"I promise to keep going to the psychiatrist if you promise to lighten up on this torture session."

Connie sniggered with malevolent glee. "Torture session? Joseph, me lad, I've only just begun."

CHAPTER 23

JOSEPH'S EYES FLEW OPEN WHEN he realized he couldn't breathe. He sat up and forced himself to focus. *It was just a dream. No need to be frightened. Relax, Joseph! Breathe!* The few seconds before his paralyzing fear released its grip on his lungs were the longest Joseph had ever experienced. Gulping air, he felt tears course down his cheeks. *Dear Lord,* he prayed, *when is this going to end?*

* * *

On his next visit to Dr. Wilder, Joseph asked if perhaps his early childhood memories had been repressed. "You know, like in cases of sexual abuse or trauma where children block out past ugly experiences."

The psychiatrist's eyebrows rose slightly. "Where'd you come up with that?"

"Here and there, I guess. I'm a science teacher, so I get a lot of input from a lot of different sources . . . which means I know very little about a whole lot."

Dr. Wilder laughed. "Well put. You certainly don't believe everything you read or hear, do you?"

"No. I like to keep an open mind, but I don't believe something just because it's in print. Still, isn't it true that 60 to 80 percent of our dreams are about being chased or falling from great heights? What I want to know is if my nightmares are just dreams or repressed memories."

"Good question. Honestly, I'm not sure I believe in the whole 'repressed memory' theory."

"Theory?" Joseph asked.

"*Theory,* because it's never been proven. Not through valid scientific means, anyway. It's a concept Freud came up with long ago to account for certain neuroses that he couldn't otherwise explain. It made sense only because there was no way to disprove it at the time."

"But what about all the books and movies on the subject?"

"Conjecture mostly." Dr. Wilder put his pen and pad aside and rested his elbows on his knees. "Because you have a science background, Joseph, I'm sure you know the importance of empirical data and reproducible experimentation."

Joseph nodded.

"The trouble with most memory repression cases is that they don't follow known facts about memory or what we currently know about brain function. See, no one easily forgets a traumatic experience. They may forget the severity of pain associated with it, but the *event* stays with most people until they die. Take childbirth, for instance. Ask any grandmother, and they'll tell you they remember it hurting, but overall 'it wasn't that bad,'" he said as if quoting.

"Sure, but haven't there been criminal convictions based on repressed memories?"

"Not convictions themselves—just explanations as to *why* the person committed the crime."

"Not guilty by reason of insanity, huh?" Joseph said flatly.

"No, no." Dr. Wilder stretched his arms then resumed his casual position. "*Insanity* is a very broad term for a valid diagnosis; memory repression is not. See, the theory is that a person—a child, usually—experiences something so vile that they unconsciously block it from their minds. The classic example, as you mentioned, is sexual abuse. Then, later in life, many of those repressed experiences surface as a mental illness or psychoses, which in turn cause the person to mimic or re-create those memories, and thus commit the same crime."

"Yeah, that sounds right," Joseph affirmed.

"Well, from everything I've read, most repressed memory is *intentionally* blocked from the mind to lessen its impact on emotions. It can spontaneously surface at any given time, but it has never been directly confirmed to cause mimicry of actions later on."

"Like a child predator claiming he molests kids because he was molested as a child?"

"Exactly. It *seems* to make perfect sense, but correlation does not prove causation."

"Never?"

"Well," the doctor snickered, "blanket statements are never a good idea in any field, especially psychiatry. I suppose there are cases where the correlation is just too strong to deny it contributed to the psychoses; but contrary to popular belief, it's not the norm. The cases that *do* tie in usually prove to be sloppy hypnosis sessions in which the patient is given—albeit unwittingly—false memories. Are you familiar with that term?"

"False memory? I've heard of it, but I don't know what it is," Joseph admitted.

"A false memory is a remembrance which is a distortion of an actual experience, or a confabulation of an imagined one. Many false memories involve mixed fragments of events, some of which may have even happened years apart, but which are remembered as occurring together. It's thought that many false memories are the result of the prodding or *leading* suggestions of the therapist. When referring to dreams, the real trouble occurs when you treat them if they were playbacks of real experiences."

Joseph mentally chewed over Dr. Wilder's comments. Could his troubled sleep be coming from the way his father had treated him as a child, or was it a mix of bad experiences from friends or even strangers who treated him poorly? He couldn't decide. Emily had told him Papa had been terrible to him, but he remembered so little of that. Then there was the dream of being held over the edge of a tall building. And all the dreams of falling. Were they connected? And if it *had* actually happened, then why had nothing been done about it? Surely Antonio would have said something.

"So does that help you or confuse you even more?" Dr. Wilder asked.

Joseph smirked. "Both."

The psychiatrist stood and moved to his desk. "Bottom line, Joseph, is that whether your dreams are of real events or not, they're still troubling your sleep. I'm going to prescribe a sedative for the next few nights."

"Doc, I hate those addicting things. And I always feel so incoherent the next day."

"Relax, Joseph. I'm recommending melatonin. It's a hormone secreted in the brain. Its function is to regulate circadian rhythms—your day-night cycle. Because you've been asleep, in a manner of speaking, for three solid weeks, you're probably still a bit out of whack."

Joseph chuckled. "'Out of whack.' Finally, a medical term I'm familiar with."

"It may do nothing but relax you. But that, combined with Dr. Olsen's exercise routines, should help you sleep like a baby."

"Most babies I know of have to be fed and changed throughout the night."

Dr. Wilder laughed. "A classic oxymoron. Sorry. How about sleeping like a log?"

"An inanimate object with human traits?"

"Anthropomorphizing. Got me again."

The two scientists shared a moment of laughter. That alone helped Joseph feel better. This psychiatrist was not your stereotypical headshrinker. Dr. Alex Wilder came across as a guy trying to help out a friend; the kind of guy who comes over to help move your air hockey table then stays for barbecue. The association was very comfortable.

The doctor wrote the melatonin order in Joseph's chart. "You still writing down your dreams?"

Joseph shrugged. "As much as I can remember."

"Good. These things can have a domino effect. I have a feeling you'll begin to remember more and more. After you get a few of them on paper, even the fragmented ones, we'll spend a session going over them."

Joseph was uncomfortable with the idea. If his nightmares proved to be real, it would open a door to experiences he had forgotten for a reason—and he wasn't sure he wanted to relive them. *And yet, if that's the only way I'm going to get over this, then I don't have much choice. Do I?*

CHAPTER 24

MICHELLE MET JOSEPH IN THE hospital cafeteria. It was between lunch and dinner rushes so the place was quiet and semiprivate. The relaxed atmosphere should have helped Joseph feel less tense about the meeting with his lawyer, but it didn't.

"Are you okay, Joseph? You seem a bit on edge."

"Really? Sorry. I guess it's being stuck here while everyone tries to figure out what to do with *my* life," he said acerbically.

She gave him a sympathizing look. "Well, I'm sure we all have your best interests at heart."

Joseph sighed wearily. He shouldn't take it out on her. After all, she *was* trying to help—and doing so on her own time. "I'm sorry for being terse. I guess I'm a bit of a control freak. Relying on others for . . . well, for everything, just doesn't sit well with me."

Michelle continued to smile softly, staring into his eyes. Joseph got the feeling she was simply trying to avoid looking at the hideous scar on his head. *And yet . . .*

"You probably don't like people prying into your personal affairs either."

"Not really," he said.

"Well, then let me apologize in advance. I've done a bit of looking into your life to date already. And I liked what I've found." She smiled with a mix of respect and embarrassment. "I assure you it was only for background on your case, Joseph."

"That's okay," he said, patting her wrist briefly. "I've had so many people checking every pore on my body that one more won't matter.

So what have you found? Any scandalous trysts with foreign dignitaries?"

"'Fraid not. Nothing but good, wholesome stuff . . . for the most part." She slid a file folder from her attaché, while she continued speaking. "Your grade school marks were less than stellar at McKinley Elementary, from K through fifth grade. There's even a record of a psych evaluation in the fifth grade. After that your academic performance gradually improved. You graduated from Santa Barbara Junior High with pretty good marks, and from Santa Barbara High with a 3.9 GPA, including some AP courses. Your college grades are very impressive, which makes me wonder why you didn't pursue a Ph.D."

"I wanted to get out and teach kids as soon as possible. I *was* looking at grad school if I couldn't find a job right away, but the Solvang position opened up, so I jumped on it," he explained.

Michelle nodded. "And you've done an outstanding job. According to your evals, you've had very high student and peer marks, not a single infraction or coaching occurrence, and your principal's comments make you sound like God's gift to the school."

Joseph rolled his eyes.

"According to county and state police records, you have no prior arrests, investigations, or even traffic citations. Even your credit history has no red flags on it. In all, you're about as squeaky clean as they come. Which makes me wonder why you're not married." In spite of her efforts to remain focused and professional, a blush colored her cheeks and neck.

Joseph shrugged. "The right gal hasn't come along, I guess. But what has all this got to do with my traffic accident?"

"Nothing really. Most of this is investigative disclosure from Stansbury, Vail, and Jenkins. They're required by law to share everything they dig up with the opposing council. As a matter of practice, I look into whatever they look into. But with your profile, they're probably sweating bullets."

"Which means what?"

"Which means this should be an open-and-shut case. I've obtained a DVD of the traffic cam showing the accident and have copies of the police and paramedic reports too." She paused as a shadow passed behind her eyes. Her brows arched in concern. "Frankly, I'm surprised you survived. Have you seen the video?"

"No. But I was there, I promise."

As Michelle tried to withhold a smile, a dimple showed in her left cheek. Joseph hadn't noticed that before. "You have a guardian angel, Joseph."

"I don't know about that. I've been going through some bad nights lately, discovering stuff from my childhood I never knew about. If I do have an angel, he certainly wasn't with me back then."

Michelle frowned. "Bad dreams?"

"Yeah."

"From your childhood?"

"Yes."

"What age?"

Joseph could almost see the wheels turning inside her head. "From about ten on back."

"Ten years old . . ." she mused, her eyes holding both surprise and delight. "That'd be about fifth grade, right?"

"I suppose," he said, wondering where she was going with this. "Why?"

She looked up, her expression suddenly infused with astonishment. Wide-eyed, she asked, "That's when you had the psych evaluation, wasn't it. Do you remember much about that?"

Joseph absently traced a seam of wood grain on the tabletop with his finger. "A bit. Social Services had us kids examined by a state psychologist after my brother died. The only thing I remember is that he had these creepy pale green eyes that bugged out of his skull—and that he scared the crap out of me. I left each session totally petrified." He shook his head. "I don't remember what he asked or anything."

She gazed blankly for a time, a slight smile slowly growing at one corner of her mouth. The smile caused the dimple to form again. Then, with her eyes wandering aimlessly from one focal point to another, Michelle began nibbling on the end of her mechanical pencil.

"What are you thinking?" Joseph asked.

She looked up and shrugged. But there was mischief in her mannerisms, pure delight in her eyes. "Oh, nothing. Not really. Just . . . oh, never mind." She shook her head and continued. "Have you ever read the report?"

"Report?"

"Your psychological eval from the fifth grade."

"No," he replied. "I didn't even know what it was for. I went in, the creepy guy hooked me up to a bunch of wires then asked a bunch of questions. I was scared spitless. Whatever the psychologist said in his report, I'm certain it wasn't favorable."

She was silent another half minute. Joseph was more mystified than curious. But he figured she was the legal expert and knew what kind of information was necessary for his case. "Would you mind if I requested a copy of it?" she asked.

"No. Go ahead. But don't be too disappointed at what you find."

"Don't worry, I won't." She smiled as if curiously amused, yet slightly delighted—as if chastising herself for something she had previously overlooked.

"What?"

"Nothing. It's just amazing what a small world this is," she said through a wide smile. The dimple was back.

Joseph just grinned yet wasn't sure why. He had no clue what she was talking about, but he trusted her enough not to question her actions.

"Don't you worry, Joseph Ramirez," she said, patting his shoulder. "We're going to have this case settled in no time."

CHAPTER 25

YOUNG JOSEPH WAS HIDING UNDER the shrubbery beside his house. He trembled uncontrollably. Sounds of brutality and abuse penetrated the walls in muffled thuds and subdued crashes.

Crouching beside him, Antonio tried to sound reassuring. "It's okay, Joseph. It'll be over soon."

"Will Mama be okay?" Joseph whimpered.

"I pray so."

After a long pause, Joseph asked, "Why does Papa do this?"

Antonio picked up a twig and snapped it in several pieces. "I don't know."

The sounds inside the house ceased for a moment. It could mean Papa had passed out, or he was simply taking a rest from his tirade. Mama usually tried to defend herself, but it never amounted to much. She always ended up with cuts and bruises, torn clothing, and a bloody lip. One time Papa had beaten her so bad she had blood seeping from her right ear for two days. She couldn't hear very well for a month afterward. Joseph had received similar punishments. But he was certain he had deserved his. Papa had said so.

"Joseph?"

"Yeah?"

"Do you love Papa?"

Joseph had asked himself that question many times. Foremost in his memory were the good times: Christmases, birthday parties, the occasional outing to the beach. Papa was caring and funny those times. His breath still smelled like beer, but he wasn't drunk, and Joseph enjoyed his antics and roughhousing immensely.

But those weren't the only images that filled his young mind. He constantly fought to rid his memory of the bad times: the punishments for no reason, the screaming and the name-calling, and the insults that tore his heart in two.

His older brothers and sister did their best to intervene when they could, but it didn't always work. Emily seemed to have the best influence in calming Papa. Xavier usually ended up yelling as much as Papa. Antonio frequently received punishment in addition to Joseph. Papa was often so wasted he didn't even know who was connecting with his fist. At those times, Papa seemed to be someone else, someone inhuman, like the kind of person the devil possessed. Father Sandoval talked about that in catechism. He said once you let the devil in, he'll take over your body and mind and make you his. The only way to purge such an evil spirit was to confess your sins and repeat the penance the Holy Father prescribed.

But Papa never went to confession. He hardly ever went to church. Joseph was convinced his father was hopelessly possessed. But to say so would be dishonoring his parents. And that was just as bad. It was a commandment in the Bible.

"It's hard to love him sometimes," was Joseph's soft answer.

"I hate him," Antonio said in a voice wracked with anger. "I wish he was dead."

"Don't say that, Antonio! It is a sin."

"Mama says she still loves him," he continued bitterly, ignoring Joseph's warning. "How can that be when he hurts her all the time?"

"I don't know," Joseph whispered, hoping to encourage his brother to speak softer.

"José!" Papa barked within the house.

Both boys flinched and sucked in breath. Neither spoke.

"José! Get in here now!" the monster bellowed.

Joseph didn't move. Antonio stared wide-eyed at his younger brother.

"JOSÉ! Come now or you'll be punished!"

Joseph screwed his eyes shut and began an urgent prayer.

"JOOOOSÉÉÉ!" his father screamed. "*Uno . . .*"

Joseph was frozen, trying his best to block out his father's raging.

"*Dos . . .*"

Tears sprang from Joseph's eyes. His body began to involuntarily tremble.

"*Tres!*"

Joseph gasped for breath that would not come—suffocating on fear.

"You are a bad boy, José! Now I *have* to punish you! I didn't want to, but you make me have to do it."

Joseph's shaking turned epileptic. Antonio put an arm around his little brother and shushed him. It did little to help. Young Joseph was terrified to the point of crippling panic.

The back door crashed open. Both boys cringed and scrunched as far back under the shrubbery as they could, their arms held firmly around each other.

"José Estefan Ramirez! Where are you, you stupid little boy?"

Joseph's praying became fervent. Tears flowed continuously. Antonio held him tighter.

"I know you can hear me, *el falla*. Come out now. If you make me search, I will have to punish you even more."

Joseph could barely restrain his raspy whimpers. Antonio placed a hand over his mouth to quiet him.

Estefan stumbled around the backyard, completely disoriented. In his hand was a dark bottle with a gold label. He growled low in his throat. "José Ramirez. José Estefan Ramirez. José is too good a name for such a silly boy. Always asking questions. Papa what is this? Papa why is that? Question, question, question. Stupid, stupid, stupid. It is an insult to say your name in the same breath as my name."

Estefan tried to take a drink, stumbled, and fell directly in front of the two brothers. Joseph loosed a scream muffled by Antonio's hand. His eyes bulged with fright, as if he'd just seen the devil himself. It wasn't far from the truth.

The drunk bumbled to his feet and brushed against the bushes under which his sons hid. "José, José, José," he spat in a drunken slur. "Your name is like a poison in my mouth. José, *el falla*. José, the mistake."

The monster tilted the bottle and drained it into his mouth. Only about half was swallowed. He then stumbled toward the side of the house and disappeared down the sidewalk.

Joseph was content to spend the night under the shrubbery, but he knew his mother must be hurt. She needed his help. When he tried to leave, Antonio stayed him. "No, Joseph. Not yet."

"Mama needs us," he whispered back.

"No, Joseph. Please stay. If Papa sees you, he'll kill you."

Joseph thought for a moment then said in all seriousness, "I'll ask God to keep me safe."

"As will I," his brother said with conviction. "But I wonder if that is enough."

* * *

Joseph awoke with a jolt and found himself scrunched under the covers at the foot of his bed. He clawed his way out and sat on the edge of his bed. Reaching for his notepad, he jumped when Clyde's voice sounded in the darkness.

"Another bad one?"

He swallowed hard. "Yeah."

"Any clues in this one?"

"Clues?" Joseph wondered how his roommate knew what he was looking for.

"Yeah. About your dad's death."

The information came as a complete shock to Joseph. "His death?"

"Well, yeah. What—didn't this last dream have anything in it about the murder?"

Joseph was wide awake now. "Wait—what in the world makes you think my father was murdered?" Joseph's surprised tone did little to conceal his angst and confusion.

Clyde didn't answer. Joseph couldn't see more than a silhouette of his roommate framed by the moon glow entering the window, but he could pick out the eerie sheen of the man's eyes staring at him.

"Clyde?"

The older man cleared his throat. "Never mind, Joe. Go back to sleep."

"Wait, Clyde. What's this about murder?"

Clyde rolled over and hiked the blankets to his neck. "Forget it, pal. My mistake. G'night."

"Hey. Clyde?"

His roommate remained silent.

Joseph clenched his jaw. He knew it would do no good to pursue the issue. Clyde was that stubborn. When he said good night, there was no turning back. The guy would be asleep in a matter of minutes.

But his roommate's incredible statement screamed for an answer in Joseph's mind. Estefan was dead? Murdered? Could Clyde be making it up? Was it more supposition than fact? And if it *was* factual, what was he basing his questions on? Or . . . or was he simply joking around?

Joseph glanced at Clyde once more, debating whether or not to wake him and insist on some answers. He sighed and let it go. It was almost two in the morning. Joseph would ask him later in the morning . . . and pray he could get back to sleep before morning came.

CHAPTER 26

EMILY AND JOSEPH SAT AT a corner table in the hospital cafeteria—the same table at which he'd met with Michelle a few days earlier. Both siblings had a small dish of blueberry cobbler in front of them; Joseph's was to satisfy his insatiable sweet tooth, Emily's was so he didn't feel awkward indulging alone. Presently, neither of them was eating.

"Dr. Wilder, my psychiatrist, he's been having me write down as much as I can remember from my dreams, but I'm not getting much. I write it the minute I wake up, but when I look at what I wrote the next morning, it doesn't make any sense."

"Like what?" Emily asked with a mix of curiosity and dread.

Joseph used his spoon to push his cobbler around the small bowl. "Well, the first time I tried it, I could barely read my own writing." He shrugged. "It was like trying to read the doctor's scribbling in my chart."

Emily smiled. "Perhaps you should have had the hospital pharmacist read it for you."

"No kidding," he chortled, then looked up with a crooked grin. "I did have a dream where I found out why I prefer the name Joseph."

"It seemed like you always did. So what was it?"

"Some lady was nice to me once and called me Joseph. With Papa always using my name like a curse word, I guess that's all it took."

She nodded. "What about the other dreams?"

"Well, a couple have been about falling from a building, and others have bits about hiding outside the house."

She shrugged. "That doesn't sound too bizarre. You often played hide-and-seek. And everybody has dreams about falling."

"True, but this is different; just a bunch of disjointed words and half sentences—nothing that spells out a definite story or plotline, and definitely nothing I remember on my own."

"Well, I'm sure your psychiatrist can figure it out from there."

"Yeah, maybe so," Joseph acknowledged. "But how do I know that what he comes up with is the right thing?"

Emily scooped a small bite of cobbler and popped it in her mouth. "How do you know the pills in the bottle the pharmacy gives you are the right ones?" she countered.

Joseph just stared at her, not understanding.

"You have to trust the expertise of the health professional. You can always get a second opinion, but for the most part, I think initial trust goes a long way in helping the therapy work."

Joseph smiled. "When did you get to be so smart, Em?"

She playfully threw a napkin at him. "Now you're making fun of me."

"No, not at all. You've always been very insightful. I constantly look up to that."

She regarded him curiously for a moment. "Is that from one of your dreams?"

He shook his head. "Not really. The dreams I do remember have had little to do with you. They're mostly about me and Antonio . . . and Papa."

"So there *is* more than just snippets. Can you tell me about them? Do any of them involve old girlfriends?" she asked, leading.

Joseph looked around the sparsely filled cafeteria. He leaned forward and poked at his cobbler. "First, tell me more about *el falla*."

Emily drew a staggered breath. Her eyes misted slightly as she stared at her brother. "I'd rather not, Joseph, if it's okay."

He looked up angrily. "No, it's not okay, Em. I think it may be the key to what's haunting my past. Please."

She paused and pulled a tissue from her purse. "It's a bit complicated. I'm not sure I know the full story myself." She sipped some water to steel herself before beginning. "As you know, most Catholics don't believe in using birth control."

Joseph nodded.

"Papa was one of the exceptions. He believed he had just as much right determining when he'd have a child as God did in sending one. Xavier was his pride and joy. Me being next was right in line with his preplanned family—a boy first, then a girl."

"Like he had much say in the matter," Joseph scoffed.

"Oh, he felt he did."

"Didn't anyone ever tell him about the whole process: the birds and the bees, sperm fertilizing egg and all that?"

"I don't know, but even if he knew, it wouldn't have mattered. He had it all planned out, and there was no altering his decision or way of thinking."

"Was he really that narrow-minded?" Joseph wondered.

Emily rolled her eyes. "*Pigheaded* is a better term. Maybe even obsessive psychotic, if there is such a thing. Whenever anything didn't go his way, he blew up. I mean really blew up—like he changed into another person and went crazy on everyone."

Joseph stabbed at his cobbler and mulled over her words. His sweet tooth had long since vanished. "Let me guess: I was supposed to be a girl?"

A tear escaped Emily's lids and traced down her cheek. "To his way of thinking, because you were born much later than he planned, you had lost your chance at life."

"*Much later?* So I was a surprise?"

"To Papa, a mistake."

Joseph leaned back and placed his hands flat on the table. The revelation didn't sadden him as much as he thought it might. Since he didn't remember much about that part of his life, it didn't affect him as it might have otherwise. Still, the thought that his own father considered him an error in timing—instead of a son—created a gaping void in his belly that ached to be filled. "But why a *mistake?*" he asked in a shallow voice.

Emily wiped her eyes. "That's what I never completely figured out. I think his plan was a child every two years. That's how much time is between Xavier and me, and me and Antonio. Then, for some reason, Mama couldn't get pregnant when Papa wanted her too. It caused all sorts of bad feelings at home. Lots of fighting and resentment. When you finally came along—what, three, four years later?—and were a boy instead of a girl, well, Papa went ballistic. That might be part of it . . . but I think there's more."

"Was Mama using birth control?"

"I assume Papa wanted her to in spite of the Church's teachings, but obviously *something* happened out of sync."

Joseph stabbed his spoon into his dessert. "And he continued to beat her for it for the next ten years."

Emily's hand shot to her chest. "How did you know that?"

"One of my dreams. Antonio and I were hiding one night while Papa was laying into her."

"Just Mama?" she asked hesitantly.

"So far. Why?"

The tears began flowing freely. "Oh, Joseph, it was awful. *He* was awful. It happened all the time, to both Mama *and* you. After he left, you never mentioned the insults or the beatings—"

"*Punishments,*" he clarified.

Emily's eyes widened, temporarily staunching the tears. "You *do* remember! We just assumed you blocked it from your memory— which was fine with us."

"I guess I did, as I'm only now learning about it." The bitterness in Joseph's voice was palpable.

Emily's eyes filled with pleading. "Please try to understand, Joseph. We didn't want you to hurt anymore. Everything was fine after Papa left."

"You mean after he was murdered," Joseph said flatly.

Emily's brow furrowed. "Murdered?"

Joseph couldn't believe that she didn't know. "Oh, come on, Em! You're saying this is the first time you've heard that?"

She nodded slowly.

"Well, I don't know for sure. I haven't had any dreams I remember or wrote down about anything exactly like that, but apparently I've been saying such things in my sleep."

"Murdered," Emily said more to herself than Joseph.

"Yeah. According to my roommate, I might have had something to do with it."

Her eyes snapped up. "You? You were only ten or so when he disappeared."

Joseph nodded. "It doesn't make sense to me either. Dr. Wilder has me scheduled for some hypnotic regression. Hopefully we'll find out then."

"Hypnosis?" Emily crossed herself. "Joseph, are you sure that's a good idea?"

He shrugged. "He seems to think it's necessary. And I'd surely like to get to the bottom of these nightmares before I lose my mind. Why?"

Her eyes had finally stopped leaking, but they still held a look of deep sorrow. "Because Papa's gone. Whether he's dead or not doesn't matter. He's gone and out of our lives." Her voice held an edge Joseph had seldom heard before. "If he was murdered, fine. I don't care. But if he's not dead, and he comes back, we're old enough now to confront him and make sure the beatings don't happen again."

"His *punishments*."

Emily's shoulders slumped. "I'm so sorry you remembered that."

Joseph leaned forward and began massaging his temples. "That and *el falla*. Strange that it's only come to me twenty years later, huh?"

"I wish it hadn't," she said quietly.

"Judging from your reaction, I'm guessing Papa had more than an anger management issue."

Emily put her tissue to use again. "Any little thing you did that displeased him made him crazy with anger, especially your questions. You were always so inquisitive," she said with a weak smile working its way through the remorse. "That's probably why you became a science teacher."

Joseph could tell this was as hard on his sister as it was on him. He smiled tenderly and took her hand in his. "It's okay, Em. I don't remember any of that—well, very little anyway. Maybe I will later on. But until then you shouldn't worry about it. I'm okay. Really. Just a little lost sleep . . . so far. I'll have a few more sessions with my psychiatrist, and if he feels there's a concern we'll deal with it then."

Emily wiped her eyes and kissed the back of his hand. "You're right. You're a brave man." A full smile finally broke through. "And smart and caring and handsome. Mama's right. You should have been married a long time ago."

"Okay, enough!" he laughed.

Emily wiped her eyes one last time, and with heartfelt tenderness, she said, "I love you, Joseph."

"I love you too, Em."

Emily Ramirez Ortega collected herself and stood. "Joseph?"

He smiled with raised eyebrows.

"Don't say anything about Papa's murder to Mama—or anyone else." And with that, she exited the cafeteria at a brisk walk, leaving Joseph with more questions than he came with.

CHAPTER 27

JOSEPH SAT ALONE AT THE large oak conference table looking through a three-year-old *National Geographic*. He wasn't reading anything; he couldn't focus long enough to finish a sentence. His thoughts were random and harried, too many concerns vying for immediate resolution. All were vital, perhaps even life-changing, but none had an identifiable resolution.

Michelle Haas entered the hospital conference room wearing a severely tailored black pantsuit and a red silk blouse. Her hair was pulled into a tight bun and held in place with two red-lacquered chopsticks. The total look said, *Don't mess with me or I'll skin you alive.*

"Wow, you look ready for blood," Joseph said, closing the magazine.

"Thanks."

"No, seriously. It's a good thing. You look great."

"You too," she said with a slight color rising in her cheeks.

Joseph looked over his baggy sweatshirt and rumpled jogging sweats with skepticism. "You're just jealous."

"Insanely."

"Yeah? Well listen, if we win this thing, I promise I'll buy you an outfit just like this."

"*When* we win this thing," she corrected him.

"When," he concurred.

Michelle placed her attaché on the table and sat next to Joseph. "How're you feeling?"

"Fine, I guess. I'm still having trouble sleeping, but the rest of me seems to be coming along okay. It's these dreams I've been having . . . particularly the ones I can't remember."

"About your accident?"

"No. The nightmares about my childhood."

She cocked her head to one side. "Have the doctors connected your accident to these bad dreams?"

Joseph played with the frayed edges of the *Geographic*. "They can't find anything *physically* wrong with me—besides the obvious. They say the nightmares might be from a bruised brain or excess blood between my skull and cranial sac, but nothing like that shows on the MRI. The good news is there's no excess pressure in there."

Michelle had her yellow legal pad out and was scribbling furiously. "How about your psychological diagnoses?"

Joseph slid the magazine across the table. "Jury's still out on that. Besides, I just started. The psychiatrist, Dr. Wilder, has a few ideas we're working on, but I don't know . . ."

The attorney stopped scribbling. "Don't know about what?"

Joseph shrugged. "Dr. Wilder's a great guy, no doubt, but, well, I just don't feel comfortable around psychiatrists."

"Because of the creepy Social Services guy?"

"I guess. Have you looked at my childhood eval yet?"

Michelle shook her head. "I haven't, but I will. In the meantime, I think it would be in your best interest to keep going to your sessions. Any patient-requested deviation in standard hospital protocol or recommendation is potential ammunition for Stansbury, Vail, and Jenkins."

Joseph sighed. "I suppose you're right."

Michelle checked off something on her notepad. "So your brother died in a gang-related incident?"

"Yeah, as far as I know."

Michelle kept scribbling. "At risk of dredging up painful memories, did you or anyone else ever look into that?"

"I can't recall. But I doubt I could get Mother to talk about it."

"Ever ask your brother or sister?"

"Yeah, but they told me the same thing I just told you."

"And your father left when?"

"A couple months after my sister Victoria was born." He paused briefly. "Um . . . is this relevant to my accident?"

Michelle smiled. "No. I apologize, Joseph. I was just curious. Let's move on, shall we?" She pulled out a plastic-sheathed document and opened it. "SVJ's second proposal here is a joke. I think they're trying to scare you with legal-speak because they cite a bunch of precedents that have very little, if anything, to do with your case. They are willing to pay for a new car of equal value to your Stanza and any incurred medical expenses and follow-up expenses up to three years from the date of the accident, plus $9,000 in lost work compensation and $50,000 for emotional duress."

Joseph gulped. "That sounds pretty complete to me," he stammered.

"It's a paltry sum. It's an insult. Joseph, at risk of any racial profiling, as an otherwise healthy twenty-nine-year-old Hispanic model citizen, you are a gold mine."

"I wouldn't be too quick with the 'model citizen' part," Brick Wiseman said from the conference room doorway.

Joseph and Michelle looked up in surprise.

"What are you doing here?" Michelle cringed as if she had just detected a nearby sewage treatment plant.

Brick remained in the doorway smiling smugly. "Oh, I just happened to be in the neighborhood. Good thing too. I was going to ask how the review of our offer is coming, but I bumped into someone very interesting instead. May I introduce my new best friend, Detective Leonard McRae of the Santa Barbara Police homicide department."

Detective McRae was a stout man with hefty bags under his eyes, a round face, and a wide, lipless mouth. To Joseph, he looked like a bullfrog. His incredibly wide shoulders stressed the stitching of his starched, plaid shirt, and his knit tie hung from a neck that resembled a tree trunk. He flashed Brick a disapproving glare then nodded at Michelle Haas. "Ma'am."

Michelle didn't move.

To Joseph he asked, "Mr. Joseph Ramirez?"

"As far as you know," Joseph said, casting a questioning look at his lawyer.

"I need to ask you a few questions regarding the murder of your father, Estefan Salvador Arango Ramirez."

Joseph's breath caught in his throat. He coughed and sputtered. How did this guy find out? Joseph had only just heard the rumor two nights ago from Clyde. He had not had the chance to expand on the conversation with his roommate and had yet to mention anything to Michelle Haas. How did the word get out, and just how many people knew about it?

"Is this your lawyer?" the detective asked, nodding toward Michelle.

"Yes, I am," Michelle said, standing. "What does this have to do with my client's car accident and current medical circumstances?"

"Nothing, I suppose," he said with a shrug.

"I'm not so sure about that," Wiseman chimed in.

The detective scowled at him. "Do you mind?" he growled.

"Hold on—you're not together, then?" Michelle asked the two men.

McRae gave Wiseman a second look of disdain. "No, ma'am. I am familiar with who Mr. Wiseman is. Just turn on the TV and you'll see his greasy, ambulance-chasing commercials. But like he said, we just bumped into each other. It's probably the only honest thing he's said all day."

Brick flinched but didn't say anything.

McRae continued. "I was just coming to ask Mr. Ramirez a couple of questions."

Michelle extended her hand across the table toward the detective. "Michelle Haas, attorney for Mr. Joseph Ramirez."

They shook cordially.

"I am currently in a meeting with my client, detective. Is this something that can wait?"

"I'd rather not, if it's all the same," he said without malice. "Besides, it'll only take a minute."

Michelle glanced at her watch and nodded. "Okay. But I insist on being present."

"Fine."

She turned to Brick. "As this is none of your affair, you may leave, Mr. Wiseman. Thank you."

"Oh, that's okay. I'll just stand in the corner, if it's all the same," he said, almost mocking the detective.

McRae said nothing, waiting for Michelle's response. He didn't wait long.

Michelle's tone was acidic. "This is a private meeting, Mr. Wiseman, not a deposition, so you have no legal precedent for being present. I've asked you to leave once. Don't make me insist."

Brick chuckled in his trademark condescending tone. "Now, now, Michelle. Let's not ruffle feathers here. We're all in this together. I'm simply interested in hearing what the good detective has to say, that's all."

"Look, Wiseman, the lady asked you nicely. If *I* have to ask, I guarantee it won't be so nice," McRae stated evenly. Although the lawyer was taller than the detective, McRae's solid form was imposing enough to circumvent questioning his sincerity.

Flustered, Brick offered his best politician's smile. "No worries, my friends. I've got to be in court soon, anyway." He waved and left the conference room without further word.

"Now, what's this all about?" Joseph asked McRae, still baffled by the man's knowledge of his father's alleged murder.

Speaking more to Michelle than to Joseph, McRae said, "We have reason to believe your client has information about the murder of Estefan Ramirez."

Joseph slammed his fists on the table. "What murder? Look—my father left my mother with four children and no means of support. We never found out where he went and haven't heard from him since. He never made much money, but at least he kept food on the table. Why would I jeopardize my family's welfare by—" He stopped short and steadied his breath. "This is ridiculous. I was only ten years old when he left. How could I have murdered him?"

Detective McRae cocked his head to one side. "That's interesting. I never said *you* murdered him."

Joseph closed his eyes and willed his temper to a civil level. "Look, detective, I have no idea where my father is. Are you saying you've found his body somewhere?"

"No."

"Joseph," Michelle jumped in, "I don't think you should answer or ask any more questions until I've had a chance to look over the police report."

"Haven't really generated a report yet, Ms. Haas," McRae admitted.

"So this isn't some cold case file?" Michelle asked.

"No, ma'am."

"Wait!" Joseph snapped. "I still want to know why you think my father was murdered."

"Can't divulge sources just yet," McRae said as he pulled out a PDA and used the stylus to pull up a screen. "He's been missing since . . . when exactly?"

"I told you: since I was ten. It was a few months after my little sister was born, maybe eighteen, nineteen years ago."

"And you say you have no idea what happened to him," the detective asked rhetorically.

"None. I've always assumed he was just a deadbeat dad—not that he was actually dead. Maybe he went back to Guatemala."

"Well, we'll see," McRae said as if it didn't really matter. "But we're pretty sure he was murdered."

"And why's that?"

"Because you admitted to killing him."

The air seemed to drain from the room. Joseph's lungs felt empty, collapsed. His mind whirled; his equilibrium vanished. When he could finally draw breath, he asked in an astonished whisper, "When did I do this?"

"A couple times. You don't remember doing so?"

"No."

"Detective McRae," Michelle said professionally. "My client is recovering from a severe traffic accident that left him with massive head trauma—the extent of which we've yet to ascertain. He's still undergoing physical and psychological rehabilitation. His release date from this hospital hasn't even been determined yet. Any undue emotional stress could seriously hamper his recovery. Therefore, unless you have a warrant for his arrest, I respectfully ask that we take this up at another time."

McRae considered her for a moment then turned to Joseph. "You're the guy who was squashed up in Solvang, right?"

Joseph coughed. "To put it mildly."

The policeman pocketed his PDA and grinned. It was the kind of grin a killer whale gives a seal just before taking a bite. "Okay. Just want you to know I'll probably be opening a file on this; but since we don't have a body . . . yet . . . I'll be taking my time. It's not every day we get someone who confesses to murder before we find a victim. I'll be in touch."

He handed Michelle his card. She accepted it with a nod.

Joseph pressed his forehead to the table and tried not to scream.

CHAPTER 28

JOSEPH WAS NOW CONVINCED HIS dreams were past experiences trying to come to the surface. They had to be. His dreams were simply too real to be pure fantasy. Everything seemed accurate, every scenario plausible. But murder? There was no way. He'd have remembered something that extreme.

Dr. Wilder read Joseph's nighttime scrawl in silence as Joseph wiped a fine sheen of perspiration from his forehead. His hands quivered even though it wasn't cold. He told himself he wasn't nervous, but his reaction to the doctor's silence spoke otherwise.

"So . . . am I capable of killing my father?"

"Are you or *were* you?" the psychiatrist said without looking up.

Joseph wanted to chuckle but couldn't bring himself to do so. "You tell me, doc."

Dr. Wilder drew a hand across his closely cropped hair. "You'd be surprised how many childhood experiences predicate our actions as adults," he explained. "But predisposing someone to be a murderer rarely happens—if ever. In your case, it borders on the impossible. I don't see anything in these snippets that says you did *anything*. Yet we can't discount the trauma you obviously experienced as a child, even the stuff you can't remember."

"But if I can't remember the rotten things I went through, how can I confront them to get some closure?"

"In a way you've already done that by repressing them."

"Yeah, but it's all coming back. And it's bringing with it a horrible act I supposedly committed. How do I begin to rectify *that*?" Joseph asked with an unmasked measure of defeat.

Dr. Wilder rested his elbows on his knees and clasped his hands thoughtfully. "First, know that it *can* be done, okay? Now, my primary concern has to be helping you remember as much as possible. That's something I can do only with your willingness to *be* helped. We'll deal with what we find later. The thing is, the procedure is not foolproof. And it's something most well-educated people consciously resist."

"What—hypnotherapy with a silver pendulum and hallucinogenic drugs?" Joseph jested.

Dr. Wilder shrugged. "Maybe later—if it comes to that. For now, just focused cognitive regression."

Joseph frowned at the psychiatrist.

"Look, it's not quite as sinister as all that," Dr. Wilder explained. "But the gist of it is helping you relax enough to allow your subconscious to dominate your conscious, and then I gently coax your repressed memories to the surface. It's at that point we can begin to resolve what's bothering you."

"*Begin* to resolve? You mean this isn't a one-time deal?"

"Rarely. Repressed memory is not something constructed as a single act; therefore, it can't be deconstructed in a single session."

"How's this different from what we've already done?"

The psychiatrist randomly scratched an eyebrow. "We've been bringing out forgotten experiences, things that for whatever reason have been pushed to the back of your mind. Repressed memories are those that you have *intentionally* blocked, so as not to relive them."

"Wait a minute. I thought you said there was no such thing as repressed memories."

"No such thing as *subconsciously* repressed memories. We sometimes deliberately block things from our minds so we don't have to deal with the guilt or sorrow they originally caused," Dr. Wilder explained.

"Could it turn out that I don't have *any* repressed memories—that I'm subconsciously making all this up to fill in the gaps of my childhood?"

"Interesting premise, Joseph, but I believe you *did* repress some of them, back when you were ten. The fact that they are disrupting the normality of your life indicates you have some emotional issues that need to be addressed."

"Recuperating from a near-death experience is not what I consider a normal life, doc."

"Okay, then—disrupting your normal sleep patterns."

"Yeah, but why?"

"It was undoubtedly the trauma to your brain that triggered the recall process," the psychiatrist said with conviction. "Where many people experience amnesia from a blow to the head, you've done just the opposite. You're now remembering things you didn't know you forgot—or, in your case, repressed."

Joseph was silent a moment as he contemplated what he'd just learned. It did not sit well with him on several levels. He had always considered himself self-assured, self-composed, and very self-reliant. He liked being in control of everything relevant to Joseph Ramirez. He wasn't a management freak, but he did feel confident he could handle any dilemma that came his way—as long as he was in charge of *how* it was handled. To have someone insinuate that his current uncontrollable problem stemmed from something that happened almost twenty years ago was tantamount to saying he had no control over *anything*.

Still, Joseph was enough of a scientist to know he didn't understand everything. He taught his students to keep an open mind—but not so open your brains fall out. He also taught them that preconceived notions were often the blinders that limited greater insights.

"But—" He paused. "But what if we find out I *am* guilty of murder?"

"Don't think that far ahead, Joseph. It'll skew the accuracy of discovery. Let's just worry about uncovering as much of your past as we can. We'll determine what needs to be done with the information later."

Joseph took a steeling breath. "Okay. When do we begin?"

"Right now," the psychiatrist said. "If that's okay with you."

Joseph rubbed his eyes. "The way I'm feeling now, the sooner the better."

CHAPTER 29

"SHOULD I HIT THE BIKES?" Joseph asked with physical and emotional fatigue straining his words.

"No. In this instance it's better for you to be as relaxed as possible."

"The couch, then?"

"Yep," Dr. Wilder said, standing.

Joseph ambled over to the long sofa while Dr. Wilder went to a wall-mounted control box. He punched some buttons, and the glass in the windows gradually began to darken to an opaque, translucent shade of gray. When a comfortable level of light filtered through the glass, Dr. Wilder drew up a chair next to Joseph's feet.

"Cool windows," Joseph commented.

"Magnetic liquid crystal–impregnated glass—kinda like the readout on a watch, only on a much larger scale. It's better than blinds because you can precisely balance the light regardless of the weather outside."

"Expensive?"

"You don't want to know."

Joseph smiled. "That pretty much answers the question. Why not black out the windows and adjust the light within the room?"

"I prefer natural light to anything artificial. It's more comforting, more relaxing." He pulled out his digital recorder and pressed RECORD. "Now, let's take this nice and easy. I'm going to ask you some very simple questions."

"Wait. Before we begin, I found out why my father called me *el falla,* the mistake." Joseph was sitting on the edge of the sofa with his hands on his knees. His knuckles blanched slightly, indicating he was not comfortable with this information.

"Okay," the psychiatrist said, leading.

"My sister told me. She said it's because I was unexpected—you know, an 'oops, guess what, dear?' child—*and* I was supposed to be a girl."

Dr. Wilder's eyebrows raised a fraction. "The 'oops' I understand. I was one of those, in fact. But what's this about gender switching?"

Joseph explained everything Emily had mentioned about their father's obsession with domination of his family, and his belief that he could control everything that went on under his roof.

"Seems pretty harsh for something totally beyond his control," the doctor said.

Joseph scoffed. "You didn't know my father."

"True. But from what we've discussed so far, neither did you."

Joseph looked up at Dr. Wilder with hooded eyes. Almost a full minute passed before he said, "You're right. I didn't. I still don't."

"Well, let's see what we can both learn, then, shall we?"

Joseph nodded.

"Lie back and get as comfortable as you can. I'm going to ask a few simple questions. I want you to close your eyes and not worry about whether your answers are right or wrong or what *I* want to hear. The key to this is total relaxation—not to the point that you're asleep but pretty close."

Joseph snuggled onto the couch and folded his hands across his stomach. He closed his eyes and willed himself to breathe slow and deep. Dr. Wilder began by asking simple yes or no questions. Are you a teacher? Do you like teaching? Do you like living in Solvang? All questions to which he already knew the answer and which would put Joseph in a positive state of mind. He then progressed to more detailed questions. What is your favorite color? What is your favorite place in Solvang? Your favorite shop? What is your favorite subject to teach and why? Next he began asking questions that Joseph would have to draw from his memory. What year did you graduate from college? From high school? From elementary school? When was the last Christmas you spent at home? What is your fondest memory of Christmas? What was your favorite thing to do with your brothers? Your sisters? What did you want to be when you grew up? And so on.

Slowly, careful not to ask questions that had a preconceived answer, Dr. Wilder softened his voice and asked Joseph to think back as far as he could. He asked Joseph to settle into that timeframe, to place himself in the actual period in his mind, to become the person he was back then. He asked Joseph to describe his home, his bedroom, his backyard. As Dr. Wilder got him talking about those memories, Joseph's voice also became softer, more childlike.

"Can you tell me your full name?"

"José Estefan Ramirez."

"That's a fine name, José. Do you like it?" he asked, knowing the answer.

"No. I like Joseph," the little boy voice answered.

"And why is that?"

Silence. Joseph scooted onto his side and began to curl into a ball.

"It's okay, Joseph. You and I are the only ones here. No one else can hear you. You're safe here. Do you believe me?"

"*Sí*."

"Good. So why do you like the name Joseph more than José?"

"A nice lady called me that once."

"What does your father call you?"

"Papa calls me José."

"Is that bad?"

Joseph nodded briskly but only moved his head a fraction of an inch, as a child might. "He makes it sound bad. He makes fun of it. In a mean way."

"Do you know why he makes fun of your name?"

Joseph's lip began to quiver.

"Joseph?" Dr. Wilder prompted.

"He says it is a . . . a stupid name, and . . . and . . ."

"And what?"

"And he says I am a mistake." The little voice was thin, strained, on the verge of sobbing. "He says I cost him too much money. He was saving his money to fix his Caddy."

"His Caddy?"

"*Sí*, his Cadillac. But Mama had me instead, and now he can't pay to fix it. It's all my fault." A single, wrenching sob broke through. "I'm sorry, Papa. I didn't mean to be born."

"Joseph, I am a doctor," Alex Wilder said in a firm tone. "I promise you no child is ever a mistake, no matter what your father says. Do you believe me?"

Joseph trembled. He stifled a couple of sobs and nodded quickly again.

"Papa says Mama had me on purpose—that she didn't ask him, and that was bad."

"Your father wanted more children, though, didn't he?"

"*Sí*, but I was too late. So Papa says I wasn't his. He didn't want to even give me a name, so Mama chose José. Papa never liked it and—" He stopped suddenly, as if sensing he was in trouble for revealing so much.

"Joseph, listen to me. José is not a stupid name. You changed it to Joseph, and that's okay. You were very smart and very brave to do so. But little Joseph is still smart and brave, and he's all grown up now. *You* are the older Joseph. Do you understand?"

Another nod.

"Very good. Now, I want you to keep your eyes closed and pretend you are at the bottom of a staircase. I want you to climb those stairs, slowly, one at a time. There's no rush, Joseph. When you reach the top, you'll be in the office of Dr. Alex Wilder, at St. Luke's Hospital in Goleta, California. You are safe. It's okay. Come on now. Are you climbing the stairs?"

"Uh-huh," he said.

"You are no longer the young Joseph of long ago. You are the older Joseph, the science teacher who is safe and happy."

"Okay."

"When you get to the top of the stairs, where will you be?"

"In your office."

"Excellent, Joseph. Are you near the top?"

"Yes."

"Good. I am going to count to three. When I get to three you'll be in my office. One . . . two . . . three."

Joseph slowly opened his eyes. They had a vacant, disoriented look in them, but no fear. He was no longer trembling, either. Joseph remained in a fetal position for a few minutes while his mind focused on his surroundings.

"Welcome back, Joseph," Dr. Wilder said with a smile.

"Thanks."

"How do you feel?"

Joseph rubbed the back of his neck. "Kind of foggy. Kind of melancholy, too, for some reason. Is that weird?"

"Not considering what we found out," the psychiatrist said, still smiling.

"Oh yeah? What?"

"You don't remember?"

Joseph concentrated but came up blank. "No."

"Apparently your father had several issues we're just discovering."

The next half hour was spent discussing what was just revealed about Joseph's past and, more importantly, how he could cope with the negative emotions generated from uncovering the truth. Dr. Wilder said it had been a very productive session. Joseph wasn't so sure.

CHAPTER 30

THE FOLLOWING MORNING, MICHELLE HAAS entered Joseph's room with a small box of pastries from Dansk Sødtbrød.

"Where'd you get that?" Joseph asked the obvious.

"Solvang. I went up to check out the accident site and then stopped in at this bakery. Why—don't you like this stuff?" The mischievous twinkle in her eyes told Joseph she already knew the answer. "By the way, the Vanden-something-somethings say hi."

"Vandenlundervaldt. It took me a while to get it right too."

"Say, whatcha got there, counselor?" Clyde perked up. He'd been thoroughly absorbed in the replay of a football game until then.

Michelle looked over at Clyde, then back to Joseph.

"Don't fight it," Joseph said. "Just let him choose one now, or we'll never get back to business."

"Atta boy, Joe." Clyde already had a napkin in hand in the short time it took Michelle to round Joseph's bed. Joseph smiled as Clyde's hand hovered over the open box, his fingers dancing. "My, my, my, my they all look so appealing. This is harder than having to choose a new wife."

"Speaking of which," Joseph sniggered, "why don't you tell Ms. Haas what you told me the last time she came here? You remember—about your first impressions of her?"

Clyde blanched. Michelle flashed Joseph a questioning glance then fixed a hard gaze on the older man. Joseph knew the poor guy was squirming under the intensity of her steely blue eyes. Wisely, he quickly shoved a large bear claw into his mouth and mumbled an apology about not being able to speak with his mouth full, and wanting to get back to his game.

"Never mind," Michelle said. "I can guess." Returning to Joseph's side, she jerked her head in Clyde's direction. "I don't think we should talk here."

Joseph chuckled. "It's okay. He's harmless." After a pause he added, "As long as he's confined to his bed, that is."

The lawyer leveled one last gaze in Clyde's direction then moved to stand with her back to him. "I'm concerned about attorney-client privilege. If a third party such as Mr. Richter overhears the details of your case, they become discoverable to anyone and may lose their effect in court."

Joseph understood only part of her explanation. He couldn't get his mind off how different she looked today. She was dressed more casually today, wearing a lustrous navy chiffon blouse that highlighted the blue of her eyes, a pair of snug jeans, and loafers. Her hair was pulled back at the sides, which accentuated her high cheekbones. She removed a manila file from her attaché and opened it.

"What if I don't care if he overhears? I have nothing to hide."

Michelle's eyes narrowed as she considered Joseph's words. "Well, I'll try to keep it simple, just in case. Obviously, we're talking about two separate cases, Joseph: the traffic accident and the disappearance of your father. But I'd be happy to help you with both, if you like."

"Absolutely," he said gratefully. "Thanks."

"My pleasure. But we should address them one at a time. The stress might be a bit much, especially since you're still recovering. I'm worried about you . . . taking on too much, that is."

"No, I'm good with it. I want to get back to normality as soon as possible."

"Okay," she said with unmasked admiration in her eyes. "You know, not many people could take on two life-altering issues at once, even when perfectly healthy. I'm impressed."

"Don't be."

"Of course, I'll probably have to bill you for the overtime. At $300 an hour, that adds up pretty quick."

Joseph stared slack-jawed, unable to speak.

Michelle tipped her head back and laughed. "Just kidding. I'm still on the firm's payroll. All this," she tapped the manila folder, "is pro bono work thus far. If you earn anything—and I believe you will—then we can talk about a contingency fee for filing charges, paperwork, etc. Made you blink, though, didn't I."

"A firecracker! Didn't I say that, Joe?" Clyde hooted. "A real firecracker."

With her back still to Clyde, Michelle pulled up a stool next to Joseph's bed and lowered her voice. "Sorry about that. I didn't think he was listening. Just trying to lighten things up. So you still don't have any idea why or when you allegedly confessed to murder?"

"No. Besides Clyde saying I mumbled it in my sleep once, the only thing I can think of is maybe it came out in a therapy session with Dr. Wilder. But I don't remember him mentioning anything like that. I suppose you could ask him."

"I just might. But even if it *did* come up in a session, it should be covered under patient-doctor confidentiality clauses. Is Dr. Wilder the kind of guy that would run to the police with something like this?

Joseph thought for a moment then shook his head. "I doubt it. And I'm pretty sure he'd have asked me about it by now."

Michelle chewed on the end of her pen, thinking. "Any chance it could have come up some other time—like someone reading one of the dreams you've written down?"

"No. I still have all those, and there's nothing there about my father's death, let alone murder."

"Hmm," Michelle pondered. "Well, let's take care of the easy before we get into the more complex." She pulled another folder from her attaché and opened it on Joseph's lap. The closeness of her torso brought with it the scent of freshly shampooed hair and a hint of perfume. Something spicy, but not like a man's cologne. This was more subtle yet definitely intriguing. "This is the proposal I want to send to SVJ and Sierra West Construction," she continued. "It covers all your medical expenses, lost wages, a new vehicle, attorney fees, and any unforeseen compensatory damages, plus a stipend in case of a relapse of symptoms or any complications that occur after your discharge. What I've left out are any punitive damages."

Joseph leafed through the paperwork with rapt attention, but he didn't understand much of what was said. It all sounded very professional, although a bit redundant too. Mostly, he didn't care to be known as "the plaintiff." He knew it was necessary legal-speak, but that didn't mean he had to like it. What he was looking for was a bottom line.

"Can you show me exactly what we're asking?" he said, feeling a bit naive.

Michelle shuffled to the papers near the back of the treatise. "Right here. Depending on the final hospital bill—which includes Santa Ynez Valley Cottage Hospital fees, St. Luke's Hospital charges, continuing checkups, and physical- and psychotherapy, in addition to Life Flight charges, lost wages, and everything else I mentioned— we're estimating a tab of just under a million bucks."

Joseph gawked then frowned. "And that *doesn't* include punitive damages?"

"No, per your instructions," Michelle said. "Would you like to know what we *could* ask if we included those?"

"I do!" Clyde sang. Apparently the football game wasn't that engrossing.

As Joseph thought for a moment, Michelle stood and closed the curtain separating the two beds. "No offense," she said plainly.

"Hey, I'm easy," the older man replied.

"Sorry, Joseph. Even if you're not concerned about attorney-client privilege, I still am."

When she sat back down, Joseph said, "I think I'll pass on knowing. Out of sight, out of mind, you know? If I knew, I'd be tempted to go for it, and like I said, I'm only interested in covering expenses. It was an accident, not intentional. I'm not out for blood."

Michelle nodded. As a smile played at the corners of her mouth, her dimple formed in all its adorableness. At their last meeting, her hair had been pulled back tightly. Now the back of it swished across her shoulders whenever she turned her head. He caught himself staring and quickly averted his gaze. "I hope that doesn't lower your commission significantly."

She shrugged. "The percentage on pro bono work is pretty easy to calculate. It could be a really nice bonus or just enough to buy a box of paper clips." In spite of her efforts to be flippant, there was a tone of regret in her voice. Joseph wasn't sure whether or not to pursue it—to ask her if everything was okay. After a moment's debate he decided to leave it alone.

"Well, I'm sorry about that. I just don't feel right soaking someone for millions when professional negligence wasn't really a factor."

"Oh, I wouldn't say that," she said with raised eyebrows. "The truck driver *was* loaded up on that energy drink and had an expired CDL."

"Be that as it may, let's just leave the paperwork as is. Are you going to have any problems passing it by the insurance companies?"

She shook her head. The hair teased again, and a few strands fell across her face. She tucked them back and said, "I don't think so. Most of what I do is contract filing, which includes clauses of every kind. It's the kind of stuff that would cure most insomniacs in one night. That's why I don't mind helping out with these 'out of purview' cases. The insurance companies will have their say, but it usually comes down to what the lawyers decide. And like I said, this traffic accident is a pretty open-and-shut case. Unless, of course, you were driving with an open container of alcohol and a minor in the car. But I can't imagine you ever being involved in something like that, even with that cute smile of yours."

Michelle ducked her head and busied herself in her attaché case, clearly embarrassed by what she'd just said.

"Thanks. And you're absolutely right, I wouldn't get involved in something like that," he said firmly. Then, a little louder, he added, "However, I can't say the same for my roommate."

"What's that?" Clyde shouted from behind the curtain.

"Nothing, Clyde. Just discussing my case."

"Well, if you was smart, you'd take 'em for all they got."

"Thanks for your input," Joseph hollered back. "Go back to your ball game."

"Vikings are whooping some Dolphin tail. Your Solvang people'll be having fish tonight."

"Mammal."

"What?"

"Never mind." Joseph smiled.

Michelle pointed to three different places to initial and one that required a date along with a signature. A slight ruddiness still colored her cheeks. "Thanks, Joseph. I'll get right over to SVJ and push this through. According to your doctor, you won't be spending much more time in here. I'd like to get everything cleared up before you leave."

"Yeah. Me too."

Michelle left quickly without further word. Joseph just watched her walk out of the room, wondering why his conversation with her had gone from businesslike to flirty to no-nonsense.

A few moments later, Clyde used a cane to slide the curtain back. "I think she likes you."

"Yeah. I like her too. She's a good lawyer," Joseph said without fanfare.

"No. I think she really *likes* you, man."

Joseph gave his roommate a blank stare.

"Come on, Joe, can't you read between the lines? Everything she said was about how impressive you are. And then the 'cute smile' comment. Man, she's got the hots for you, buddy."

"Whatever," Joseph said, grabbing a magazine and opening it to a random page.

Clyde chuckled knowingly. "Yeah, *whatever* indeed."

Joseph flipped through the pages, not seeing a thing. The memory of the movement of her hair and the scent of her perfume addled him. Now, his already overloaded things-to-be-concerned-about list had a new demand on his attention.

CHAPTER 31

DR. WILDER GREETED JOSEPH IN his office wearing a yellow oxford button-down and hunter green Dockers. "I decided to go for a casual look today. We both need to be relaxed for this." Pointing to the couch, he said, "Go ahead and have a seat there."

"Don't you want to see what I wrote from my dreams first?" Joseph asked, holding up a few sheets of paper.

"Nope. That would skew how I lead you through hypnosis. I want this as fresh as possible. We're going to take you back again, just like we did last time. Only I'll ask some more specific questions this time. Don't try to second guess an answer. Just let it come from within your mind. Okay?"

Joseph nodded nervously.

Using the technique of slowly leading Joseph into a state of complete relaxation and minimal external stimuli, Dr. Wilder fully regressed Joseph within a few minutes. He started with simple questions and progressed slowly to ones that required more complex answers.

After a few minutes of questioning, Dr. Wilder asked, "Joseph, how old are you right now?"

"Nine," he answered in a small voice.

"You're a very brave boy for only being nine. Let's talk about something that happened when you were nine, okay?"

Joseph shrugged.

"I believe you've had many happy experiences as a nine-year-old. I know you love feeding the ducks at the bird refuge, don't you?"

"Uh-huh," was his boyish response.

"I believe you also had many experiences that weren't so happy."

Joseph remained silent. His brows furrowed, and he bit at his lower lip.

"It's okay, Joseph. You're safe now. But I would like you to remember a sad time."

Joseph shook his head as a child might, exaggerated, forceful. A thin sheen of sweat appeared on his forehead as he continued chewing his lip nervously. His breathing increased in tempo and coarseness.

"Don't be scared, Joseph," the psychiatrist said in a tender voice. "Where are you now?"

Joseph mouthed some words, but no sound came out.

"I'm sorry, Joseph, but I can't hear you."

"In the living room," he whispered.

"Is everything okay?"

He shook his head. A tear trickled from the corner of his eye.

"Are you alone?"

"No."

"Who's with you, Joseph?"

No words came. His lower lip trembled as his jaw quivered. His hands were clasped tightly across his chest, his elbows tucked snugly to his sides.

"Joseph, no one can see us or hear us. You can tell me what's happening with no fear of being punished, okay?"

Joseph drew in a gasp to suppress a sob. "'Kay."

"Who is with you?"

"The monster."

"The monster?"

"*Sí.*"

"Does the monster have a name?"

"*Sí.*"

"Can you tell me?"

Joseph remained silent. His jaw continued to quiver.

"Don't be afraid, Joseph. You can whisper it if you want to."

In his little boy voice, he whispered, "It's Papa."

"Is anyone else in the room with you and Papa?"

"Antonio."

"You're doing great, Joseph. You are a very brave boy." Dr. Wilder paused a moment. "Tell me what is happening right now."

After a couple of ragged breaths, Joseph said, "He wants to show me a punishment."

"Are you being punished?"

"No. Antonio is."

"Why is Antonio being punished?"

Joseph went silent. His eyes conveyed vacancy and fear. Another tear escaped down his cheek. He hid his eyes in the crook of his elbow.

"It's okay, Joseph. Why is Antonio being punished?"

A sob burst from young Joseph. "Because I didn't empty the trash."

"Because *you* didn't empty the trash?"

"*Si.*" He sucked in a lungful of air and cried out, "No, Papa, don't!" Joseph flinched harshly and tucked into a tight fetal position. "Stop it! Please make him stop!" Tears were flowing freely now.

"What's happening, Joseph?"

"I—I want Papa to stop hurting Antonio. I want to tell him to stop, but I can't."

"Why not?"

Joseph's head whipped back and forth as if trying to rid itself of something instead of simply saying no.

"Joseph?"

"I can't say it."

"Why not?"

"I can't speak."

"You can't speak? I don't understand."

Joseph made a gagging sound, as if drowning. Catching his breath, he whimpered, "Papa put duct tape over my mouth to stop me from crying."

"I see," Dr. Wilder said, trying to remain neutral in his reaction.

"Papa always tapes my mouth before he punishes me. So the neighbors won't hear."

"Are you being punished too?"

"*Si.*"

"Why are you being punished?"

Softly, Joseph said, "Because I—I forgot to empty the trash." Then much more earnestly: "I'm sorry. It won't happen again, I promise."

"But you said Antonio is being punished because the trash wasn't emptied."

"*I* forgot to empty it. It was my job. When Papa told me to get the tape, Antonio knew he was going to punish me and tried to make Papa change his mind. That got Papa even madder."

"I see. If you *could* speak, what would you say to your father?"

Joseph began whimpering in long, drawn-out mewls as he curled tighter into a ball. "Stop it, Papa! Stop hurting him. It isn't his fault. I will empty the trash, honest. I won't forget, ever again! Don't punish him for my mistake. Don't punish him because I am a mistake." Joseph barked out a single high-pitched bleat and then broke down into sobbing.

"Okay, Joseph, it's all right. You can leave your living room now. Antonio won't be hurt. It's time to come back. The past is over. The monster is gone. No more punishments, no more hurting." Dr. Wilder was going to bring Joseph back to consciousness but paused and very slowly, very earnestly said, "You are not a mistake, Joseph. Do you hear me? You are not a mistake."

* * *

"Hello, Joseph," Dr. Wilder said softly.

Joseph looked up and slowly uncurled himself. "Wow. That felt strange."

"Yeah? How so?"

"It was like . . . I don't know. Like having a dream, I guess, yet I knew where I was the whole time. Only . . . only it *felt* like I was back in my house in Santa Barbara."

"Do you remember what we talked about?"

Joseph sat up. "Wow, that's even stranger. I . . . I guess I don't. I know that I was afraid. It had something to do with my brother Antonio. And . . . I can't remember much more." He wiped his face and was shocked to find tears. "Was I crying?"

Dr. Wilder reached out and patted Joseph's knee. "You did great, Joseph. We covered more ground than I thought we would. Now, let's see what you've written from your dreams, and we'll try to match them up as best we can."

CHAPTER 32

JOSEPH KNEW HE WAS DREAMING again. He also felt he could simply wake up before it developed into anything. But he let it play out—just as Dr. Wilder said to do. He needed resolution to this whole mess. And the only way to achieve that closure was to let it open.

* * *

The beachfront was extra crowded that day. That's because it was Sunday, and every Sunday a large portion of Cabrillo Boulevard was lined with artists and photographers and tradesmen selling their creations. It was an open-air bazaar that attracted hundreds of tourists every weekend. The distance from the Santa Barbara bird refuge to Stern's Wharf—another popular tourist spot and the far boundary of the art show—was about three miles. Young Joseph loved walking amongst the artisans and admiring the paintings, drawings, and sculptures, when the crowds were light. But when they grew into a churning throng of strangers, it frightened him.

Today was one of those days. Holding Antonio's hand tightly, Joseph followed a few paces behind the rest of the family. Mama was pushing a stroller holding two-month-old Victoria with one hand and holding little Emily's hand with the other. Xavier was at work. Papa walked a few paces ahead holding a paper bag wrapped tightly around a bottle. He marched like he was in a race.

"Keep up, boys," Papa called over his shoulder.

Every half a block he'd bring his paper bag to his lips and take a nip. Emily and Mama were jabbering away, talking about the pretty pictures and the variety of people. Antonio mostly kept to himself, making only an occasional comment on a particular painting or photograph when asked.

Joseph, on the other hand, was full of questions, most of them without simple answers: How did that guy make the water in his painting look so real? How long did it take these palm trees to grow so tall? How many people were here today? How far away were those islands on the horizon? How long did it take to build the wharf?

With fire in his eyes, Papa stopped and turned. "Stop it! Stop asking so many questions, José. You give me a headache."

"José, do what your father says," Mama scolded.

They walked in silence until they passed a flock of pigeons strutting around the legs of easels holding photographs of shoreline sunsets. Their cooing was mellow and their quirky bobbing gait was funny. Still, Joseph moved to the far side of the sidewalk to avoid them.

"How come those birds walk like that?" he asked Antonio.

"I don't know."

"It looks silly."

"Sure does."

"Some of their feathers shine. Why are they all colored differently?"

"Maybe they had different parents," Antonio guessed. "But even if they have the same Mama and Papa, they can still look different. I mean just look at how different you and me look."

Joseph thought about that. "We look a little different, but we have the same hair color and—oh, look, there's one that's almost white."

"Ew, he's kind of creepy looking," Antonio sneered.

"Why are they down on the ground instead of up in a tree?" Joseph wondered.

Antonio shrugged. "Lots of people usually mean lots of food. They're probably just looking for scraps."

"Oh. That makes sense. Do you think they're very smart?"

"Yeah, I guess so."

Estefan slammed his foot down and spun around. "Question, question, question! They are just dumb birds, José. Pigeons. They are stupid. They only know how to eat and make filthy messes. But even as stupid as they are, they are smarter than you because they don't ask question after question!"

"Papa!" Emily snapped. "Be nice."

"Why? Why should I be nice to a mistake?"

"Papa, it's not his fault," Mama offered in defense.

Estefan pointed a finger an inch from her mouth. "Close it," he growled.

Mama went silent as he took a long swig from his paper bag then started down the sidewalk without further comment. Consuela trotted after him, pushing the stroller and dragging Emily behind her. Antonio stood with Joseph's hand still in his.

"He didn't mean that, Joseph." Antonio spoke as if he didn't believe his own words.

"Yes, he did. He always calls me a mistake, you know that."

"Yes, but he is only kidding."

Joseph shuffled his feet aimlessly. He knew his brother was only trying to protect his feelings. Joseph had come to accept that his father considered him a mistake, but he didn't understand it. He tried extra hard to be good, to do everything that was asked of him. Sometimes he just couldn't remember to not ask questions. He had so many of them. His fourth grade teacher said he had an "inquisitive" mind, whatever that meant. Xavier told him it meant he always had a lot of questions. But apparently Papa didn't think that was a good thing.

"Come on," Antonio said, leading the way with Joseph in tow.

After jogging almost a block to catch up, they fell into step behind Mama, Emily, and the baby. Papa was several paces ahead of his family.

"You know, Joseph," Antonio whispered after they caught their breath, "I think you are very smart. You see things that no one else sees. Just because you ask questions doesn't mean you are stupid. In school they encourage us to ask questions."

"I know."

"Just don't ask Papa any more questions."

"Okay," Joseph said. "But . . . why?"

"Because it always makes him mad. You already know that."

Joseph nodded. "I'll try. But sometimes I forget."

Antonio squeezed his hand extra hard. "I know. But one of these times, when he's really drunk, he's going to *really* hurt you. I don't want that to happen."

"Me either."

They walked in silence for a time before Joseph asked, "But what if I forget again?"

Antonio was quiet for a few moments before he looked off at the horizon and sighed heavily. "I'm hoping something will happen before you do."

"Will Mama leave him?"

Antonio's head snapped around. "How do you know about such things?"

"Lot's of kids in school have only a mama or only a papa. It happens all the time, I guess."

Antonio shook his head. "Mama will never leave. She says the Church doesn't believe in divorce."

The little group came to a halt because Papa had stopped to look at a painting of a girl lying in a suggestive pose on a couch. Antonio pulled his brother off to one side behind a very wide palm tree.

"Listen to me, Joseph. I hate the way Papa treats Mama. I hate the way he treats you. He's okay to me and Xavier . . . most of the time. The only one he seems to like is Emily. But that doesn't matter. Mama won't do anything about the way he is. Xavier is always gone, and Emily isn't as strong as you and me. The whole family would be better off if Papa were gone. That means it's up to us to take care of things."

Joseph stared at his brother with minimal understanding. What Antonio said made sense, but he had no idea what they could do about it.

"But this has to be our secret, Joseph. You understand? No one can know—not even Emily, and especially not Mama. Okay?"

Joseph nodded.

"No, say it. Say, I understand."

"I understand."

"We'll only be okay after we do something about Papa, right?"

"Right. What are we going to do?"

Antonio hugged his brother quickly. "I don't know yet. But I have an idea I'm working on. I've got some friends at school. They want me to be part of their club. If I join, maybe I can get them to help, and we—"

* * *

Joseph sat upright in his bed. He was sweating, but not in a panic this time. His heart rate was steady. His breathing was deep and controlled. But his stomach churned and stung as if he'd just swallowed a hornet's nest. Grabbing his pen, he wrote frantically. His dream had been clear and revealing . . . mostly. Unfortunately, it created almost as many questions as it had answered.

CHAPTER 33

THE LINGERING HALF-LIGHT OF dusk filled the hospital room with a purple-amber hue. A steady breeze played with the treetops outside the window. The birds had long since ceased their singing for the night.

Using a cane, Joseph ambled from his bed to the bathroom. He moved slowly in the low light. He could see just fine; his main concern was balance. Connie had told him that the more practice he got walking, the better his equilibrium would become. And he craved any chance he got to practice.

After washing his hands, instead of returning to his bed, Joseph headed toward the door.

"Where're you off to?" Clyde asked, looking over the top of his magazine.

"Just going for a walk. Thought I'd go take in some evening air. You wanna come?"

The older man shook his head. "I thought you got enough exercise from that Nazi physical therapist. I know she's kicked my trash a time or two."

"She *is* very persuasive," Joseph agreed, "but it's for your own good."

"Says you. My old-school doc says bed rest is the best thing for liver disease. I don't see how stressing my body will do anything but wear me out."

"I believe the operative term you used is 'old school.' Times have changed, my friend."

Clyde waved him off and went back to his reading.

"In any event, I can't sit around all day doing nothing. I've got to get moving. Maybe burn off some of this nervous energy so I can sleep tonight."

Tossing his magazine to one side, Clyde grabbed his TV remote, pointed, clicked, and sneered. "Yeah. Good luck with that."

Joseph was going to ask about Clyde's sour mood but decided not to open that can of worms. Over the past three days, his roommate had become increasingly agitated and standoffish—except when it came to food. Otherwise, Clyde's remarks were clipped and delivered with a barbed edge to them—no more than a one- or two-word answer.

Joseph softly harrumphed, moved past the doorway threshold, then stopped short. Across from the door sat a uniformed police officer. The young man looked up with a flat, hard stare. His badge read OFFICER GREENSTREET. "Do you have an appointment somewhere, Mr. Ramirez?"

"Um, no," Joseph replied, very confused.

"Then I have to ask you to remain in your room, sir."

"Why?" he asked.

The officer stood and moved to block Joseph's exit. "You are under house restriction, sir. Please step back into your room."

"What? Wait—when did this happen?" Joseph was more confused than angry, but both emotions fueled each other much like gasoline feeds a fire.

"Since just this afternoon, sir."

For a time, Joseph was speechless. "Why wasn't I notified? Aren't you supposed to read me my rights or something first?"

"You know now," Officer Greenstreet said straight-faced. "And you're not under arrest. It's just a restriction."

Joseph bristled. "This isn't right."

When he returned to his bed, he noticed that Clyde looked more smug than usual. "Oops," the older man said with a smirk.

"You knew about this?" Joseph asked.

"I met him when I came back from dinner. Seems like a nice kid."

Joseph sat down hard. "He's holding me against my will."

"He's just doin' his job," Clyde said evenly. His attention was currently fixed on a major-league baseball game, but Joseph knew he was watching him out of the corner of his eye.

"I'm no law expert, but this has got to be illegal." Joseph grabbed his cell phone.

"You sure you want to do that?" Clyde asked.

Joseph paused. "Why?"

He shrugged. "Seems to me when a man's got himself in this much trouble, it's best to keep quiet until the dust settles, you know."

"What trouble?"

Clyde leveled a caustic glare in his direction. "Like you don't know."

"I don't!" Joseph snapped. "I believe it's within my rights to know what I'm being accused of."

Clyde scoffed and snorted. "Yeah. Keep playing the 'bad memory' card. Maybe it'll work with some folk."

"But not with you?" Joseph was livid. He thought Clyde Richter was his friend. The man now came across as prosecution, jury, and judge.

When Clyde said nothing more, Joseph called Michelle Haas. Her answering machine picked up with a brief message about leaving detailed information or she wouldn't return the call. Joseph left a rather terse recording and hung up.

Clyde was still smiling.

Joseph was not.

CHAPTER 34

"WHO AUTHORIZED THE HOUSE ARREST?" Michelle demanded of the young cop.

Officer Greenstreet shrugged. "It's not an arrest, ma'am, just a restriction."

"That means the same thing to me," she shot back. "Who told you to do this?"

"My lieutenant. You can ask him."

"Do you have a warrant for my client's arrest?"

"No, ma'am."

"Do you have any paperwork authorizing this action?"

"No, ma'am. But it's ten o'clock at night. Where's he going to go—"

"I'm well aware of the time, officer," Michelle cut him off. "And I can assure you these are not my normal office hours. You can also rest assured that I will bill your department for the overtime charges my client has incurred because I had to come down here to correct a blatant breach of the law. If you don't want a personal suit filed against you, Officer Greenstreet, for holding a citizen against their will without probable cause, I suggest you call your supervisor immediately."

The young man's face twitched a bit, but otherwise he remained impassive. Joseph was impressed with the mettle of his nerve. Greenstreet unclipped a microphone from his shoulder and called into dispatch.

As the officer relayed a message to headquarters, Michelle turned to Joseph. "If you want to go back to bed, I can take it from here."

"And let you have all the fun alone?"

Michelle allowed herself a brief smile. The dimple was subdued. "You sure?"

"Heck yes. Besides, I'm too worked up for sleep right now. Did McRae ever get back with you?"

"No. I have his card, but I was going to wait until he brought me some real evidence before I got too excited about anything."

"But . . . it's a *murder* charge," Joseph said, still not believing it.

"No, it's not. And don't let him or anyone else pressure you into thinking otherwise. The last time he was here, he only said he had questions about your father's murder—not that you were the one accused of committing the crime."

"But apparently I admitted to killing him."

"Says him. He never produced any proof that you did."

Joseph thought about that for a moment. She was right.

Officer Greenstreet cleared his throat, interrupting Joseph's thoughts. "Seems the paperwork got lost somewhere. No one's sure when the order was given. I told HQ you weren't a threat and that you probably wouldn't be fleeing the country anytime soon." It was a poor attempt at humor, and no one was laughing.

Michelle turned to Joseph and smiled. "You best get some sleep now. I'll follow up on this in the morning." She reached over and squeezed his hand. "You gonna be all right?"

Joseph was touched by the sincerity in her voice—and her touch. *She's just being friendly,* he reasoned. *Just showing she cares.* But when she didn't release his hand, he felt some color rise in his face, which caught him off guard. He never blushed. He squeezed her hand and held on. "Yeah, I'll be fine. Sorry about getting you out of bed."

"Who said I was in bed?" She smiled.

Joseph tried to hide the goofy look he knew was pasted on his mug. It was silly to think her actions were anything more than professional concern for a client. And yet . . .

"Well, you folks have a good night," Greenstreet said, tipping his hat before walking away. Joseph and Michelle watched him walk the distance of the hall before making a sound.

"Thanks for coming tonight," Joseph said, finally releasing Michelle's hand. "I'm sorry I made such a big deal of things."

"Nonsense. I told you to call me anytime. It was the right thing to do."

"Well, thanks again. You'll call me tomorrow?"

"If I find anything. I'm pretty swamped at work right now. We're in the middle of budget cuts because of the new bill the legislation just passed. Seems someone in Sacramento doesn't see the need for music classes in middle school anymore."

Joseph rolled his eyes. "Don't get *me* started on that. I have a litany of reasons not to drop the classes they deem unnecessary—and can even think of a few PC courses they *should* drop."

"Yeah. Well, I'm glad we agree. Good night, Joseph." Michelle turned and walked away. Her walk was not as brisk as usual. Joseph figured she was just tired. He brought his hand to his nose and sniffed a lingering hint of her perfume. *What was with the hand holding?* Not that he had minded. But what did it mean—if anything?

Returning to his room, he noticed Clyde was fast asleep—or was pretending to be. He wondered again about his last conversation with him. The man was downright . . . accusatory. Joseph shrugged. He was too beat to care anymore. Right now he simply wished to go swiftly to sleep.

And to *not* dream.

CHAPTER 35

"Dis hospital give me da creepies," Consuela Ramirez said as she entered Joseph's room.

He chuckled. "Why? Are you afraid of needles or something?"

"I jus' don' like it here. Da only happy time I e'spen' in a hospital was having *mi hijos*."

She handed Joseph a Tupperware container filled with a caramel-colored pudding coated with a dark brown sauce. "Here's a treat for ju. I know dey don' feed ju enough in here."

"They feed me just fine, Mama, but thanks. I love your flan."

Consuela settled into a chair and set her huge purse in her lap. "But jur e'still lookin' so tin, *mi'jo*."

"I've always been thin."

"*Sí*. E'still, jur head es lookin' better. Jur hair almost cover da e'scar. An' jur face isn't black an' purple an' e'scary anymore."

"Thanks," he said again, cringing at his mother's fumbled attempt at a compliment. He glanced at Clyde's empty bed and was grateful his roommate had left for a consultation.

"So, ju goin' to try da flan? Es *muy delicioso*."

Joseph's eyes narrowed. "It's not from Yolanda, is it?"

Consuela sighed heavily. "No, no es from Yolanda. She e'still concerned for ju, José. But this flan Victoria make. She tryin' to learn to cook. She not bad, but e'still needs practice. She miss ju very much."

"I miss her too. Emily visited me last week, but I'd like to see Victoria too."

"I tell her, but e'she run 'round like crazy all da time. I worry about her e'so much."

Joseph was tired of small talk. Normally he loved to hear his mother prattle on about nothing, but he wanted to ask about the strange remembrances he was experiencing—the ones Emily had confirmed and the ones coming out in his hypnosis sessions. Especially those revealing his father as less than the ideal dad. He didn't want to come right out and confront his mother about Estefan, but he had to find out more. He knew it was crucial to his sanity—perhaps even to solving the murder mystery. Besides, Mama was known to clam up when encountering direct confrontation. She was a person prone to reaction rather than action.

Broaching the subject from an odd angle, Joseph said, "You worry about Victoria? Why? She's a good girl. Besides, Papa's gone now, so he can't punish her for making choices he might not approve of."

Consuela's breath faltered as her eyes fixed on Joseph. Her expression went flat, leery. It was a look of trepidation—a look of caution spawned by . . . *what*? Fear? "She es runnin' roun' with e'some bad kids at da e'school," she said coarsely. "I do not like it, and neiter would Papa."

Maintaining the focus of his inquiry, Joseph said, "Huh. Emily told me Victoria's meeting lots of new kids all the time in her a cappella choir class. Apparently, it's a large choir filled with kids from several ethnic backgrounds. She's very happy . . . but you're right, I'm sure it's the kind of thing Papa wouldn't think is right."

"*Sí*. I know Papa would no like the boys she e'seeing, I know dat for chur."

"You know that for sure, huh? Well, too bad he's not around to ask him face to face, isn't it," Joseph stated more than asked. The segue to his father wasn't progressing quite like he wanted, and it was irritating him.

She tipped her head to one side. "Are ju tryin' to be disrespectful, José?"

"I don't think so. I mean, how can I be disrespectful to someone I don't even remember?"

Consuela didn't say anything for a long time. Her eyes seemed to be searching Joseph's. For what, he couldn't tell. But he knew he had struck a nerve. He had to proceed with caution, but it was hard for him. Nothing but bitterness filled his heart when he thought of his father. He loved his mother very much and didn't want to bring up memories that might be painful to her too. But she deserved some of the blame. If horrible things did happen, and she did nothing to prevent them, then she was guilty by association. Still, this was *his* battle, not hers. How she chose to deal with the issues of their past was her affair. No need to drag his loved ones through *his* misery. As Connie said, you have to push through the pain before the healing can begin. And if his pain unavoidably involved the pain of others, then possibly hurting them was the only way he could get the healing *he* needed.

Joseph broke the silence by saying, "I'm sorry, Mama. I don't mean to be disrespectful. But recently I've been learning things about Papa that are not good. My psychiatrist says I may have intentionally repressed memories of him because of the things he did."

She waved a hand dismissively. "I don' even know what ju mean."

Joseph took a breath and held it. "Emily told me that Papa was very mean to me. All the time."

Consuela bristled. "Papa was very firm. He demanded respect— jus' like da Church. He was no differen' dan other faders."

Joseph tried to stare down his mother but couldn't. He saw defensiveness in her eyes, a mental wall that hid a deep-seated pain— perhaps even guilt. "Mama, I'm sorry if this hurts you, but I have to know." He paused and looked down. "Papa used to beat me, didn't he."

She drew a gasping lungful of air, as if utterly appalled by his question. "He was e'strict wid his children. Dat is all."

"Mama, I know that's not true. He used to drink a lot. And when he got drunk he—"

"He drank no more dan oder men. He was a good man all da oder times."

"Was he?" Joseph felt his eyes begin to sting. He willed the tears back. "I'm so confused, Mama. I *need* to know the truth. I remember some good times with him. You know, at the beach, at Christmas. But in my dreams he is always mean and hurtful." He paused and swallowed the lump constricting his throat. "I even dreamed he was beating you once, maybe more. I remember the cuts and bruises, Mama, but until now I never knew where they came from. It was Papa, wasn't it."

Tears threatened to spill from her eyes as well as his. It wrenched Joseph's heart to be the cause of them. But he had to know! "Mama, I've learned that he used to call me *el falla,* the failure—the mistake. Do you remember that?"

"Where did you hear that?" she snapped.

"It's been in my dreams several times." Joseph blinked to staunch his tears. He wasn't ashamed of them, but at the moment they seemed like a sign of weakness. "Apparently, I was not supposed to be born. He hated me for that, didn't he, Mama? He hated his own son."

"Oh, José," she moaned. Consuela pulled a hankie from her purse and leaned her face into it. Her shoulders trembled, her body quivering like a spring wound too tight. "No, no, no, no," she mumbled through the cloth.

"What, Mama?"

"No. I no can e'say." Her voice was strained, choking.

"Why, Mama? Why did he hate me?"

"I no can e'say," she repeated. It was a whisper now, barely audible.

"Please," Joseph pleaded.

"I just no can tell it. Es better to not remember. It's over, Joseph. Ju been happy for e'so long. Please. Es for da best."

Joseph hated seeing his mother in tears—hated the fact that he had brought her to it. And she called him Joseph. That meant she was serious about not wanting to discuss it. Emily had also said to leave it alone—to go on being happy and just forget about the past. Perhaps they were right. Nothing could be done about it now. The only thing it would do was bring up sorrow, remorse, and pain. Things were good now. He had a career he loved. His new religion brought him unfathomable happiness. Why poke a stick into a potential hornet's nest?

"Never mind, Mama. I'm sorry. I didn't mean to make you cry."

She waved him off a second time and blotted her eyes. "Ju was a good boy, Joseph. An' ju turned into a fine man. Isn' dat enough?"

Was it? Joseph reached his hand out to his mother. He wanted to explain so much, but he was at a loss for words. Seeing his mother reduced to tears so quickly had unnerved him. But could he simply leave the past in the past? He'd been able to before his accident. Why couldn't he just continue?

Why? His mind argued. *You know why. Because there's something else going on. Something deeper than a lousy father and a dysfunctional childhood. Something that implicates you personally. Something that involves murder.*

Then a new, more disturbing thought entered his mind. *What if Mama was . . . involved?*

CHAPTER 36

DR. LINDLEY SPENT A GOOD deal of time examining Joseph that morning. He gave him a battery of diagnostic tests that were exhaustive but necessary—according to him. A series of MRIs, a CBC, UA, and PSA panel, an EKG, an EMG, and a host of other acronym-labeled tests Joseph endured because he had to. The litany kept Joseph poked, zapped, and drained until well after lunchtime. A quick meal in the cafeteria was followed by his last session with Dr. Connie Olsen. She ran him through a regimen of balance and coordination trials as wells as strength tests and a well-earned full-body massage. An hour later he was sitting in her office on an ergonomically designed chair. To Joseph the chair felt like something designed by the Spanish Inquisition.

"You've healed remarkably well, Joseph. Now, the key is to maintain your health through continued exercise and smart eating," the PT said.

"I was doing that before I came here."

"And that's partly why you healed so quickly."

"Yeah, I was hoping you'd say that," he said, squirming to adjust himself on the strange piece of furniture.

"What's the matter? Don't you like that chair?" She smiled.

"Not really."

"It's designed to force good posture while sitting. Most people slouch while sitting, which bends their spine in the wrong direction. That ergo chair tilts your hips forward so that even while sitting, your spine is postured as if you were standing. Less backaches by day's end with that bad boy."

Joseph twisted again. "Says you."

She laughed. "Perspective, Joseph. Along that line, how're things going with Alex Wilder?"

"We're making progress, but nothing earth-shattering has come out yet, except a dysfunctional childhood and an abusive, drunk father."

"Is that all?"

Joseph favored her with apathetic eyes. They masked what he was really feeling inside. Or tried to.

"But you're still learning about your past, right? So it's not a total loss."

"Oh yeah. It's just swell."

A warm expression softened her features. "Dr. Wilder knows his stuff, Joseph. I bet from his perspective you're doing great. You still have appointments with him, don't you?"

"Yes. We're trying to unearth the stuff I blocked out twenty years ago. He's convinced it's stuck in there somewhere," he said, tapping his forehead.

"Well, from my perspective, you're 99 percent better. But as the patient, you're the final judge. Is there anything you have questions about or anything you'd like to ask me?"

He thought for a moment. "Yeah. Would you come out to my school and teach the kids about the need for getting enough exercise and eating a good diet? It's my understanding that childhood obesity is on the rise in this world."

"In the world, true—but especially this country! It's our wonderful computer age that's doing it. Well, that and fast food. But the fact that this generation spends its playtime in front of a monitor instead of out riding bikes or playing kick-the-can is causing kids everywhere to develop adult-onset diseases and liver disease in adolescence. It's a travesty."

"I agree. So can I count on you?"

"You bet, Joseph. Just tell me when, and I'll head on up to Solvang."

"Thanks," he said, standing. "You've been a great help, Connie. I truly appreciate the *perspective* you've given me."

She held up both palms. "Hey, I did nothing. *You* put in all the effort. I just gave you direction. So don't slack off now, promise?"

"Promise," Joseph said, crossing a finger over his heart.

* * *

When Joseph returned to his room, he was surprised to find Michelle Haas sitting on the edge of his bed, chatting with Clyde Richter.

"Hey, Joe, come here," Clyde said with a Cheshire cat smile. "Did you know this gal of yours writes romance novels?"

"Clyde, you promised!" Michelle cried.

Joseph sat next to Michelle. "No way. Romance novels? You're not another John Grisham wannabe, then?"

"Hardly. Law is my career, writing is my escape."

"That's super. So how many are in print?"

She ducked her head. "Just one."

"A best seller, no doubt," Joseph said confidently.

"Hardly. I went through a commission publisher who did zero advertising, in spite of what the contract said. Plus, they keep all royalties until the production costs have been covered—another tidbit left out of the contract."

"Hmm. Sounds like you need a good lawyer. I have a personal 'in' with the famous Attorney-at-Law Brick Wiseman if you'd like an introduction."

Michelle slugged him in the shoulder. Hard.

Clyde drew a sharp breath between his teeth. "Ouch—careful, Joe. Don't get her dander up. Remember, this one's got claws."

"Stop it, you two. It's no big deal. I haven't made any money on it. It's not all that good anyway, so I really don't care." Joseph could tell she was trying to cover up a letdown that still bothered her, despite what she claimed. The forced smile did little to negate the crestfallen tone in her voice.

"So where can I get a copy?" Joseph asked.

"Oh, it's out there and still available, but none of the big stores carry it. You might check out an online used bookstore. But I'm guessing you're not really into romance novels anyway, are you?"

Joseph shrugged. "I am a voracious reader, and I devour just about everything—especially when I know the author. What's it called?"

Her face flushed crimson, and she immediately busied herself in her attaché case in a poor attempt to avoid answering his question. "Let's see . . . I think I have some papers in here . . . I need a signature on . . ."

"Michelle?"

"Hmm?" she mumbled.

"Your novel?"

"Oh, nothing. I need to talk to you about the latest desperate attempt from SVJ." She whipped out a file folder and held it out.

"*Forbidden Lust,*" Clyde said in a drawn-out, throaty voice.

"Really?" Joseph mused openly.

Michelle flashed the older man a scalding glare. "*Forbidden Trust! Trust,* Clyde! Like I *trusted* you not to say anything to anyone. Thanks a lot."

Clyde was laughing too hard to respond.

"*Forbidden Trust* doesn't sound bad," Joseph commented. "As long as it's not one of those novels where one false breath and the gal on the cover falls out of what little she's wearing, or where every noun is proceeded with *throbbing* or *pulsating* or *savage.*"

Michelle slapped the file on Joseph's lap and scowled. "Not hardly. It's very tastefully written. I don't do smut."

"I wouldn't have thought otherwise," Joseph demurred.

"Too bad." Clyde grinned. "I bet your imagination can get pretty toasty."

Michelle jumped to her feet and closed the room partition with a brutal tug.

"Okay, I can take a hint," Clyde called from the other side.

Lowering her voice a bit, Michelle said, "Let's forget about the novel and get back to business."

Joseph sobered and said okay.

"This is joke number two or three now," she said, tapping the folder in Joseph's lap. "I can't keep up. But it's typical of a big firm to shuffle and delay as much as possible, especially when they know they've got no hope."

"What kind of delay this time?"

"Well, I don't know how they got a hold of this information, but they're trying to say you had suicidal ideation stemming from remorse over your alleged involvement in your father's murder."

Joseph frowned. "I was trying to kill myself?"

"That's what they're saying."

"That's nuts! I didn't even find out about my father's murder—if that's really what happened—until a few nights ago. My family doesn't even know about it."

"SVJ is claiming you acted alone in the crime—that's why you're the only one affected with such overwhelming remorse."

"I was ten years old!" Joseph cried. "My father was a mean, heartless drunk, but there's no way I could have killed him—even if I had wanted to."

"I know that, Joseph," she soothed. "Don't worry about it. They're reaching for straws again. They have no proof."

Joseph took a couple of deep breaths and forced his temper to abate. "So what do we do now?"

"I may just file a reverse suit for defamation of character. Until then, they may request a psych eval from one of their medical cronies. It's pretty common. But we've got Dr. Wilder's eval on file giving you a clean bill of health."

"Clean bill of health, huh? We're not even close to being done with my sessions."

"So? Since your dreams didn't begin until after your accident, he says the two are definitely not germane."

"Meaning . . . ?"

"As far as your accident goes, you had no previous mental limitations, repercussions, or disabilities."

Joseph stared into his open hands for a time. His mind was fraught with vignettes of the terrible events from his past. His thoughts focused on the regressions he'd had, many of which revealed a dysfunctional childhood due to a very abusive father—all of which was confirmed by his older sister. Maybe he had *subconsciously* wanted a release from the past. Maybe his psyche was instructing his body to self-destruct before his repressed memories began to surface and cause intolerable emotional disabilities.

He scoffed inwardly. No—that was nonsense. Dr. Wilder had said there was no proof repressed memories dictated current mental processes or actions. There was no way he had *intentionally* driven in front of the cement truck. He was a happy, successful science teacher. He had lots of friends and was respected by his peers. He wasn't crazy. He didn't have any habits or addictions that might be construed as childhood repercussions. It was common knowledge that children often followed in their parents' footsteps—for good and bad. For whatever reason, Joseph had come out amazingly stable. Lately, he had wondered why. The more he learned about his troubled past, the more he was surprised at how well he had adjusted and progressed.

In spite of all that, one question still plagued his mind. It was a question he was loath to answer, because it would affect the rest of his life—potentially in a very bad way. *Talk about a repercussion!* What if his upcoming regressions revealed that he *had* murdered his father? What if they showed—

"Joseph?" Michelle interrupted his thoughts.

"Oh, sorry." He shook his head to clear the jumble of thoughts within. "A clean bill of health, did you say?"

"Yes."

Joseph closed his eyes and exhaled slowly. "I sure hope so."

CHAPTER 37

JOSEPH WAS GETTING BETTER AT being regressed. Dr. Wilder was able to lead him into a deep conscious sedation in a matter of minutes. Joseph's remembrances became crystal clear. It was as if he were experiencing his past for the first time. And even if he could not recall what came out in the regression, Dr. Wilder had a digital recording of each session. When played back, it was like listening to old-time radio theater—each show filled with mystery, suspense, and horror.

* * *

Papa was drunk again. Young Joseph could hear him screaming at Mama from the kitchen. Joseph pulled the covers over his head and turned his back to the noise. Despite his best efforts, he was already crying. He hated that. He hated being weak. Even though he was only nine, his papa said it was important for him to start being a man.

Antonio shared the bedroom with him. So did Xavier, but he was at work again. Joseph knew his brothers would do what they could to distract Papa . . . if it came to that. Joseph looked to his brothers for everything, from friendship to learning to protection—especially Antonio. But when Papa got like this, even Antonio admitted to being frightened.

"It'll be okay," Antonio whispered with forced confidence. "He doesn't sound too bad this time."

Joseph's voice was tremulous, weak. "I'm scared."

"Me too. Shh, just close your eyes and put your pillow over your head."

Joseph's eyes widened even further. "I won't be able to see."

"I'll watch out for you," Antonio said, trying to sound brave.

A spark of hope flickered in Joseph. "You promise?"

"Cross my heart."

He visibly relaxed. "You're way brave, Antonio."

"No, *you* are, little brother."

Just as Joseph hiked his pillow over his head, Estefan Ramirez burst into the room. The backlight from the hallway transformed Papa's tousled hair and rumpled shirt into the image of a hideous beast. It wasn't far from the truth.

"Get up, boys. Now!" he bellowed.

Joseph bolted from the bed and stood straight as a board. Antonio was quick to follow. How Joseph wished Xavier were here now! His oldest brother was almost as big as Papa and was not afraid of him anymore.

Wide awake, terrified at the forthcoming punishment their father regularly gave for spending all *his* money on food and clothing—even though little more than rags hung from their undernourished bodies—Antonio and Joseph fought to keep their knees from knocking together.

A horrifying silence sucked the air from the small room as Estefan stared into the darkness, trying to focus on something on which to vent his anger. The Ramirez boys dared not breathe. Joseph wondered if their sisters were already awake. They must be. No one could sleep through one of Papa's tirades.

The drunk weaved slightly. He placed a hand against the doorjamb to regain his balance as he continued to stare, totally disorientated. "Boys!" he yelled again.

"*Sí,* Papa?" Antonio answered softly.

Estefan shook his head, trying to clear the alcoholic tsunami currently saturating his brain. "Come here," he said, turning from the dark bedroom.

The Ramirez boys followed their father into the family room. Their mother lay in a crumpled heap on the floor. She was whimpering. Already large red bruises were swelling on her neck and arms. Her left sleeve was torn. One shoe was missing.

"Sit," the drunk commanded his children, pointing loosely at the couch.

The boys silently complied. Emily was already there, staring at the floor, hands folded tightly in her lap. Victoria was crying in another room.

"Somebody shut that baby up!" Papa growled through clenched teeth.

"I will." Emily bolted up and ran to their bedroom. Within a few seconds, little Victoria stopped crying. Except for Mama's tiny whimpers, silence stifled the air. Joseph knew better than to make any sound. Yet upon seeing his mother, he couldn't hold back his tears.

The monster stood over Mama, struggling to maintain his balance. "I come home from a lousy job to a house where I am fed lousy food made by a woman who's a lousy cook, a lousy housekeeper, and a lousy lover," he grumbled.

Emily entered the living room cradling Victoria on her narrow shoulder. "But *I* made supper tonight, Papa," she said in defense of her mother.

"*Cállate!*" he snapped at his daughter. The effort taxed him, and he jostled to maintain his balance. In doing so, he brushed a foot against his wife's shoulder.

Consuela Ramirez let out a panicked chirp and recoiled from his touch. Estefan straightened and scowled at his family. "You all need to learn a lesson. I am the man of this house! I should be respected! I demand to be honored as the Bible teaches!"

"We'll try harder, Papa," Emily promised.

"You bet your life, you will!" he hissed. "Because I'm gonna show you what happens when you don't."

He reached down and yanked his wife to her feet by a clutch of hair. The children gasped. Consuela whimpered in pain. Her face was a mess of bruises; one eye was swollen shut, blood trickling from a split lip.

"Now," the drunk continued, "she got a punishment for each stupid thing she's done just to make me angry."

Estefan began to list infractions, one at a time. It didn't matter that few of the "stupid things" had ever occurred. It didn't matter that the ones that had were of his own doing. With each infraction his anger intensified. Whenever the children turned away, Estefan would bellow at them, threatening the same punishment if they didn't watch and learn.

Although Joseph kept his eyes on the gut-wrenching scene, he forced his mind elsewhere. In his imagination, he ran along the beach, discovering the wonders of each tide pool, trying to mentally match each creature with a picture book he'd seen at school.

He did it quite often. It was the only way he could survive.

* * *

Shivering from a bone-deep chill, Joseph didn't want to open his eyes. He knew where he was, what he'd just experienced, but he was hesitant to reenter reality. Lying on his side, curled in a tight ball, he was frustrated at his lack of recall. He knew he'd just gone through something terrible, some memory that was heart-wrenching, bitter, shocking. So why couldn't he remember it? He knew his psychiatrist would share it with him when he was ready. But how could you ever be ready for something like this? To wake up knowing that you had a horrible childhood, that your father was a monster? Of course this session could be different, but he doubted it. The regressions he'd had were all the same depressing experiences. *Why bother continuing them?* he wondered. *Why? Because I still need to find out what happened to my father.*

Joseph moved his head to a more comfortable position. The pillow on which his head lay was soaked. His jaw hurt from being clenched. His head throbbed to the point he could hear the blood pumping past his eardrums. He felt a comforting weight settle on his legs, shoulders, and up to his neck. He knew Dr. Wilder had placed a blanket over him to quell his chill.

"Joseph?" It was Dr. Wilder's deep, soft voice.

Yes, he felt himself say, but no sound came out.

"Joseph, you are safe now. You are in my office in St. Luke's Hospital."

He nodded. "'Kay," he whispered.

"Do you need a few minutes?"

"Please."

"Take your time. I'm right here if you need me."

Snippets of the regression harassed his mind: His brother and sister crying. Baby Victoria screaming. His concern for his little sister. Papa was very upset. Something despicable was happening. Something that no child should ever have to experience. Something—

He shook his head. He didn't have to relive the memory again. He knew the doctor would share what he felt he needed to know. There was little that could be done about it now—unless it had something to do with his father's supposed murder.

"Anything new?" he asked in a shallow voice.

"Some. Would you like some water?"

"Yeah. Thanks."

As Dr. Wilder got a bottle of water from a small fridge in the bookcase, Joseph struggled into a sitting position. His head was still pounding but less so. He opened his eyes to a shadowy room. The psychiatrist handed him the open bottle and he drank deeply.

"More abuse in this one, Joseph. Nothing about falling or murder, though. Sorry," Dr. Wilder explained.

Joseph wiped his brow with the blanket. "How are we going to get any information if I never go there in my regressions?"

Dr. Wilder played with the tassel of his loafer crossed in his lap. "There is a way, but I hesitate to do it."

"How come?"

"Because it involves *leading* you through hypnosis. Remember when we discussed this on your first visit? Making suggestions or directing with specific questions often ends in false memories. There's really no way to know if the information we gather will be the truth or not—especially in childhood trauma cases such as yours."

Joseph considered that for a moment. "I still want to try. If anything, it'll give me a starting point to look into on my own—even if we don't take the results at face value."

After a pause, Dr. Wilder said, "Okay, Joseph. We'll try a bit on your next visit. But if I detect we're heading into an area that'll cause an emotional relapse, I'm stopping."

Joseph stood on wobbly legs and finished his water. "That's all I ask, doc."

CHAPTER 38

JOSEPH WHEELED SLOWLY TOWARD THE admissions desk at the hospital. He felt a strange sort of melancholy knowing he was actually heading for home this time. Sure, he'd come back for his appointments with Dr. Wilder, but he'd no longer have trained hospital staff at his beck and call. St. Luke's had given him a pager in case of an emergency, but it was little consolation for the 24-7 care to which he had grown accustomed. With a tornado of lead butterflies in his gut, Joseph acknowledged that from now on he'd be on his own. If it weren't for his nightmares and the mystery surrounding his father, that'd be fine. Obviously, he still had a few deep-seated issues to resolve. But the thought of handling them on his own suddenly made him feel very isolated, very much alone.

It was a curious emotion—one he'd never had before. He never considered himself a loner. He had his classes at school, and they more than made up for any lack of social life. But now, for the first time in his life, he wished he *was* married, or at least in a steady relationship, so he could have the emotional support he'd need to make it through. *Mama would be so happy to hear that.* He smiled inwardly, knowing the likelihood was next to ridiculous. He bit his lip and continued toward the hospital's main entrance.

"Checking out of our hotel, Mr. Ramirez?" the receptionist asked playfully.

Joseph shifted his bag of clothes, get-well cards, and other souvenirs off his lap and stood. "Yep. It was a very pleasant stay, the room service was excellent, but you really need to talk to your chef."

She laughed heartily. "Fair enough. Now, let's see, I have a note here that says all charges are to be sent to the Santa Barbara School District in care of Michelle Haas?"

"Yes. She's the attorney handling all insurance issues and bills."

"Oh yes, I see that now. It says I'm also supposed to send a copy of everything to the offices of Stansbury, Vail, and Jenkins, too?"

Joseph shrugged. "If Ms. Haas says so."

The receptionist turned her flat screen so that Joseph could see it. "You signed a HIPAA release authorizing them access to all your records at St. Luke's. It that still okay?"

Joseph looked at the scanned image and half-remembered Michelle instructing him to sign it. "Yes, that looks like my chicken scratch."

She beamed. "Excellent." Pointing to a small, flat rectangle on the counter, she said, "Please sign the electronic pad. It says you are leaving the hospital with no questions or concerns."

Joseph chuckled. "I have plenty of those but none relating to this facility. I'll be coming back for a visit in a few days."

The receptionist clicked her mouse and read something on her monitor. "Oh, I see. You have a schedule of appointments with Dr. Wilder."

"That's right."

"Well, if anything else comes up, you don't hesitate to call, okay?"

Joseph thanked her, sat back in his wheelchair, and allowed himself to be wheeled out of the hospital per their stipulations. He smiled at the silliness of it all as he covered the mere thirty-foot distance to the entrance.

Emily was standing beside her car, holding the door open. He closed his eyes, tipped his head back, and inhaled deeply. An offshore breeze brought a slight tanginess from the nearby beach. It was glorious.

Victoria saw him first and came running up. "Here he is," she sang to whoever was in earshot. "Our own *milagro santo.*"

Joseph snorted. "A holy miracle? Hardly. I was just lucky."

Emily joined in. "Come on, Joseph, you have to admit it was more than just luck that you're *walking* out of the hospital with barely a scratch just four weeks after being run over by a cement truck."

"Seven weeks. Don't forget the three I was in a coma." He tipped his head down and parted his inch-long hair. "And I'd hardly call this a scratch."

Emily examined him as if unsure of what she was trying to find. "What?"

"Oh, come on, Em, you can see the scar just fine. You're just trying to be nice. Granted, it's no holy stigmata, but it's way more than a scratch."

Emily kissed him on the cheek and hugged him tightly. "Let's ask Mama. I bet she'll see an image of the Virgin Mary in it."

"No, no," Victoria chimed in. "She'll see da Vinci's *Last Supper,* with all twelve apostles breaking bread across his scalp. That way he can claim his dandruff is just left over Eucharist."

"Victoria!" Emily gasped.

Joseph shook his head and got into the front passenger seat without a word. He loved his sisters' irreverent banter.

Pulling onto Hollister Avenue, Emily asked, "Was your roommate sad to see you go?"

"Clyde Richter? Yes and no. He's going to miss the pastries I got from the Vandenlundervaldts—"

"And from Yolanda Vasquez," Victoria interrupted in a singsong tone.

Ignoring her, he continued. "But he's not going to miss the sleepless nights. Toward the end there, he was acting pretty ornery."

"Are you still having nightmares?" Emily asked, concern softening her voice.

"Yeah. And I'm beginning to remember more and more of them. Nothing's come perfectly clear yet, but the parts I do remember are not the happiest of times."

Emily glanced in the rearview mirror. Victoria had inserted earbuds and had her iPod cranked up. She bobbed and swayed to the beat, mouthing the words to whatever was playing.

"And your psychiatrist sessions?"

"Even worse. I'm discovering we didn't have a very nice dad."

Emily checked the mirror again. In a lower voice she said, "No, we didn't. But what we did have was each other."

Joseph nodded. "That's what I'm learning. I guess Antonio and I were very close . . . before he died."

Emily's eyes misted. She blotted tears away before they could streak her mascara. "I was close to him, too. But we probably shouldn't discuss this while I'm driving."

"Okay. But when? I have a feeling the more I discover on my own, the more my dreams and therapy will reveal."

"Really?"

"Yeah. It's like one thing leads to another. You know, a snowball effect."

Emily didn't say anything. Joseph noticed a slight quiver of her chin. This wasn't going to be easy. But it was necessary. No—more than that. It was paramount to his recovery. Perhaps even to his sanity. He just didn't want to cause more scars than were already there—especially for his loved ones.

"Well, we've got time for that later," he said.

"Thank you, Joseph," Emily whispered through a throat constricted with emotion.

CHAPTER 39

JOSEPH'S HOMECOMING WAS LOW-KEY but still more extravagant than he wanted. Consuela had more food laid out than any two neighborhoods could eat, even though there were only about a dozen people at her home. Everyone wanted to see Joseph's scar. He received many condolences and oohs and ahs, and overall, much more attention than he could stomach.

He excused himself from recounting the "accident story" for the twenty-third time and made a beeline for the backdoor. He loved his mother's backyard. It was a small triangle-shaped plot with a large jacaranda tree at the apex. In the spring, the tree was a riot of tiny purple blossoms that rained down with each gentle breeze and released a fragrance that was as intoxicating as the plumeria flowers he loved so much.

Nothing much had changed since his last visit four months ago. The junk cars and car parts of Papa's days were long gone. That was good. The small fenced area was now cluttered with religious bric-a-brac. The focal point was a large statue of the Virgin Mary ensconced in a tall, narrow half-dome painted with vibrant colors and surrounded by a legion of cement saints and plaster angels. Joseph smiled in spite of himself. His mother had always been a worshipful woman, but in the last twenty years she'd become obsessed with religious artifacts and sacred decor.

"Hello, Joseef."

Joseph cringed and slowly turned around. Yolanda Vasquez stood with her head ducked and her eyes looking out from under lashes coated with enough mascara to make a raccoon look bland.

"Hi, Yolanda." Joseph knew he should say more but couldn't think of anything that wouldn't initiate a conversation.

"How are you?"

"I'm fine. Thanks for asking."

"I am happy for you."

The vacuous silence that followed her last statement was compounded by the austere, Vatican-like surroundings, making the yard feel like holy ground on which one should speak in hushed, reverent tones—until two cats started fighting in the next yard.

"So you stay at home awhile or you going back to Solvang?" she asked loudly.

"I'll be going home to Solvang. I have to get back to my classes," he said in a raised voice.

"Oh."

Silence immediately followed. The cats had apparently reached a truce.

"Did you try my taquitos?"

"No. I'm sorry. I'm not very hungry."

More silence.

Then a familiar yet unexpected voice filled the vacuum. "There you are!"

Joseph turned. "Michelle! I didn't know my mom invited you."

"She didn't. Emily did."

"Emily? When did you talk to her?"

"I called her. I hope you don't mind. I needed to ask her some questions, and she said to come for your celebration."

"That's great." Joseph was smiling until he saw Yolanda's snubbed expression. "Oh, I'm sorry. Yolanda Vasquez, this is my attorney, Michelle Haas."

Michelle extended her hand first. "Pleased to meet you, Yolanda."

The shy girl took her hand in a weak shake and quickly dropped her hand to her side. "You too." She then turned and trotted into the house.

"You are a savior," Joseph said just under his breath.

Michelle looked at the door Yolanda had disappeared behind and grinned. "An ex-girlfriend?"

"Old schoolmate and longtime neighbor. Mother continues to hold out hope for us, in spite of my assurances that the pope is more likely to make a personal visit than me marrying Yolanda Vasquez."

Victoria entered the backyard just as Joseph finished speaking. "My brother the heartbreaker," she teased. "Yolanda's been after him since grade school, and Mama keeps encouraging it. She wants Joseph to marry someone with Hispanic roots because she's so entrenched in tradition, she thinks marrying outside her culture is the same as befriending the devil."

Michelle laughed. "I'll keep that in mind."

"I'm Victoria Ramirez, Joseph's little sister," she said, extending her hand.

"Michelle Haas, Joseph's lawyer. I bet you break a number of hearts yourself, Victoria. You're gorgeous."

Victoria eyed her suspiciously for a moment before turning to her brother. "I like her, Joseph."

Joseph chuckled. "Does that mean I get to keep her?"

"Is she housebroken?"

"I haven't asked, but I assume so."

"Hey!" Michelle cried. "Don't I get a say in this?"

"Sure," Victoria said. "But only if you let me ask you some questions."

Michelle looked from Victoria to Joseph and back again. Joseph's expression showed he had no clue what his little sister was up to. He folded his arms and waited.

"Okay . . . ?"

Victoria's ironclad confidence softened a little, as if shyness had found a chink in her extrovert armor. "I really want to be a lawyer someday. Could you give me some advice on how to go about it?"

Michelle's wary expression melted in an instant. "Of course! Just let me know when."

"Oh thank you, thank you, thank you!" Victoria gushed. She grabbed Joseph in a tight hug and whispered in his ear, "I *really* like her. Don't lose this one."

Joseph held her at arm's length and smiled. "She's just my lawyer, sis. She's stuck with me until my accident case is settled."

"Um, objection," Michelle said. "Until both cases are settled."

Victoria blinked in confusion. Joseph flashed Michelle a stern look then turned his sister toward the house. "Legal jargon. You'll understand when you're a lawyer. Now go bring Ms. Haas a glass of Mom's cactus punch before you say something that will truly embarrass me."

Victoria jogged into the house, her long black hair shimmering with lustrous highlights as it danced in the sunlight.

"She is *really* pretty," Michelle said.

"And she knows it," he laughed. "So is this a social visit?"

"Yes and no. I need to know if you're staying here or are heading back to Solvang, in case I need to contact you."

"Stay here? With Yolanda two doors up the street and Mama with a church altar on permanent reserve? No. I'm hoping to leave this evening."

She shook her head in mock chastisement. "I never figured you for a chauvinistic profiler."

"You don't know the secret combination Mama has with Yolanda. It's a blood pact not unlike the Mafia's."

"Okay, I get it," she said with hands held up in truce. "How're you getting home? Do you have a car you can use?"

"No. I was hoping my lawyer wouldn't mind billing me for the mileage by giving me a ride in an hour or so?" He paused thoughtfully. "On second thought, I'd rather not wait until this evening."

She gave him a mischievous smile that weakened his knees. "As a lawyer, I'll have to bill you for mileage *and* the hours."

Joseph extended his hand. "Deal."

CHAPTER 40

MICHELLE PARKED IN THE DRIVEWAY of Joseph's home and killed the engine. Sitting in the passenger seat, Joseph had a confused look in his eyes. "Are you okay?" she asked softly.

He didn't respond right away. His eyes searched the small bungalow and drifted around his yard. Fall was coming on quickly. Even though Solvang was only 500 feet above sea level, the pocket of valley in which it sat seemed to welcome the season sooner than its neighboring communities. Joseph had a silver maple in his front yard that was already tinged yellow and orange, and the burning bush euonymus bordering his house was in full red splendor.

Michelle removed her keys and opened her door.

"Hang on," Joseph said. "Give me a minute."

She closed her door, opened the windows a crack, and folded her hands in her lap.

"Thanks again for the ride."

"Sure thing."

"No, I mean if you hadn't driven me home, I would've had to have my mother or sisters drive me, and I don't think I could have handled it."

Her brows furrowed. "I thought you got along well with your sisters."

"I do. It's just that, well, I think she's hiding something from me."

The furrow deepened. "Emily or Victoria?"

"Emily."

"You mean hiding information about your past?"

"Yeah. But I can't get her to come right out with it, and it's just . . . awkward being around her, knowing that she knows . . . something."

"I see."

Joseph kept his gaze fixed on the front of his house for a full minute. The silence was soothing and strangely comfortable. A few birds competed with a soughing breeze as the only external noises. The late-afternoon light was soft, the temperature just right.

"What if I am guilty?" Joseph asked without preamble.

"*If* is a very big word normally, but in this instance, I don't think it even applies. You were a minor when your father disappeared. To date there is no evidence that he's passed away; he's just missing. So far no one in your family corroborates the murder theory, right? So the only proof is one man's word that you confessed to it."

"What?" That was news to Joseph. "Which man?"

Michelle pulled out a document from her attaché and handed it to Joseph. "This is a hearsay testimonial claiming you admitted to murdering your father. I believe it's the only proof you actually made the confession."

Joseph scanned the paper. It stated that the accused, Joseph Ramirez, admitted to murder in the first degree. The accused offered his confession while talking in his sleep. The realization of who swore to this hit Joseph even before he saw the name and signature at the bottom of the document.

Clyde Richter.

"Clyde said this? It was him all along tipping off Wiseman?"

"Apparently," Michelle answered as if unconcerned. "And Wiseman was passing it on to the police."

Joseph was flabbergasted. "Why didn't Clyde say anything to me?"

She shrugged. "My guess is he was sworn to secrecy until the facts were validated or disproven. I haven't asked him because it doesn't really matter."

"It doesn't?" Joseph felt his temper coming to a boil. He felt cheated, stabbed in the back, betrayed.

"No, Joseph, it doesn't. People talk in their sleep all the time. They vocalize their nightmares and happy dreams, and even fantasies.

That doesn't make them real . . . but it does get a lot of spouses in trouble." Her attempt at lightening the mood fell on deaf ears. When Joseph didn't smile, she continued. "A confession made while asleep is not admissible in any court. And even if McRae finds something in his investigation, I doubt it'll hold water because of the statute of limitations."

Joseph gawked. "So McRae *has* opened an official investigation?"

"Yes." She ducked her head. "I should have told you sooner. But I honestly didn't think it mattered."

Joseph got out of the car and leaned against the roof. The cool breeze striking his face helped to clear his head but did little to resolve the conflict within.

"Are you sure you're okay?" Michelle asked, also exiting the car.

"No, I'm not okay," he snapped. "It seems I can't trust anyone anymore. My psychiatrist won't tell me what he's thinking about my case—says it's 'not the right time.' My sister won't tell me what really happened during my childhood because it's 'better I don't know.' My mother claims I'm being disrespectful every time I ask questions about my dad. My ex-roommate was hiding information from me—and so were you, for that matter! What's next? Are you going to tell me we can't win the traffic accident case because of a technicality? That I'm now being charged for the emotional duress of the truck driver?"

An offended twitch crossed her face. "I'm doing everything I can for you, Joseph."

"Well, apparently it's not enough. I'm still under investigation, which means I can't go back to work until I'm cleared from this mess. Plus, I won't receive any payment from SVJ until it's resolved to *their* satisfaction. And who knows when *that* will be. What do I live on—my good looks?"

Tiny crinkles formed at the corner of her eyes. "You'd be living pretty large if that were the case."

He harrumphed. "Gee, thanks, counselor."

Michelle stood rigid, staring at the roof of her car as Joseph paced up and down his driveway. After a few moments he mellowed and looked more sheepish than angry. "I'm sorry for snapping like that. I have no right to yell at you."

She nodded but kept her eyes fixed on the roof of her car. "Fine. But I'm not sure what it is you want me to do," she mumbled with a tight voice.

He had obviously offended her with his outburst. Joseph rounded the front of the car and took her in a tender hug. It surprised both of them. He let go and stepped back quickly. "I—um . . . I don't know why I did that. You sounded like you needed a hug, I guess."

She tucked an errant lock of hair behind her ear. "I think we both did."

He sighed heavily. "Okay. So what do we do now? I can't simply sit around and wait."

She thought for a moment. "I'll look into what Detective McRae is doing with his investigation. I'll also urge the judge assigned to your case, Judge Nathaniel Record, for a settlement. SVJ knows how to bluster and stall, but Judge Record recognizes delay tactics when he sees them, and he hates them."

"Thanks, Michelle. I really do appreciate it. So . . . what can I do?"

"Continue to heal and keep your appointments with Dr. Wilder."

Joseph's shoulders slumped. "In other words, just sit around and go nuts while everyone else tries to figure out if I *am* nuts."

She laughed. "That's one of the things I like about you, Joseph: you have a great sense of humor."

"I was being serious."

She laughed even harder. "See what I mean?"

He couldn't help but give a half smile. "Whatever. But don't plan on me just sitting around waiting."

"Fine. Where should we start, then?"

He blinked. "We?"

"As long as I'm with you, I'm on the clock. So where do you want to go?"

He was smiling fully now. "Out to eat. It's almost dinnertime—you choose the place."

Michelle reached out and touched his shoulder. "Joseph, are you offering to buy me dinner?"

He cocked his head to one side. "Technically, I'm still in recovery, right?"

"Well, yeah . . ." She hesitated.

"We'll just put it on SVJ's tab."

She covered her mouth to suppress the laugh bursting out. "You know that borders on the unethical, don't you?"

"Haven't a clue."

She pulled her keys from her purse. "When I'm this hungry, the border *does* get a little blurry for me too."

CHAPTER 41

"No, Mama, you don't need to come here and cook for me," Joseph said into the handset of his home phone.

"But ju still e'sick, *mi'jo*. An' ju been gone e'so long, ju have no food dere. What ju gonna eat?"

"Michelle took me shopping before I came home. Everything's fine."

"Michelle? Michelle who?" Consuela asked with a tone of suspicion.

"Michelle Haas. She's my—"

"Haas. That's no e'Spanish name, José."

"I know, Mama, she's m—"

"Ju should marry a nice e'Spanish girl. It's what da Church e'say ju should do."

"Mama, just let me expla—"

"Jur brother, he marry Anna Maria Hernandez and give me tree grandchildren. She come from a nice family. Emily, she marry Miguel Ortega, and dey give me five grandchildren. *Cinco!* Miguel es a hard-working man an' always go to Mass. Now Victoria es e'seeing a gringo at her e'school and now ju are e'seeing—"

"My lawyer," Joseph interrupted.

The line was silent for a couple of seconds. "Who?"

"Michelle Haas is my lawyer. She drove me home and took me shopping yesterday, and it's all covered by the school district insurance until Sierra West Construction's insurance pays up."

"She's not jur girlfriend?"

Joseph took a steadying breath. "That shouldn't matter to anyone but me. She's a very nice woman and is helping me out a lot, so I don't want you saying anything bad about her."

"Es she *bonita*?"

"Yes, Mama, she's very pretty. And smart, too. But more importantly, she's a very good lawyer. And that's exactly what I need right now."

As if catching the frustration in his voice, Consuela asked, "Why ju need a lawyer? Are ju in trouble, *mi'jo*?"

Joseph fought the temptation to bring out everything he was learning, to lay it all on the table so that there was no question he knew his father was not a good man. Or, worst case, *had not been* a good man, and that Joseph, as a youth, had done something about it. But he was dealing with his mother—a woman prone to rapid mood swings, often of a pious nature, and one who frequently adopted self-imposed vows of silence. If he came right out and asked about how Papa treated her and her children and, more importantly, what had become of the man, she might clam up and hang up. *Better leave that one alone for now,* Joseph decided.

"I'm not in trouble, Mama. The construction company's insurance is stalling on admitting blame and agreeing to any payment."

"How come?"

He bit his lower lip, debating. Mama always read so much into whatever he said and rarely got it right. "They think I may have planned it," Joseph finally said.

"Ju *plan* to be almos' killed? Like e'suicide or e'someting?"

"Yeah, or e'something."

Consuela's voice hardened, unbelieving. "José, ju really try dis?"

"No, Mama."

"E'suicide es agains' da Church, ju know."

"Yes, Mama. It is in my church, too," Joseph said wearily. He shook his head and decided he'd had enough. "Look, Mama, I just called to tell you I'm okay, and you don't have to worry. I have food, my house is fine—the Vandenlundervaldts took good care of it—and I will be coming back down to Santa Barbara next Monday. I'd like to see you to talk about some things."

There was a pause filled with mistrust on the other end of the line. "Ju *are* in trouble wit' da law, aren't ju," she snapped.

Steeling himself, Joseph said, "There's some question as to my involvement in Papa's disappearance."

He heard a sharp intake of air on the line. "Who e'say he disappeared?" Her voice was hard and strangely accusatory.

He chortled forcefully. "Well, he *did* suddenly vanish, didn't he?"

"I tought ju no remember dat."

"Mama, I—" He stopped short, closed his eyes, and said a quick prayer. *Just get it over with, Joseph.* "I am very confused about many things in my childhood. Mostly, why it is I can't remember anything before a certain age. But my psychiatrist is working on that with me. And also on the strange dreams I've been having." He paused and took a breath. "And a lot of the questions I have seem to deal with . . . um, they seem to *relate* to Papa's leaving."

"Oh," was all she said.

Sensing her trepidation, Joseph said, "A number of my questions really need answering. It's been bothering me ever since I started having these dreams. My psychiatrist thinks maybe we can figure this out through hypnosis sessions."

"Joseph. Dat es not a good idea," she said in a low voice, almost a whisper.

'Joseph,' now? "Why not?" he asked, hearing her anxious tone increase.

"It just not a good idea!" she cried. She sounded on the verge of tears now. "Please. Just e'say ju no remember no more and be done."

This was getting stranger by the minute. He had never heard such fear in his mother's voice. Deciding to let it go for now, he said, "Well, that shouldn't be too difficult, because I don't remember anything anyway. At least nothing before Papa left."

"Dis es good," she said, still quite wary but sounding relieved.

Confused, but willing to postpone his questions, Joseph sighed. "Okay, Mama. I'll see you next week, then, okay?"

"*Sí.*"

"I love you, Mama."

"I love ju too, *mi'jo.*"

CHAPTER 42

THE FOLLOWING MORNING, JOSEPH DRESSED in sweats and went for an early walk. The sun had yet to crest the eastern Sierra Nevadas, but it lit up the sky with a metallic brassiness and highlighted the random wispy clouds with bold strokes of pink and orange. The air bit at his face as he walked to the corner and headed toward town. In twenty minutes he was close enough to town to smell coffee brewing and baked goods just out of the oven. He hadn't planned on a particular destination but soon found himself approaching Dansk Sødtbrød. The Vandenlundervaldts opened their doors at 7:00 AM, well ahead of the other shops in town. As a result, the place was frequented by shopkeepers, business people, schoolteachers, and others wanting a quick breakfast before they trundled off to their respective businesses. It was always a warm, friendly atmosphere that Joseph loved.

An obnoxious cowbell clunked, announcing Joseph's entrance into the pastry shop. Helga looked up and bellowed, "Goede morgen, Yoseph. Gern, Yoseph is back."

The swinging door to the kitchen about left its hinges as Gern Vandenlundervaldt burst through, rounded the counter, and lifted Joseph off his feet in a crushing bear hug. The pressure from the big man's arms was not unlike the crushing force of the Sierra West cement truck. "Zo goede to see you, Yoseph. Auch, ve missed you zo!"

Regaining his footing, Joseph had to take a few deep breaths to expand his lungs to their proper size. But he did so with a smile. "Thanks. It's good to be back."

"Vhen did you return?" Helga asked.

"Two days ago."

She was clearly appalled. "Vhat? Two days? And vit us next door? Vhy didn't you come over?"

"I didn't want to bother you. Besides, I had a lot of catching up to do with mail and bills and cleaning and such."

"But you should take it easy," she argued. "You are still recoverink, yah?"

He shrugged. "I'm supposed to go slow, but believe me, I've had plenty of rest. What I haven't had in a long while is a decent blintz. Can you help me?"

"Strawberry cream cheese?"

"Is there any other way?"

She laughed heartily. The windows rattled. "Ach, Yoseph, you are a happiness to have around. Gern, get back to ze kitchen and make our son some strawberry blintzes."

"Yah, Mother."

Joseph spent half his day in the pastry shop talking with the Vandenlundervaldts as well as other townsfolk with whom he was acquainted. They talked of many things, but mostly about his accident and current state of health. All the while Helga made sure he had soup, sandwiches, cakes, and pastries in front of him. By the time he left Dansk Sødtbrød, he felt like he wouldn't have to eat again for a week. Although ready to burst—or purge—he was very, very happy. He'd missed his little town more than he had realized. Seeing many old friends had been comforting, joyful, and therapeutic.

* * *

It was young Joseph's favorite birthday treat: a strawberry-flavored cake with thick white frosting and multicolored sprinkles on top. Mama was so good at baking cakes and treats. The table was decorated with homemade starbursts and confetti, with a single red balloon tied to Joseph's chair. For dinner, Mama had made a *paella*—a traditional Spanish dish cooked in a large open skillet, with rice, onions, peppers, tomatoes, spices, and two kinds of meat. Joseph had his dinner with a big glass of root beer, a rare treat for the kids. Papa had his with real beer, his usual.

After a rousing chorus of happy birthday, Mama cut into the cake and gave Joseph a large slice. In spite of how good it looked, he waited for everyone else to get a slice before digging into his. He wanted to be on his best behavior today. He wanted his parents to be extra proud of—

"What's wrong with it?" Papa snapped.

Joseph sucked in his breath. "Nothing," he said in a soft voice.

"Then eat it. Mama went to a lot of trouble making it."

"Papa, he's just being polite," Antonio said in Joseph's defense.

Papa harrumphed and took a pull at his beer.

The slices were soon divvied out, and everyone dug in. Moans of joy sounded around the table and eyes brightened. "This is delicious." "Very, delicious." "*Sí, delicioso,*" many voices sang as if in a round.

"The icing is too sweet!" Papa grumbled. "It gives me a headache."

"I love it!" Joseph cheered. "I could eat a whole bowl of it."

"Don't be stupid. No one can eat a whole bowl of this crap," Papa snarled. He stabbed his fork into his half-eaten slice of cake and shoved his plate into the center of the table. "Get me another beer, Mama."

As Consuela moved to the fridge, Emily said, "Of course he can't eat a whole bowl, Papa. He was just speaking figuratively."

Joseph gawked at his sister. He had spoken *figuratively*? He was speechless, astounded that he had done something so intelligent without even knowing he had. *Figuratively*. Whatever that meant, it sure sounded smart. Maybe he wasn't all that stupid.

Estefan's bloodshot eyes fixed on his daughter. "Are those the kind of words they teach you in the gringo school? Figur . . . figa . . . figora . . . whatever it was."

The fifteen-year-old huffed. "It's not a gringo school, it's a public school, and kids from all nationalities go there."

"It's okay, Em," Joseph said. "I didn't mean to speak figuremen-tally. There's no way I can eat a whole bowl of that frosting. I'd get sick. But it sure is good! And the cake tastes like real strawberries. How do you make it taste like real strawberries, Mama?"

Estefan slammed his beer down with such force it cracked the bottle. Luckily, it didn't shatter, but beer began to seep everywhere. The man growled in anger and turned to Joseph. "Another question? Why can't you just eat it and be quiet? You don't hear Antonio or Emily ask about every little thing."

Joseph sat frozen. He stared at his cake and willed himself not to cry. That would only make things worse. It always made things worse.

No one around the table said anything. Papa wasn't drunk—yet. But when his temper flared, as it often did without warning, then it was best to become unnoticeable, to blend into the background.

Papa held up the leaking bottle and rotated it appreciatively, as if examining the complexity of the crack. "How old are you today, José?"

"Ten," he said proudly.

"Wow, ten years old. That's almost a man."

Joseph said nothing. He wasn't sure what Papa wanted to hear.

"I think ten years old is old enough to learn why you are so different from your brothers and sisters."

"Papa!" Mama blurted.

"What?" he snapped back. "Don't you want him to know why he was a mistake?"

"Papa, we've talked about this," Mama said. Her eyes blazed with a heat Joseph had never seen before. It had come on so fast, it scared him to look at her. But there was also fear in her eyes. And that frightened him more than the anger.

"I am head of this house!" Estefan bellowed.

"Papa, please," Emily said tenderly. "It is José's birthday. Let's not spoil it."

He scowled at his daughter. "*You* don't even know the truth. No one here does because I promised. But I was tricked." He stood and shook his fist at Mama. "I was tricked!" He then hurled the leaking bottle of beer against the wall.

Everyone held their breath. Joseph forced a smile, even as a tear trickled down one cheek. "Thank you for my birthday, Papa," he said bravely. "I'm sorry you don't like my cake."

Estefan's eyes momentarily softened. Conflict distorted his face; anger and remorse, pity and blame. When he finally spoke again, his voice was constricted. "Happy Birthday . . . *el falla*."

* * *

Joseph stared at the ceiling of his bedroom. His thoughts were harried and cut deep. Papa had almost revealed why he felt Joseph was a mistake. Emily had said it was because he was a surprise baby—that neither Mama nor Papa had planned on him coming when he did. She also hinted that he had wanted a girl as their fourth child. But something in his dream told him it was more than that. That he *was* a mistake. And not just because he was unexpected. Perhaps he was unexpected in an unexpected way . . .

Grabbing his notepad, Joseph scribbled his thoughts as legibly as he could. He'd wait to talk to Dr. Wilder at their next appointment. Until then he'd do his best to get back to the way things were before his accident—before he realized he had such an ugly past.

CHAPTER 43

IT FELT TRULY GOOD TO be home. There was security and assurance in familiar surroundings. With the solace in which a thick down comforter envelops the body, Joseph luxuriated in the soothing embrace of his little home. He didn't live in a grand palace, but then, he didn't want to. His 1,100-square-foot bungalow was just the right size for him. His furnishings were functional, his decor understated and tasteful.

Joseph had spent the weekend cleaning, organizing, and readjusting to life at home. The hard work felt good, satisfying. Michelle Haas had arranged a rental car for him until SVJ and Sierra West Construction came through on his claim. There was no telling how long *that* fiasco would continue. Until then, he was happy just to be able to get around without relying on the charity of others. Church went about as expected: lots of questions, lots of concern, lots of dinner invitations. Joseph was very gracious but declined all offers. He simply wanted to relax at home watching a David Attenborough nature DVD. Maybe two or three.

Monday was spent cleaning his yard, preparing it for winter. Snow rarely fell in this part of California, but rain was plentiful, and he wanted to get all the dead foliage cleared and his little garden tilled under. That evening, he had just added a dollop of salsa to his Denver omelet when his phone rang. Glancing at the wall clock, he wondered who would be calling him so late on a Monday.

"Joseph, I have three items of great news," Michelle fairly sang over the phone. "I got a call from Judge Record this morning, and he asked me to come to his office at four o'clock today. So I went, and he had your file laid across his desk and a very forlorn Brick Wiseman sitting in a corner, like he was in time-out or something . . ." She paused and giggled like a young girl.

The mirth in her voice was delightful. She sounded very happy. Joseph pictured her face on the other end of the line, with a smile stretching ear to ear, eyes dancing, the dimple showing. He marveled at how simply hearing her voice was refreshing. She was such a multi-faceted woman. While deep-thinking, intelligent, and serious, she could sometimes come across with teenaged whimsicality. He loved her unpredictability. What's more, she was pretty, very pretty. Joseph shook his head and concentrated on her words.

"Okay?" Joseph prompted.

"So I walk in, and he says to take a seat in front of his desk, then sits behind the desk and starts to shuffle your file back into the folder." She paused as if indicating Joseph should find something astounding in the judge's actions.

"Okay?" he said again.

"Don't you see? He left Brick in the corner. It's customary to have both attorneys side-by-side at his desk when he delivers a ruling or a mandate or whatever, but he just asked *me* there! Apparently, Brick had already been raked over the coals, and he was sitting in the corner silently licking his wounds."

"Brick Wiseman reduced to silence? That I'd like to see," Joseph mused.

"Exactly!" she cheered. "Anyway, Judge Record said, 'I've looked over your client's case, Ms. Haas,'" she said in a low voice, mimicking the judge's gruff timbre, "and frankly I am very disappointed.'"

"How come?" Joseph asked.

"That's what *I* wondered, but I didn't get a chance to ask. He went on to say that the treatment of your file was below standard—even for SVJ's standards—and that he was upset that he had to waste time on something so obviously frivolous."

"Getting run over by a cement truck is frivolous?" Joseph balked.

"No, wait," she urged. "I've replayed this so many times in my head I have it memorized! He said, 'This is an open-and-shut case,

Ms. Haas. I have reviewed arguments from both sides and examined the evidence. On your side you have an outstanding young man from a poor neighborhood who worked hard and made something of his life. He has no criminal record—not even a speeding ticket. He is a respected middle schoolteacher and a model citizen in every way I can see. And you have detailed video tape of the accident, which clearly shows fault on the part of the Sierra West truck driver. On the SVJ side we have *nothing*. A few unsubstantiated claims and a lot of hearsay. Therefore, this case is clearly open-and-shut. I assure you and your client you will not have any more delays from Messers Stansbury, Vail, and Jenkins in receiving compensation from Sierra West Construction. Accordingly, I have ordered a settlement of three million dollars to one Joseph Ramirez of Solvang, California, payable immediately via SVJ law offices.'"

Joseph could hear her hold her breath on the other end of the line, as if awaiting his reaction. Frankly, Joseph was holding his breath too, though not intentionally. He moved to a chair next to his kitchen table and fell into it. "Could you repeat that, please?"

She laughed. "The whole thing or just the three million part?"

Searching for something to say that would not come out blithering or obtuse, he asked, "What did Wiseman say?"

"Nothing. I turned and looked at him, but his head was hung so low I could see the bald spot forming on the back of his scalp."

Joseph was in shock. *Three million dollars?* What in the world would he do with that kind of money? It was crazy. Obscene. He was a science teacher at a middle school, for heaven's sake. He wasn't *worth* three million bucks!

"Can, um . . . can the judge do that? I mean, can't SVJ appeal it or something?"

"Oh sure, they can request that a higher court look at it, but they won't. They know they don't have a leg to stand on, and at this point, they'll gladly pay just to have it out of the limelight."

"The limelight? Great. You mean now I'll be hounded by paparazzi—not to mention every first, second, and third cousin I never knew I was related to?"

A loud guffaw preceded her next revelation. "That's the second bit of great news. You won't! Part of the agreement is that this will *not* go public. It's an undisclosed settlement, Joseph."

"Per Judge Record?"

"No, per SVJ and Sierra West Construction. Neither of them want this egg on their face, so you have to sign a release saying *you* won't go public with the settlement. I told them you'd think about it."

"What?" he cried. "The last thing I want is for everyone to know I just got three million dollars. Geez, Michelle, you know I don't want that kind of money! We already talked about that."

"Of course I know that," she countered. "But *they* don't. I said I'd get you to agree to it only if there was no delay in payment on the settlement."

"What kind of delay?" Joseph wondered, staring at his cold omelet, realizing he was no longer hungry.

"Oh, you know, paperwork, insurance regulations, filing requirements, review of hospital charges, that sort of thing. That's the kind of garbage that can withhold payments for months, sometimes years."

"Super."

"But Judge Record assured me that won't be an issue. He ordered a check to be cut this coming Wednesday before the close of business."

Her excitement was contagious. Joseph couldn't help but smile. His hands trembled, and his head felt lighter than it had in weeks. Months. Heck, in years!

Through a warble of mirth, she was barely able to say, "And then he added, 'Eastern Standard Time.'"

"Can he do *that*?" he asked, struggling to regain a modicum of rational thought.

"I don't know. But he did. And Brick didn't say a thing about it. Not a peep! He just sat there like a ruffian in the principal's office."

Joseph laughed at the simile. As a teacher, it was a picture with which he was very familiar.

"That's the third bit of great news," Michelle went on. "You'll have a check by Wednesday afternoon. Can you come to my office day after tomorrow, say around four?"

"Uh, sure. I have an appointment with Dr. Wilder at about one, so I should be done in time."

"Good. You know where my office is, don't you?"

"Yeah. You work in the school district offices, just off Santa Barbara Street, right?"

"Yeah," she said, finally calming down a bit, apparently forcing herself to be more professional. "We'll go over the paperwork and get the required signatures. Then, you'll let me take you out to dinner to celebrate. Do you like steaks? We could go to Chuck's."

Joseph's head was still spinning. He shook it again and furrowed his brow in concentration. "What if I don't want all the money?" he asked hesitantly. "What if I just want the bills covered?"

Michelle was silent for a moment. "I figured you were going to ask that. Listen, we'll discuss that over dinner. Don't make any rash decisions right now. Sleep on it. We'll talk about it Wednesday."

Joseph nodded to the phone. "Okay. But on one condition. You let *me* buy dinner. I mean, I'm almost a millionaire now, right?"

She chuckled. "Since I don't get a percentage of this settlement, I was hoping you would say that."

"Great. See you Wednesday."

Joseph hung up and leaned against the wall. He was confused and annoyed with himself—annoyed at his lack of memory and his inability to get clear answers. He should be happy, for heaven's sake! *Happy? Overjoyed. Ecstatic.* Three million dollars was more money than he could imagine—more than he had ever *dreamed* of having. Yet, in spite of that, he couldn't shake from his mind his other dreams. He was still plagued with nightmares. He still awoke each morning in a cold sweat. He still needed closure to something he couldn't even recall suffering through.

More importantly, he still needed to learn whether or not he was guilty of murder. After all, what good would three million dollars do to a soul burdened with that?

CHAPTER 44

"D<small>ID YOU BRING A CHANGE</small> of clothes?" Dr. Wilder asked.

"Yeah. I'm still not sure why."

"Because we're going to go deeper into your past than before. Quite often the body responds to that in strange ways, sometimes with lots of sweating, sometimes loss of bladder control."

"Super."

"Okay, Joseph, we need to do this right. I'm going to lead you into more detail as you regress. As before, just go with it. Don't try to anticipate where I'm headed. And don't be afraid of what we find. Can you do that?"

"I'll try," Joseph answered.

"No, we're not going to try," the psychiatrist said. "We're going to accomplish. We're going to get through that mind block of yours and show you there's nothing to fear anymore."

Joseph nodded, reclined on the couch, said a silent prayer, and let Dr. Wilder lead him into a deep, complete regression.

* * *

The young boy was leaning over a precipice: the rooftop ledge of a tall building. He knew if his knees buckled, he'd fall. If he trembled too much, he'd lose his footing. If he cried out, the man holding him by his shirttail would let go.

He didn't want to look down. He tried closing his eyes, but his lids refused to shut. Abject fear held them peeled back. From this height, his view was unobstructed. He was downtown, atop the

Granada Theater, perhaps the tallest public building in Santa Barbara. To his right he could see up State Street to the Arlington, the famous theater whose interior resembled a Spanish courtyard. To his left, lots of red-tile roofs lining State Street straight to the beach and onto Stern's Wharf. But the panorama was anything but pleasing. At this dizzying height, gravity seemed to pull with amplified force. The slightest breeze felt like a tornado. The pigeons cooing merrily on the roof's edge sounded malicious, threatening, as if mocking him with hollow laughter.

The man holding the boy adjusted his grip, causing him to lurch forward. Gravity tugged with tenacious force. Despite his best efforts, his gaze was drawn downward. The sidewalk looked so far away. It was early morning—so early the sun had yet to crest the eastern mountains. State Street was empty—no one milled about, window shopping in the downtown area. A street cleaner crept along the faux cobblestones, leaving a moist trail in its wake like a noisy, monstrous snail.

Someone cried out—not the boy, but another equally young voice—something about stopping, and not being mean, and promises of trying harder to be good.

The man's voice fractured the soft morning air. Harsh words in Spanish. He'd had enough with disobedience, with conspiring with their lazy mother, with everyone going behind his back. He was going to teach the whole family who was in charge.

Suddenly, Joseph's perspective changed. He was the boy leaning over the edge. It was a punishment.

Antonio was clinging to his father's leg. He was fourteen years old, pulling on Papa's knees with all his might. Papa was crazy drunk and blind with rage. Antonio was trying to save Joseph from Papa's anger—Joseph *knew* it. He'd do the same for him.

Antonio yanked on Papa's pant leg again, trying to pull him—and his kid brother—away from the ledge. The sound of ripping fabric filled Joseph's ears, but it wasn't Papa's pants. His shirt was tearing apart! Papa was still swearing, oblivious to the terrifying sound and what it meant.

Joseph's breath caught. Antonio's grip on Papa's pants faltered.

Joseph's eyes locked with his brother's. His thin flannel shirt gave way again, the threads separating like a zipper opening. Papa was glaring down at Antonio, spitting one vile curse after another. He couldn't see what was happening. Antonio pointed at Joseph and yelled for Papa to turn around. Papa ordered him to shut up or he would be next. Antonio let go and lunged toward the edge.

A final rending tear, and, in the next instant, Joseph felt himself fall. He did not scream, did not cry out. He sucked in a huge breath, his eyes squeezed shut. Ten seconds of agonizing silence passed where no breath was drawn, no breeze ruffled a shirt, no birds called to each other. Joseph finally realized his fall had been stopped.

He opened his eyes and saw emptiness below him. He heard his brother yell to him to grab onto something. Because the Granada had decorative cement work on its front, Joseph was able to latch on to a narrow lip of trim and look up. Antonio was dangling halfway over the edge, hanging onto Joseph's collar with one hand. Sapping all their combined energy, Antonio helped Joseph over the edge, and the two fell exhausted onto the rooftop.

Looking up, Joseph saw his father staring in dismay at the scrap of fabric in his hand. Slowly, Papa looked back at young Joseph. The man's eyes were filled first with shock then sorrow then with raw hatred. He released the shard of Joseph's shirt and pointed over the ledge. When he spoke, his voice hissed like a snake, his words slow, accusatory, and dripping with malice. "You weren't supposed to live. You have a devil's blessing. The devil possesses your soul."

Joseph was petrified. He couldn't speak, couldn't breathe, couldn't blink. He started shaking his head—more in fright than denial. How could he be possessed of the devil? He didn't believe he was. He went to church every Sunday with Mama. But then, since he couldn't remember what he'd done to make Papa mad, maybe he *did* have a bad spirit making him do bad things.

Estefan inched to the edge and peered over. He immediately recoiled with a look of pure horror distorting his face. "The devil has you now, *el falla*. He has you forever because I couldn't finish what needed to be done! It is a sign. You are *evil*!"

* * *

Joseph woke suddenly to find himself sitting at the far edge of Dr. Wilder's couch, with his legs pulled tightly against his chest. He couldn't breathe. Even though his mouth was wide open, no air traveled in or out. His lungs screamed for oxygen. His clothes were soaked in sweat. His head pounded with unimaginable intensity. His gaze shot randomly about the room, focusing on nothing.

"Breathe, Joseph."

Joseph flinched as if he'd been struck by lightning. Wide-eyed, pupils dilated, he gawked at Dr. Wilder.

"Breathe, Joseph," the psychiatrist gently repeated.

Sounding like a chorus of lost souls, Joseph's lungs finally complied and drew in a huge volume of air. The release of the lungful was even noisier, filled with a cry of remorse, of pure agony. Joseph immediately began to cry, his shoulders lurching with each gasping sob.

"It's okay, Joseph. Just let it out. You're safe again. You're in my office, safe and sound. Go on and release your sorrow. It's been pent up inside of you for twenty years. Let it out. Let it all out." Dr. Wilder's deep voice was extra tender, extra caring, full of compassion and understanding.

With his knees still drawn tightly to his chest, Joseph fell to one side and sobbed, letting his emotions flow out, purging his soul.

* * *

Joseph had no idea how long he had lain there. Dr. Wilder was at his desk, typing softly on a laptop. Joseph cleared his throat and tried to sit up, but his body refused to comply. It was as if he had lost all muscle tone and strength. What's worse, he hurt from head to toe. It felt like he'd been run over by another cement truck.

"How long have I been out?" he croaked through a parched throat.

"About two hours," the psychiatrist replied as if the time were inconsequential.

Joseph groaned as he forced himself up and rubbed the back of his neck with both hands. "Sorry about that. I hope I didn't make you miss a later appointment."

"Don't even worry about it. I scheduled plenty of time for this. Do you remember much?"

Joseph just stared blankly as fresh tears filled his eyes. "I almost wish I didn't."

"On the contrary, it's important you do. I think this may be the murder you were dreaming of. Your father tried to murder you, but he tried to make it seem like he didn't. He blamed it on your association with the devil, and thus made you feel all the more guilty of being bad. Do you understand, Joseph?"

Joseph nodded but still had trouble accepting the information. It was easy to understand why he would want to block such a despicable event from his mind. It was easy to see why guilt had tortured his subconscious for twenty years. It was a wonder no one else had ever found out about the incident. Or had they? Did Antonio tell anyone before his death?

"Do you think my mother knows about this?"

Dr. Wilder slid his hand across his closely shorn scalp, pondering. "No. I don't think so. Your father was the kind of man who could not accept blame of any kind. He had almost killed you—whether intentionally or accidentally, I'm still not sure. But if he claimed it was your fault, he must have believed it in his mind. As far as Antonio, your father probably threatened him into silence, as well as you, and then never spoke of it again."

"Wow. Did that come out in my hypnosis?"

"No. You snapped from the regression before we got that far. But it doesn't matter."

Joseph wiped his face on his sleeve. "So this whole thing about my father being murdered is really about *my* brush with death?"

"It's a strong possibility."

"So . . . what should I do with this information?"

Dr. Wilder exhaled a long, slow breath. "I'm not sure there's much you *can* do. We're talking about filing a police report on an event that occurred twenty years ago—implicating someone who's been missing for nearly two decades. I suppose the police *could* send out an APB on your father, but I doubt it'd get much attention."

"But he tried to kill me! Shouldn't I do . . . *something?*"

Dr. Wilder stood and drew a chair up to his patient. "Joseph, let me reiterate something. It may come across as harsh, but it's something you have to consider."

Joseph nodded, not sure he wanted to hear this but knowing he had to.

"I believe your regression was accurate. I believe your recall was not sullied with false memory or confabulation. However, the possibility remains that it was. That's why hypnotic regression is so . . . flawed, even dangerous. There's no guarantee of accuracy."

"I don't understand. You're saying I could have *made* this up?"

Dr. Wilder nodded. "Another possibility is that your father killed your brother—and to deal with the loss, your mind created the rooftop scenario."

"But Antonio's death was gang related."

"Was that proven? Were any arrests made?"

Joseph's mind whirled again, reaching, grasping for an answer that would prove the psychiatrist wrong. He came up blank. "I . . . I can't remember."

CHAPTER 45

JOSEPH WALKED INTO THE SANTA Barbara school district offices just before four. He had taken a shower at the hospital and changed into fresh clothes. And although he was greatly refreshed, he still felt unsteady. The emotions he'd revisited with Dr. Wilder had drained him emotionally and physically.

"Mr. Ramirez?" the receptionist asked.

"Yes?" he responded, mildly surprised by her recognition.

"Ms. Haas said to be expecting you. She asked that you wait in her office. She had to run downtown to the courthouse for a moment but said she'd be right back. Right this way, please," the woman said, heading down a hallway.

Michelle Haas's office looked like the aftermath of an earthquake. Her bookshelves sagged from excess burden, and stacks of files, file boxes, and manila envelopes grew from the floor like fragile stalagmites. Her desktop was just the opposite. Where the floor and shelves were an avalanche waiting to happen, her desktop was pristine and clutter-free. A single green-glass banker's lamp illuminated a writing blotter that was placed with such precision, Joseph wondered if Michelle had used a ruler to determine its exact position. A pen, pencil, and Post-it set sat in perfect repose at the top of the blotter, an African violet in a terra-cotta pot rested next to a three-tier letter organizer in one corner of the desk, and a burnished-brass picture frame occupied the other corner.

"Please have a seat," the receptionist said pleasantly. "Can I get you anything to drink? Coffee, water, soda?"

"No, thanks," he replied.

She nodded and left Joseph alone. There were four chairs in the small space in addition to the desk and bookshelves. Each chair had its own stack of files and papers. The only available seating was Michelle's high-backed office chair. Joseph considered standing until Michelle showed, but his fatigue was getting the better of his stamina, so he weaved through the paper monoliths and plopped into her chair. Soft light filtered through the blinds behind her desk and cast a diffused silhouette across the blotter. The African violet had a half-dozen deep purple blossoms that glowed in the light of the desk lamp, and the dark brass frame housed a happy photo of—

Joseph's breath caught. The photograph was taken outdoors, on a beach, and showed an adorable little girl with dark wavy hair, a dimple in one cheek, and big blue eyes. She looked familiar. Joseph knew it was a picture of Michelle as a young girl, but the familiarity he felt with the child went beyond age-deferred recognition. The photo also showed an older woman, clearly a relative, standing behind little Michelle, with her arms wrapped around the front of her in a tender embrace. Was the woman her mother? The resemblance was close but not quite similar enough. And although the woman had as much happiness in her eyes as the little girl, there was also a preponderance of sorrow—dark circles under her eyes that spoke of suffering and fatigue. The woman wore a bandana on her head. Not uncommon for a day at the beach, but there was something strange about it. The cloth appeared to lie tightly against her scalp, as if there were very little hair underneath to give it volume. Joseph didn't know what to make of the photo.

"Sorry I'm late," Michelle said, stepping into her office with a satchel over one shoulder and her attaché in the opposite hand.

Joseph jumped from her chair as if guilty of some infraction. "Oh, that's okay. Sorry about sitting in your chair. I didn't have much choice."

She smiled sheepishly. "Yeah. Sorry. My legal assistant has been out with the swine flu for two weeks, and I haven't done a good job keeping up."

Joseph stepped to one side as Michelle doffed her satchel and took her chair. "Swine flu, huh?" he asked.

"Yeah. The whole district is reeling from it. Haven't you heard?"

"No, I've been . . . preoccupied the last little while." He grinned.

She blushed. "Sorry." She pulled a thick file from her attaché and placed it on her desk. Opening the file, she slid a green cashier's check toward Joseph. "This should help you feel better." It did just the opposite.

Joseph was abruptly speechless. He was sure his eyes were bugging out of his skull. *Three million dollars payable to Joseph Ramirez.* His skin went cold, clammy. He could feel his heart pound against his sternum with such force he was sure his ribs would crack. He reached for the check but couldn't make himself touch it. It couldn't be real. If he got too close, it'd disappear in a wisp of vapor. *Poof!* He blinked hard and looked again. *Three million dollars payable to Joseph Ramirez.* He tried to swallow but found his mouth suddenly bone dry.

It didn't seem right. It was an accident! He'd learned long ago to turn the other cheek. He'd done it several times throughout his life—or had he? Could he honestly forgive his father for the countless harms, the countless *crimes* he'd committed against him—and against his mother, brothers, and sisters?

"Joseph? Are you okay?" Michelle asked with a concerned tremor.

He shook his head as if shivering. "I still don't know about this, Michelle. It doesn't feel right."

Michelle stood and told him to take her seat. He did.

"Okay, listen to me. You are not doing anything wrong here, okay? This is perfectly legal, and what's more, it is perfectly *right.* Judge Record could have insisted on a lot more, but he knew your reservations about getting too much money for an unintentional event. He actually told me that he respected and admired your decision. That's *huge* coming from him. But he did order the payment, and SVJ agreed to it. Unless you want this to drag out until next summer two years from now, I suggest you sign these papers and be done with it."

Joseph went to say something, but Michelle cut him off by holding up an index finger. "If you decide you don't want the money, fine. You have the option of signing the check back to SVJ Law offices—not that that pack of hounds deserves a penny of it. You can donate it to your church. You can use it to buy new textbooks or even a huge aquarium for your classroom. Heck, buy a whole new school! I don't care. It's *your* money, Joseph; you can do whatever you want with it. Okay? But there's also a secondary concern. You are still under a great deal of stress regarding your father. Anything that adds to that stress could cause serious emotional damage, which in turn could destroy your health. To have your bills paid, your house free and clear, would certainly eliminate a lot of stress, right? And just think what you could do for your brother and sisters. Victoria wants to go to law school. How's she going to pay for that?"

Joseph picked up the check and read it several times. *Three million dollars!* His inner turmoil still raged, but he could see the logic in her argument. The ruling had already been made. He couldn't change that. Slowly, he allowed himself to accept that fact. He liked her metaphor, calling SVJ a pack of hounds. Oh well. *Might as well let sleeping dogs lie,* he decided. He smiled.

"You are my lawyer, and I trust you implicitly," Joseph said officially. "I appreciate your expressing my concerns to Judge Record. Please tell him I appreciate his consideration. Now, tell me how I go about setting up an account to pay off those hospital bills?"

"Your hospital bills? What bills? Those are already taken care of."

"But I thought the settlement was this large to pay off my hospital expenses."

Michelle laughed and placed her hand on his shoulder. "I'm sorry, Joseph, didn't I mention that? The judge awarded you that sum *after* your expenses are covered."

Joseph's head began to spin again. The pangs of guilt began to creep back into his heart. It was still too much. Way too much.

"But before you get all magnanimous and send the money back, I'd like to ask one favor," Michelle said, her hand still resting on his shoulder.

"What—you need a loan?" Joseph asked, half kidding.

"Nope. I'm just like you: I like to work for my living. No, what I was hoping is that you'd still take me to Chuck's. I've been craving a juicy porterhouse all day!"

He looked up at her and couldn't hide his surprise. "You can eat an entire porterhouse steak? One of those things weighs as much as you do! You're not one of those people whose eyes are always bigger than their stomach, are you?"

She punched him in the shoulder. "That sounds like a challenge."

Joseph shrugged.

"Let's go," she said, heading for the door.

CHAPTER 46

THE SEMI-POLYNESIAN ATMOSPHERE OF Chuck's and the aroma of freshly grilled steaks was just the tonic Joseph needed to feel better about things. But the presence of Michelle Haas across the table was an even stronger medicine. More powerful. More intoxicating.

Having had her bluff called, instead of a porterhouse, Michelle ordered the house special, an eight-ounce tenderloin that she could cut with her spoon. Joseph had the top sirloin—the biggest they offered. Both were savory, grilled to perfection.

"I guess I'll never get used to the idea of having so much money," Joseph said for the umpteenth time.

"You know one of the things I like most about you?" Michelle asked. "You are honest to a fault. And you're friendly and kind and . . . and just a . . . a *good* man. Regardless of what dirt Brick Wiseman tried to throw at you, you came out spotless, squeaky clean. You always have."

"Now you're the one throwing stuff around, and it ain't dirt," he scoffed.

"No, seriously. You're good-looking, you have an honorable career, you have no vices or addictions that I can detect. Even without all that money, you're like every girl's dream come true." Her mouth clamped shut too slow to stop the last words from escaping. A deep, delightful blush colored her cheeks. It was easy to spot, even in the dark restaurant setting.

Joseph toyed with the idea of teasing her about the Freudian slip but decided he liked what she said too much to make light of it. What's more, he felt the same way about her.

"Thanks," he said humbly. "But I think you're exaggerating a bit much, even for a lawyer. I think we'd better talk about something else before we both say something totally mortifying."

"I couldn't agree more," Michelle said, struggling to regain her composure. "Can you discuss what you and Dr. Wilder found today?"

Joseph took a sip of water. He didn't want to go through that emotional roller coaster so soon after getting off. "Yes. But if it's all the same . . ."

"You'd rather not."

He nodded.

"Too painful?"

"For now." He forced a smile and leaned forward. "You know so much about me. How about I learn a little about you?"

She blushed again. "There's not much to know."

"How about that picture on your desk? I'm guessing you're the little girl in the photo. So who's the woman with you?"

Michelle's eyes immediately dropped to her plate. She reached for her water and tried to take a casual sip, but her hand trembled too much to hide her emotions. She dabbed her mouth with her napkin and took a couple of shallow breaths. "Next question, please."

Joseph was surprised at her response, and a bit disappointed, but he didn't force the issue. "Oops. Sorry. How about this one: now that I got the check, what happens next?"

The relief on Michelle's face would have seemed comical had it not been for the deep sorrow Joseph had seen only moments before. "I will make several copies of the settlement documents, give you a set, and deliver the rest to all parties involved. The hard part is done. All that's left is some paper shuffling. Oh, you probably want to get a good financial adviser and perhaps a savvy tax guy, too. If you invest your settlement wisely, you'll save a fortune on taxes."

"Good advice, counselor."

"My pleasure. Within a week to ten days, the whole thing should be behind you."

Joseph set his fork down and pushed his plate away. Grumbling, he said, "I wish. There's still the matter of my father's death and my nightmares." Joseph was instantly sorry for his remark because of the hurt expression that crossed her face.

"I'm sorry, Joseph. I should have been more thoughtful—"

"No, it was me," he interrupted. "I know how much you've done for me, and I truly appreciate everything. But, Michelle . . ." He paused for another sip of water. His throat felt curiously raspy. "I wonder how much of my past will change your opinion of me."

"It can't be *that* bad."

Joseph finished off his water and folded his napkin. When the waiter stopped by to refill his glass, Joseph asked for the check, which the young man produced on the spot.

Outside the restaurant, the air had cooled considerably. When Michelle shivered, Joseph removed his jacket and wrapped it around her shoulders. Lost in their individual thoughts, they drove back to the school district offices listening to light jazz on the radio.

The parking lot was empty. Joseph parked next to Michelle's car and switched off the engine.

"You know how Clyde says I confessed to murder?"

Michelle answered with a soft yes.

Staring straight ahead, he asked, "What if the murder committed wasn't my father's?"

Her look was one of bewilderment. "I thought your dreams indicate your *father* is dead."

"So far, they indicate he's missing. And that's something we've known all along. The dreams that mention his death are the ones I can't remember. And Dr. Wilder has yet to find anything that links Estefan's death—if he is dead—to me."

She continued to stare blankly, expecting more.

Joseph sighed heavily. "What would you say if the person who was almost murdered was saved at the last, and then made to feel like it was *his fault*?" The last two words came out in a coarse whisper. "And false guilt is what's plagued him all this time?"

"You?" she asked, disbelieving. "You're saying *you* were almost murdered?"

He nodded and gripped the steering wheel with both hands, blanching his knuckles. "I don't know for sure yet. Maybe. I have another session with Dr. Wilder on Friday. But something like that might have given me the incentive *to* murder. If not—if my mind *created* the incident—then that means I'm not guilty. Just psychotic. What would you think of me then?"

Michelle was quiet a long time. Joseph sensed that her lack of response was a valid answer. He could feel her discomfort radiating from her silence. He hated putting her in such an awkward position. But he knew he had feelings for her beyond their contractual agreement. And he was pretty certain she felt the same way. Still, that was all secondary to his current dilemma of finding the whole truth. Whatever his past revealed, he really couldn't blame her for walking away just to avoid dealing with the mess.

Just as he was about to say never mind, Michelle turned to face him.

"The girl in the photo is me. The woman was my mother."

He waited quietly, respectfully.

"That was the last picture she took before she died. The bandana was covering her baldness because of the radiation and chemo. She had breast cancer that metastasized before it was detected. It all happened so fast. They tried everything to stop it, but it was too late." She paused to gather her emotions. "We were very close. My dad had left us the year before. I took both losses pretty hard. My *supposed* friends in grade school treated me like a disease. They said everyone around me always died. '*Don't get to close to Michelle or you're next,*'" she sang as if quoting nine-year-old school kids.

Joseph's hand reflexively moved to her far shoulder, and he drew her into a hug. "I'm so sorry," he whispered. "I wish I could have done something for you back then." He said it as a way to convey his remorse for her. But what she said in return caught him completely off guard.

"You did. And I've never forgotten it."

Joseph blinked and pulled back. "Excuse me?"

"McKinley Elementary. Mrs. Cuthbert. Fifth grade. You were the only kid in the class who was nice to me. You were the only one willing to sit next to me at lunchtime and play games with me at recess. We actually became pretty good friends. Do you remember?"

Joseph blinked again and shook his head rapidly. He tried to picture what she would have looked like back then. *But I already have!* The photo on her desk. The full recollection came instantly and hit him hard. His eyes grew as big as saucers. "Wait—I *do* remember. Michelle Haas. I remember that! You were so quiet. The kids *were* always picking on you. We were both loners. You were one of my best friends back then."

"After my mom died, you were my *only* friend," she said with tears brimming on her lashes. "Kids can be so cruel at that age, so uncaring. But you cared. Even at that young age I could feel the depth of your compassion. You *saved* me, Joseph—saved me from . . . from doing something terrible. McKinley was right next to that pedestrian bridge over the freeway. It would have been so easy . . ."

"I had no idea," he breathed. "I was just being friendly, and you looked like you needed a friend."

She nodded silently.

"But . . . but what happened afterward? You stayed in school for a while, then you disappeared."

"I stayed with my dad and his girlfriend in Goleta. They kept me at McKinley because it was too much bother to transfer with the school year almost over. But Dad's girlfriend never liked me, and she treated me like dirt. At the end of the year, I moved to Ventura to stay with my mom's sister. They were pretty well-to-do and could afford another mouth to feed. They were kind and generous but very self-centered and had little time for me. I got too little attention when I really needed it most. I thought about you a lot. Then, while they went off on extravagant vacations, I'd spend summers in Solvang with my grandma. She encouraged me to become whatever I wanted. She taught me that regardless of your circumstances, the only one who puts limits on you is yourself. She taught me never to take education for granted, because you can never learn too much."

"I like her already," Joseph said.

"She was great. Since my aunt and uncle in Ventura could afford to send me to good schools, I took Grandma's advice and excelled in my classes and got into law school at UCLA after just three years of undergrad college. I passed the bar on my first try and hired on with the Santa Barbara School District because I liked helping people who help kids learn."

She smiled softly. Her eyes no longer held sorrow but were filled with contentment. "Don't you see, Joseph? We've come full circle. You helped me so much back when I truly needed a friend, and now I get to help you."

He smiled. "As a lawyer or as a friend?"

"Both, I hope."

He pulled her into a second hug and whispered, "Good. I could use a new best friend."

CHAPTER 47

JOSEPH RETURNED TO THE SCHOOL district offices the next day. In spite of it being lunchtime, Michelle was at her desk, absorbed in a stack of files. That was good. He rapped on her door frame and leaned half his body in. "Hello?"

She looked up over narrow reading glasses. "Joseph. What are you doing here?"

"I was wondering if you'd had lunch yet?"

She removed her glasses. "No. I'm way too busy. But I'm glad you're—" She stopped suddenly. "Do I smell pizza?"

Joseph entered the rest of the way carrying a large box and a stack of napkins from Rusty's Pizza Parlor. "I hope you like the deluxe combo."

"'Like' doesn't quite cover it."

Joseph moved to a chair with the fewest folders and set them on the floor. He handed her a couple napkins and said, "I took your advice and saw a financial adviser this morning. When I told him my 'problem,' and that I wanted his help, he about jumped over his desk and kissed me. Seems I'm making new best friends everywhere." He opened the box and handed Michelle a generous slice of the pie. "He seems to think I could retire and live off the interest alone."

"Let me guess, you told him you weren't going to quit teaching."

"See how good you are?"

With a large bite of pizza in her mouth, Michelle looked back to her papers and made a notation on one. Joseph realized he had intruded on a very busy person and instantly regretted not calling ahead. "I'm sorry. You're swamped. I should come back later."

"Nonsense," she said before taking another bite.

Just then her phone rang. She washed her bite down with a swig from a bottle of Dasani and answered with a smile. Soon after saying hello, the smile left her face.

Joseph watched as she gave short one- and two-word answers to the questions posed. The concern on her face was tangible. He closed the pizza box and sat on the edge of the chair. Something wasn't right.

"Okay. Okay, thanks. Yeah, he's right here. Yes. Okay, we'll be right there. Yeah. About ten minutes? Okay. Bye."

She hung up and stared at Joseph with hollow eyes.

"What's up, counselor?"

"That was Detective McRae. He says he's got something we might find very interesting."

"What?"

"He wouldn't tell me over the phone. He wants us to come down to the station right now."

Joseph used a napkin to wipe his fingers. But despite how hard he rubbed, they never felt completely clean. Wondering what dirt the detective could have unearthed, the more he rubbed, the greasier his whole body felt. Greasy, soiled, polluted. He scoffed inwardly and threw the napkins in a trash can. He had nothing to hide. It was silly to feel that way.

"Joseph? Are you okay?" Michelle was staring at him with worried eyes. "We don't have to do this, you know."

"I know. Let's go."

McRae's office was on the second floor of the police department complex on Figueroa St. The detective was at his desk looking over a sheet of paper. Michelle knocked, even though his door was open.

"Come in," he said with a flat smile. "Take a seat."

Joseph and Michelle helped themselves to two cheap office chairs in front of McRae's desk.

"Sorry about the accommodations," the detective began. "Budget cuts affect everyone."

Michelle nodded but said nothing. Joseph thought it best to follow her lead.

"You've got quite a . . . a remarkable past, Mr. Ramirez."

"Remarkable?" Joseph asked.

"Remarkable in that you've come through it unscathed," McRae said.

Joseph thought about his last session with Dr. Wilder and thought *unscathed* couldn't be farther from the truth. "Thanks," he said.

"I want to go over some of the history on your family I've pulled up. If anything doesn't sound right, let me know. Mind if I record this conversation?"

"I'd like a copy," Michelle said.

"You bet." He clicked on a cassette recorder and slid it to the edge of his desk. "Now, Joseph, your father, Estefan Salvador Arango Ramirez, born in Quetzaltenango, Guatemala, immigrated to the United States at the age of eleven with his parents. They lived in L.A. for a time then moved to Oxnard, and eventually ended up in Santa Barbara. He married Consuela Guadalupe Emalia de Hernandez and had five children: Xavier, Emalia, Antonio, José, and Victoria. All children were born at home except Victoria, who was born at Cottage Hospital." He looked up. "So far so good?"

"Yeah," Joseph acknowledged.

"Estefan worked odd jobs growing up, attended school only to the sixth grade as far as I can tell, and ended up at Pacific Heating and A/C for roughly eleven years before he disappeared."

Joseph nodded. "He was a sheet metal worker."

"I have record of several drunk and disorderly conduct charges, a handful of arrests for public intoxication, and half a dozen DUIs. Records show a number of domestic disturbance calls but no charges ever filed. Can you tell me about that?" McRae asked.

"First off, detective, you should know I've never had any memory of anything before my tenth birthday. Since my accident, I've been experiencing flashbacks of events dealing with my father. None of them are pretty, as you might guess. I'm currently going to a psychiatrist to help me sort things out. We're finding some . . . disturbing things. One of those is that he regularly beat my mother and probably beat his children too."

Detective McRae took everything in with a deadpan expression. "Okay."

"Why my mother never filed charges, I don't know. She could have been threatened, I suppose, either personally or having a threat leveled against one of her children. My guess is that she assumed her church would not condone a wife complaining about her husband."

"Could your father have had something to hold over her? Like a secret or something that she'd want to keep hidden?"

"My mother? She's an open book, detective. The only secrets she holds are family recipes. She'd protect those with her life."

Joseph smiled. McRae did not.

The detective made a notation and continued. "Anyway, about twenty years ago things really began to go haywire. Your brother Antonio was found dead in an alley behind Santa Barbara Junior High, supposedly the victim of gang violence. That was when gangs started initiating inductees with hazings that sometimes went too far."

"Yeah. I think I remember a little of that. But . . ." Joseph hesitated.

"But what?" McRae prompted.

Joseph held his breath his moment. "There's a possibility Antonio's death wasn't gang related."

McRae folded his arms and leaned back. "Okay?"

Joseph condensed the session he'd had with Dr. Wilder for the detective. McRae chewed on the information with narrowed eyes. "Your dad was quite a piece of work. I'll look into what happened. If your father was involved and ended up running, I'll find out. No one just drops off the planet." He absently scratched his chin. "How accurate would you say this hypnosis is?"

"Dr. Wilder says it's pretty good. But he doesn't give it more than an 80 to 90 percent reliability."

"And you personally? What do you think?"

"Joseph, you don't have to answer that," Michelle jumped in. "You can refuse any question that'll self-incriminate. Fifth amendment."

Joseph nodded. "It's okay. I believe it's 100 percent. When I was under hypnosis, the images were crystal clear. It wasn't like a dream or a foggy memory—it was like I was actually there. It was bizarre, but I have no doubt I was reliving something that actually happened. It's probably also why I was saying I murdered someone in my sleep.

Clyde Richter obviously mistook my confession to mean *I* had killed my father."

Detective McRae leaned forward again. "Oh, there's no mistake there," he stated. "It's very clear who you were talking about."

"From one man's testimony," Michelle said.

McRae shook his head. "From Mr. Ramirez's own mouth. We have it on tape."

CHAPTER 48

"WHAT TAPE?" MICHELLE HAAS ASKED.

"When Joseph began actually forming sentences in his sleep, Mr. Richter started recording them, on the off chance he'd say something humorous. He thought it'd be fun to play back to Mr. Ramirez the next day. What he didn't expect to record was this." The detective pulled a pocket recorder from his desk and punched PLAY.

The recording was fuzzy and filled with background hums and white noise. The rustling of bedsheets could be heard, along with someone groaning, a man's voice. Only, the voice was speaking in falsetto, as if mimicking a young boy's voice. "No. Don't take me there. I'll be good, Papa. I promise. Please." Silence filled the recording for a time. Then, "Papa, why are we here? There aren't any ducks here at night. What are we doing, Papa? No. Papa, don't make me go there. It's dark. It's too dark. I can be a good boy. I can stop asking questions. It's scary there. I hear strange things there. There . . . there might be monsters. I'm afraid. Ow! Please don't hit me, Papa. I can't help being scared. Ow! Please don't. I'll try not to cry, I promise." More rustling obscured most of the words through the next section, but it was clear Joseph was crying out from physical abuse, from a punishment. "Stop, Papa! Stop it, please!" Some rapid breathing followed, like that of a little boy scared to death. "It's dark here. I can't see. I don't want to get out of the boat. Please don't make me. It's cold here. What about the birds, Papa? What if they attack me when I'm asleep?" A moment of silence followed. Suddenly Joseph screamed, "NO! Don't leave me! Please, Papa. Don't leave me here all alone! Wait!" A series of harsh grunts came next—the sound of Joseph flailing in his bed, crying. Intermittent words, sentences came: "Ow! Please stop! Ouch! Stop hurting me! Stop it, stop it, stop it."

Joseph had his eyes closed. He was trying to concentrate on the words, not on what was being played out. But he couldn't. He felt his body trembling. He clenched his jaw forcefully. He heard himself breathing rapidly, taking panicked short breaths. Macabre images crowded his thoughts. Dark, spectral forms reached in from the recessed corners of his mind. Joseph wanted the recording to stop. But he didn't dare ask. He needed to hear this.

"Stop, Papa! Why do you hate me so much? Wait—don't leave. Papa! You—hey . . . hey, look out. It's sinking. Papa, hurry, over here." His young voice turned urgent, afraid for someone besides himself. "You can do it. It's muddy but you can—ow! No, Papa, I didn't break the boat. I promise I didn't. Ow! OW! Stop, Papa, please stop." His recorded voice suddenly stopped. His breathing was still coarse, still rapid, but it was different now. It sounded like he was . . . running. "Oh no. It's so dark. I can't see! I can't—uh-oh. He's coming. A stick, he grabbed a stick. He's going to kill me. I know he's going to kill me this time. He's—"

The recording went silent once more. No rustling of sheets, no rapid breathing, no crying. Just when Joseph thought it was over, the young voice came back. Only this time it was remorseful, bitter, speaking with a constrictive huskiness. "I killed him. I killed my father. I have committed the worst sin ever . . ."

The little voice then began reciting the Lord's Prayer in Spanish. Halfway through, Joseph realized he was mouthing the words with the tape. When it finished, both Joseph and Michelle reflexively echoed amen. Then in a voice barely above a breath, the young Joseph said, "I have killed my own father. He was right: I *am* a mistake."

The recording ended.

Detective McRae switched off the player and folded his hands. He looked from Joseph to Michelle and back again. In a tone filled with unexpected understanding, he asked, "Well . . . what do you think?"

"I think I'm going to be sick," Joseph whispered.

Michelle moved to the edge of her seat. "Detective McRae. Thank you for sharing that with us. I believe it clearly shows a case of self-defense. I'd like to get a copy and have it analyzed, but I'm confident a voice expert will come to the same conclusion."

McRae nodded. "My thoughts too. I can't find fault in it. I think—" He stopped and looked closely at Joseph. "You okay, Mr. Ramirez? You look like you've just seen a ghost."

Joseph looked up slowly. "I just did."

McRae absently scratched his chin. "Look. If it's any consolation, this comes close to an illegal wiretap. Mr. Ramirez did not give Mr. Richter permission to record his . . . conversation. If you want to press charges . . . ?" He left the sentence unfinished, allowing his visitors to fill in the blank.

"How'd you get the tape—if I may ask?" Michelle said.

The detective smirked. "Mr. Richter was released from the hospital just yesterday. Turns out all this time he was trying to sell the tape to Mr. Wiseman and his firm. But Wiseman wasn't buying. Seems you guys had already reached a settlement? Anyway, so he brings it to me and hits me up for some cash. I told him if it *did* point to murder, then it's the state's evidence, and he was required by law to hand it over." He snorted and smirked again. "Richter swore up a storm—used cusswords *I* ain't even heard—and then tossed the tape on my desk and left. I'm thinking he and Wiseman are two of a kind. You know—always lookin' for an angle to ream the next guy out of a couple bucks."

Michelle agreed. Joseph was shocked. *All that time Clyde was just scheming?*

"So," McRae continued, "if it's any consolation, he ended up empty-handed."

"They both did," Michelle said, adding Brick to the summation.

Michelle and McRae talked for a few more minutes discussing various aspects of Joseph's case, but Joseph did not participate. He was lost in a quagmire of crippling thought. The harder he struggled, the deeper he sunk. The more he tried to forget the images of his past, the more they haunted him.

It was going to be another very long night.

CHAPTER 49

"Joseph, it was *definitely* self-defense," Michelle reiterated for a countless time. "If you *did* kill him, no court in the world would blame you. Even Detective McRae said he felt you were not at fault."

Joseph looked up from his chair in Michelle's office. "I don't know. He also said they have no record of my father after the night he 'left.' I was listening to every word," he grumbled, his voice rising with each sentence. "He said he's still going to investigate Papa's disappearance. 'No one just drops off the planet,' he said. What if he uncovers something that proves I deliberately killed my father? Since I can't remember any of it, anything he comes up with is plausible."

"Dr. Wilder said dreams are not proof of anything because they are subject to so many other factors," Michelle said, moving from her desk to stand behind him. Grappling with his shoulders, she began to rub the knots from his neck and arms. "It could be you made up the whole thing. It could be it never happened. You said your dad used to threaten to leave you out on one of those little islands at the bird refuge all the time, right? It could be your dream filled in the gaps, when in reality nothing happened."

Joseph looked out the window at the sodium vapor lamps casting cones of hazy yellow light on the empty parking lot. It was late. He should have gone home long ago but didn't trust himself to drive. His nerves were shot, his emotions unstable. He hated feeling so weak. He hated being so vulnerable—especially in front of Michelle. But what could he do? He was a wreck. Irrational. Indecisive. Pathetic.

"Maybe you should take a sleeping pill," Michelle suggested. "I know you don't like them, but you've got to get some rest."

"My pills are at home," he said in defeat.

"You want me to drive you?"

He looked at his watch. 11:47 PM. With a pang of embarrassment, he realized they had not eaten dinner. They'd come straight from the police department to her office. He had sat in her office like a vegetable, not talking, not existing. In fact, he couldn't remember what he'd done all that time, but he knew he hadn't moved an inch.

"Joseph? Can I drive you?"

"No. It's too far away. You wouldn't get back till after two." He forced himself to stand. He hurt worse than after one of Connie Olsen's physical therapy sessions. "You go home. I'll get a motel or something."

"No, you won't," she said authoritatively. "Let me pull in a favor." She dialed a number on her cell and had a brief conversation with someone on the other end before terminating the call.

"You're in no state to be left alone," she said. Joseph opened his mouth to object, but Michelle cut him off. "Don't argue with a lawyer. The duplex adjacent to mine has been empty for months, and the owner who's trying to sell it said it would be fine to let you crash there for tonight. That way I can keep an eye on you without giving the neighbors their diet of gossip for the week. I insist. Now let's go."

Joseph couldn't help but smile. He let Michelle lead him to her car and fell into the passenger seat. He couldn't believe how drained he felt. But in spite of that, his mind was still whirling a thousand miles an hour. He doubted he'd get any sleep that night.

The drive to Michelle's small duplex was a blur. If asked to repeat the route or find her house some other time, he'd have no clue how to get there. She helped him into her place and sat him at her kitchen table.

"Do you like tea?" she asked.

"Just herbal tea," he heard himself say.

"Great. I've got some chamomile and valerian tea that'll have you relaxed and in slumber land in no time."

Joseph closed his eyes and opened them to find a steaming cup sitting in front of him. How or when it got there he hadn't a clue. "Thank you," he mumbled.

He sipped the herbal tea and let the hot liquid burn down his throat. It felt heavenly to have something register in his system like that—even if it hurt. He sipped again, hoping the herbs would quickly knock him out.

He let Michelle show him to the adjoining duplex, to the master suite. It was still furnished very luxuriously, and he sat on the bed and let her remove his shoes and socks. She turned down the covers and fluffed his pillow. In the shadowy room, Joseph found her hand and had her sit next to him. Looking into her eyes, he wondered, *Where did this angel come from?*

"You going to read me a bedtime story too?" he jested groggily. The tea was already kicking in.

"Sure. What do you want to hear?"

He grinned mischievously. "*Forbidden Lust.*"

She smacked him on the shoulder. "Just for that, you aren't getting *any* story tonight, and just nasty cold cereal in the morning." Then, very tenderly, she laid him down, pulled a comforter to his chin, and kissed him on the forehead. "Good night, Joseph. Sweet dreams."

Sweet dreams? he mocked. *Not likely.* He knew it was going to be one of the roughest nights of his life.

CHAPTER 50

THE NIGHT WAS CLOUD-COVERED and eerily dark. Enraged and mindlessly drunk, Estefan tried to drive his precious Cadillac from his home to Cabrillo Beach. Joseph sat in the passenger seat holding the door handle with viselike force as Papa weaved, careened, and screeched along the dimly lit streets. Joseph's tears had dried out long ago. It was all he could do to keep from opening the door to dive for safety as Papa nearly missed one obstacle after another. Joseph wanted to cry out, to ask Papa to slow down, to not drive drunk, but the tape across his mouth allowed little more than grunting. Then, instead of heading for the waterfront, Papa turned into the parking lot of the bird refuge. The place was completely empty. Joseph was pulled from the car and led to the shore.

It had been an unseasonably warm day, and the stench of decay from the placid estuary thickened the air. Dim light from Cabrillo Boulevard penetrated the gathering fog, limiting their visibility, but it also masked their movements. Estefan stumbled and tripped but kept moving in the general direction of the small bungalow used as an office during the day. The tiny building had a single incandescent bulb attached to its roof that remained lit all night. A few feet in front of the office, a small dock extended some twelve feet into the lagoon.

"Keep up," Papa growled at Joseph. "Don't make me any angrier."

Joseph wanted to ask what he had done, but he didn't dare remove the tape from his mouth. He knew he had made another mistake. He had done something to make Papa furious. He didn't know what it was, but then he rarely did. Emily had tried to stop Papa from giving another punishment, but he'd ignored her. Or maybe he was just too drunk to hear her. Papa got that way. He drank so much that he could only hear what he wanted to hear. His mind was made up, and nothing could change it. When Emily persisted, Papa had knocked her against a wall. She hit her head hard and crumpled to the floor. Victoria was asleep in her crib. Mama and Xavier were at work.

Staggering onto the dock, with a bottle in hand, Papa went directly to the end where a two-man dinghy was lying upside-down. He stopped and stared at it in confusion, as if trying to figure out what was wrong with it. He wavered and blinked hard several times. Joseph stood by his side shivering, knees trembling, eyes stinging. Papa had dragged him out of the house and into the garage, not even seeing that Joseph wore only his pajama bottoms and a threadbare T-shirt. Papa drained the remainder of the bottle into his mouth then cast it into the lagoon. The splash sounded somewhere unseen in the fog. He turned sharply and glared at Joseph then turned back to the small boat and glared at it. He repeated the movement twice more, clearly disoriented and bewildered.

"What did you do to the boat?" he demanded of Joseph.

Joseph didn't answer, *couldn't* answer.

"You ask so many questions. You always want to know. Now you don't answer me?! You show me disrespect like this? You are a mistake. I knew it from the start. Do you know why?"

Joseph shook his head. It was all he could do.

"No. Of course you don't. No one has ever told you. But I will. Sit here!" he growled, and forced Joseph onto his knees.

Estefan turned to the dinghy and tried to turn it over, but he couldn't focus his efforts enough to accomplish the task. Something was restricting its movement. He shook his head and rubbed his eyes. Joseph watched him weave in place and a couple times thought he might fall over.

Estefan then dropped to his knees and began searching around the rim of the boat. At the back of the little craft, he found a small padlock securing it to the dock. He yanked on the lock a few times, but it wouldn't open. He bumbled to his feet and kicked it. The lock whipped against the dinghy but still did not open. Infuriated, Estefan laid into the lock with one vicious kick after another, cursing, spitting, blind with rage.

Joseph cringed and scooted backward to the opposite edge of the small dock. He heard the splintering of wood and saw the screws securing the hasp work their way out of the time-rotten wood of the dock. One final kick sent the lock and hasp combination sliding along the dock and over the edge.

Estefan then leaned against the dinghy and heaved until it too slid off the dock, flipped once, and landed upright in the lagoon. He shuffled to the edge and looked down. The dock was no more than two feet above the water, and the small boat bobbed only a few times before steadying itself.

"Ha! You see? I am always right. I always know what is best." He sneered at the craft, as if it could understand him. Turning to Joseph, he hissed, "Get in the boat."

Joseph crawled over and looked down. It was dark in the boat, but he could still see a plank across the bow and one across the stern that formed seats, and two oars secured to the seats with metal clamps. In a flash he realized what Papa was going to do. He was going to take him to one of the little islands and leave him there overnight. Maybe even longer. Maybe forever.

"I said get in!" Estefan bellowed as he kicked Joseph's backside, sending him tumbling into the small boat.

Joseph landed hard and let out a muffled wail of pain through the duct tape.

Estefan then shuffled to the edge, sat, and carefully slid into the dinghy. "Sit there, in the back," he ordered.

Joseph crawled onto the rear plank and sat. In doing so, his feet created a splashing sound. Looking down, he saw water sloshing in the bottom of the boat. Searching for a source, he found a crack in the fantail, running from the bottom of the boat to the place where the padlock used to be. Apparently, Papa had damaged more than the lock when he repeatedly kicked that area. Wide-eyed, Joseph turned back to Papa, pointed, and mumbled through the tape. Estefan had unclasped the oars and was securing them in the oarlocks.

"Stop mumbling!" he barked at his son as he began rowing out into the dark lagoon.

Joseph became silent and sat with his feet drawn up. He breathed hard through flared nostrils as the boat moved further into the blackness. The water was creeping around Papa's feet now, but he seemed oblivious to it. When they were well away from the dock, the dinghy had taken on nearly an inch of water in the bottom. Thin fog had encircled them, leaving them in a murky void that had neither dimension nor substance.

"I am sorry, *el falla*," Estefan began, "but I have to make a decision. As head of my house, I have to see that everything is as it should be." He stopped rowing and let the boat continue to drift through the fog. He leaned forward and yanked the tape from Joseph's face. Joseph let out an uncontrollable yelp but quickly quieted. "You may wonder why I call you a mistake. I promised your mother I would never tell, but I cannot live with the shame anymore. I am the man of my house. I should not have to live with such embarrassment!"

Risking a slap, Joseph said, "I'm sorry, Papa. I didn't mean to be your son."

A heated flash of anger filled Estefan's eyes. "That is because you are *not* my son!"

Joseph didn't know what to make of his father's statement. Was Papa kidding him? He knew Papa never called him son, like he did to Xavier and used to do to Antonio, but he never worried about it. Mama called him son all the time, so he figured it meant the same for both parents.

"Did you hear me?" Estefan shouted. "You are not my son!"

Joseph nodded. "I know I was not supposed to be born, Papa. You told me that before."

Estefan clenched the oars until his knuckles turned white. He screamed deep in his throat. "You are so stupid! You can't understand plain language. You—are—not—my—son!" Estefan violently spit out each word as if expelling poison. "Your filthy mother had a boyfriend I did not know about. She got pregnant by him and had you. Have you never wondered why your eyes are green and your brothers and sisters all have brown eyes? Have you never wondered why you are shorter than your brothers and sisters? You are always asking questions—why have you never asked *those* questions?"

Joseph was dumbstruck. He was just a little boy, but he understood what Papa was telling him. Papa was not his real papa. Someone else was. But . . . but did that really matter? In catechism he learned that we are all brothers and sisters. Even Jesus was his brother. Joseph had friends at school who were adopted into their families, and it didn't matter to their fathers. Papa was right, Joseph *didn't* understand. Maybe he *was* stupid.

"You have nothing to say?" Estefan spoke as if shocked. "The boy who will never close his mouth because of all his questions? Perhaps . . . perhaps you have known all along?" The anger in Estefan's eyes turned resentful, filled with loathing and contempt. In a voice thick with betrayal, he breathed, "You *did* know, didn't you!"

"No, Papa. I didn't," Joseph replied fervently.

"Yes, you did!" Estefan screamed. "You did, and you have been lying to me all this time. Now I must punish you again!" Estefan's glare reflected the diffused light from the bungalow with an eerie, animal-like glimmer. His countenance took on a seething hatred, his face twitching with raw emotion, and spittle flecked his lips and chin as he ejected each word with venomous wrath.

Joseph had seen this transformation before. He knew what was coming, and his stomach cramped in agony at the knowledge. Papa was turning into the monster again.

"I am the head of my house, but no one honors me as such!" Estefan continued to bellow. "I am responsible for everything under my roof. I work long and hard to support my family, and what do I get in return? Dishonor. Disrespect. And lies. I tell you, I have had enough! ENOUGH! I must do what is necessary to bring things back to order. I must correct all mistakes. *All* mistakes, José. *El falla.* Your Mama will not do what is right—what she should have done when she carried you—so I have to. It is my responsibility." Estefan looked behind him then returned to rowing toward a large black shape distorted by the fog.

Joseph did not know what to say. Papa was right. He *was* a mistake. He wasn't supposed to have been born. But . . . what could he do about it now? He couldn't very well go back to live with God again. Could he?

"What should I do, Papa?" he asked in a hollow voice.

"You should be quiet for now," was his father's curt response.

Estefan rowed in silence for a time, the only sound the dip and trickle of the oars as they entered and exited the black water. Fog swirled across the surface of the lagoon surrounding them in a clot of haunting white shapes and muffled noises. Ahead, the black shape loomed larger.

It must be the big island, Joseph thought. "Papa?" he whispered.

"*Sí?*" There was a strange softness in his father's voice. Like he was at peace with his decision to correct his mistake.

To Joseph, Papa sounded sad. *Perhaps I should try to make him happy.* "Even if you are not my papa, is it okay if I still love you?"

Estefan stopped rowing. He stared at Joseph with a confused expression. He opened his mouth then closed it. A curious battle raged across his face. Sorrow was replaced with bitterness, followed by remorse then anger then tenderness then anguish. He opened his mouth again. "José. I need you to be quiet. This is hard for—"

Just then, the dinghy scraped against a partially submerged root just off the dark, tree-choked island. Startled, Estefan turned—and smacked his face into a broken branch. The sharp end of the branch dug a jagged slice along his cheek. He flinched and grabbed the branch with a trembling hand. Blood poured from the gash. He cursed angrily through the pain.

"Are you okay?" Joseph asked softly.

"Shut up! This is *your* fault. You distracted me and now look," he screamed, holding out a hand covered in blood. "Don't make another sound, or the tape goes back on."

Dragging the dinghy from branch to branch, he circled the small island until he found a break in the vegetation. Pulling the boat into the small gap, he was able to drag it to a spit of earth between a tangle of branches and roots. A few birds screeched and flew into the night-blackened fog. He stepped from the boat and turned to Joseph. The angry resolve was back in his eyes. His face was contorted in hatred and pain. Blood still poured from his cheek and dripped onto his shirt. "We're here," he hissed.

Joseph was more scared than he'd ever been in his life. The dark branches seemed to claw at him, wanting to tear his flesh as they had his father's. The screeching of the birds had sent his nerves into a frenzy. His heart pounded in his frail chest, and his vision blurred. He looked to his papa for comfort, but all he saw was . . . evil. A blood-soaked monster filled with pure anger. A beast that wanted only to punish and hurt and destroy.

Reaching for his son, Estefan cackled. "Welcome to your new home."

Estefan told Joseph to get out of the boat. Moving from the stern to the bow necessitated stepping into the hull, which was now filled with about four inches of water. Papa was so drunk he didn't even notice. That surprised Joseph. He knew Papa didn't have a fear of water, but he also knew he couldn't swim. And being so completely plastered, if he fell in, Papa would not be able to save himself.

The thick tangle of plant life made movement difficult for Joseph, but there was enough room to shuffle sideways between the trees and branches. His shoes were soaked through, and water squished from them with every step. It was cold, and the water smelled like rotten eggs.

"Estefan Salvador Arango Ramirez may not be a perfect man," Papa stated as if giving a public speech, "but when he makes a mistake, he admits it and corrects it." He looked directly at Joseph and scowled. "*El falla*. I knew from the start I should not have allowed Mama to keep you. You were her mistake, and then you became mine. But no more! Tonight, I correct my mistake."

With one foot in the dinghy and one on a tree root, Estefan pushed off from their meager landing and drifted backward into the lagoon. From the narrow shore, Joseph watched in terrified silence. At first he hoped Papa was playing a joke on him. Then he hoped maybe Papa was just being extra harsh, to give Joseph time to think, then would let him back in the boat.

He shivered. *No*—that wasn't going to happen. The look in Papa's eyes convinced Joseph that Papa *had* turned into the monster again. Only this time, much worse. There was something *final* about the way Papa spoke—something that unmistakably said *I'm leaving you forever.*

"Papa, I'm sorry. I won't ask any more questions, I promise," Joseph cried.

"I cannot hear you. You are no more. I have corrected my mistake," Estefan said without making eye contact.

The realization of what was happening finally hit Joseph, and his knees buckled. "Papa! Wait, please!" He was now shivering uncontrollably, both from fear and the chilling cold. New tears wet his face, and the cramp in his stomach spread outward with debilitating pain. "Papa!"

The fog swirled around Estefan as he continued to drift away. As if entering a magical transporter that quickly dissolved his body into nothingness, Papa faded into the gray fog before Joseph could cry out again.

Then stillness.

He saw a movement to his left. His eyes opened wide and his breath stuck in his throat. The only sounds were the faint lapping of water against the branches and roots, and the occasional rumble of a large wave pounding the shore of the beach in the distance. He could hear the sharp chitter of insects, but no other life beyond the panicked thumping of his own heart. Maybe that meant no birds. Or maybe they were silently waiting for the right opportunity.

Joseph crouched into a ball and screwed his eyes shut. The creeping fog penetrated his skin, the cold touching his bones with icy fingers. He forced himself not to whimper, not to cry, but that did not stop his tears. Why was he born? Why did God send him to Papa's family? He knew Xavier and Antonio were his brothers, Emily and Baby Victoria were his sisters. He knew it in his heart. But was he *their* brother? Their *real* brother? He drew a quick breath and swallowed. Perhaps this was God's punishment for possessing the devil—even though he didn't mean to. Maybe Papa was right: if he hadn't been born, or if he didn't let the devil live in him, then everyone would be happier. Maybe even Antonio would still be alive.

"Help!" a muffled cry came from the blank, fog-covered estuary. It sounded like Papa. "The boat is sinking!"

"Papa?" Joseph called. But his little voice was strained and weak. The emotions, the crying, the cold all conspired to close his throat and dampen any volume. He could see nothing in the churning fog. Darkness had encircled him, had become a thick cloak that pressed down with suffocating weight.

"Help me!" the cry came again. Out there, somewhere. "I—I can't swim!" Papa's cry was getting weaker.

He must be near the center of the lagoon, Joseph reasoned. Filled with sudden guilt, Joseph hid his face in his hands. He should have warned Papa about the leak in the boat. He should have said something. But Papa had told him to be quiet. He had ordered him not to make a sound.

Splashing now. The frantic attempt of someone trying to stay afloat. Papa was drowning! *Should I swim out and try to save Papa?* Like his brother and sisters, Joseph could swim quite well. It was a wonder that Papa had never learned.

"José! You did this! You made a hole in the boat!" Estefan gagged and choked. "You tried to kill me!" He splashed and struggled. "Help me!"

More splashing, grunts of pain, and gasping, more choking on thick, stagnant water. Joseph thought of the ugly catfish he'd seen so long ago and wondered if Papa was fighting it or some other hideous creature living under the black water.

Then, quite suddenly, the commotion stopped. The sounds of struggling ceased.

Joseph mustered his strength and what little courage he could find and crawled higher onto a collection of roots, using thin branches to pull himself up. The cold stung his skin like a thousand wasps. His heart pounded anew. He fought to quiet his own desperate gasps for air. Then he heard the sloshing of water again. But it wasn't desperate anymore; it was slow and steady. It was . . . it was someone crawling up the muddy shore! He peered into the dark gray fog, seeking any movement, but dreading what he might find. *Wait. What's that?— there!* Someone or some *thing* was crawling onto the island. He could just now make it out. It was—*oh no!* It was the monster!

Panic reached up with bile-coated claws and clenched his throat.

Joseph tried to look away but couldn't. A burning gorge rose from his stomach, and he vomited acidic liquid. His head spun. Fatigue, panic, cold, and fear all combined to narrow his vision and jumble his thoughts. He felt his grip loosen on the tree branch. Blackness encroached. The monster was closer now, slowly crawling over the roots toward him. It gasped and grunted, sounding like a hungry, vicious beast. Having lost all strength, Joseph felt himself falling. He tried to hang on but couldn't. He hit the ground with a painful jolt. Breath burst from his lungs. He somehow got to his feet and began crawling into the thickness of the island, away from the monster. He couldn't run—there were too many branches, too many roots, and he had too little strength.

The monster followed right behind. Joseph could almost smell its foul breath. He heard it speaking his name. Mustering energy, Joseph tried to crawl faster, but his foot caught in a tangle of roots. He stopped cold. The monster smiled. It had a wicked, evil grin. Its eyes glowed with rage. Blood ran from a jagged gash in its cheek. With a gurgling laugh, it grabbed a narrow, upright branch and snapped it off. It broke with a loud crack, separating from the tree a couple feet off the ground. Joseph cringed. The monster took a step forward and swung. The stick whistled through the air and struck Joseph on the shoulder. He cried out in pain. "Ow! Stop, please. Don't hit me! I'm sorry, I'm sorry!"

The monster swung again. Joseph flinched as the blow landed across his back. He screamed in agony. The monster struck again. And again. With a desperate surge of adrenaline, Joseph yanked his foot from the knot of roots and tried to stand. As the monster wound up for a severe, final blow, Joseph slipped, fell against the beast, and knocked it off balance. The monster's muddy shoes skidded along a wide root, unable to gain purchase. It twisted, fell backward, and landed on the broken branch from which it had gathered its weapon. The sharp, pointed stick rising from the ground pierced the monster's chest, fastening the creature to the ground. The monster gave a terminal wheeze of dismay and then went silent.

Joseph stared in shock. What had he done? Had he actually . . . ? Papa looked dead. He had to be dead. Joseph had seen the same sightless eyes, the same blood and gore on TV when people died. Papa stared upward with the same empty gaze. He wasn't breathing. But neither was Joseph. He couldn't believe he had done something so terrible.

I killed my father.

Joseph sat by his father's body for what felt like hours. He was in shock. He couldn't think straight. Finally, the cold brought him to his senses. He crawled around his father and worked his way to the narrow shore. He entered the lagoon and began to swim. The thick, black water washed over his face and into his mouth. He felt creatures swimming beside him and underneath him. Tears flowed from his eyes, but he kept focused on the dim light from the office bungalow in the distance. Images of bloodthirsty underwater monsters filled his young mind. He felt his muscles failing. He fought for every stroke, struggled for every breath.

Just at the end of his endurance, Joseph reached the dock and pulled himself to the shore. Crawling up the muddy bank, Joseph's one thought was reaching home. He got to his knees, tried to stand, and fell on his face.

Then everything went black.

CHAPTER 51

JOSEPH AWOKE WITH A SCREAM. He opened his eyes wide and sucked in huge gulps of air.

What the—? Where am I?

His question was answered when Michelle came running into the room. She immediately took him in a tender and sure embrace and held him until his breathing steadied. She stroked his hair and shushed him with calming reassurances. When Joseph stopped trembling, she turned to his nightstand, switched on the light, and pulled a pen and pad of paper from the drawer. Handing them to him, she patted his leg and then left the room. Neither person said anything. Nothing needed to be said.

By the time Joseph was done transcribing what he remembered from his dream, his hand was shaking, and tears stung his eyes. He remembered *everything* that happened that night at the bird refuge. It all came back to him with disturbing clarity—with one exception. Had he killed his father?

Joseph recognized that as a ten-year-old boy, he could never have overpowered his father. But Estefan had been drunk. The night was dark and dank and slippery. Joseph's mind battled with accusation and rationalization. Should he have warned him about the leak in the boat? Perhaps. But Papa's goal had been to leave Joseph out there—possibly for good. And he had commanded him to be silent. The sinking boat and subsequent near-drowning had weakened Papa but hadn't stopped him from beating Joseph with a stout tree branch. Joseph was certain Papa wouldn't have stopped until he was dead.

He had tried to run but slipped and fell. He didn't intentionally push Estefan onto the broken branch. It was an accident. But Papa *had* ended up dead. Of that he was certain.

* * *

The following morning, Joseph spent a few minutes in the bathroom doing what he could with a comb and water. His growth of beard, his bloodshot eyes, his sagging skin, and his puffy lids did anything but create a handsome visage. What's worse, the embarrassment of crying out last night had his self-esteem at an all-time low.

Joseph made his way to the adjoining duplex, finding Michelle waiting at the kitchen table with a plate of pancakes, a bottle of syrup, and a carton of milk. She looked freshly scrubbed and ready for the day. Her smile was warm and welcoming. And . . . something more?

"Good morning," he croaked, entering the kitchen.

"Good morning, Joseph."

He rubbed his eyes. "I thought you said it was cold cereal for me this morning."

"I changed my mind."

She loaded his plate with pancakes and slid butter and syrup in his direction. "Coffee?"

Pushing against the bags under his eyes, he said, "No, thanks. I know I look like I could use an IV of it, but I don't drink coffee."

"Oh, that's right," she said, mildly embarrassed. "You're Mormon."

"Yep." Joseph sat and stared at the breakfast. "You sure I'm up to this?"

She laughed. "It's okay if you're not. I won't be offended. But since you missed dinner last night, I thought you'd be extra hungry."

Joseph drew a steady breath and held it. "Maybe just one. I have a feeling my stomach won't be settled until we finish this mess."

Michelle sat next to him and placed a hand on his arm. "Did your dream reveal what you needed to know?"

He looked at her with his warmest expression. "Oh yeah. And I . . . well, thank you for being there for me. I'm sorry I ruined your sleep."

"I was pretty much awake all night. I suspected you might have a rough one. The look in your eyes when you heard Clyde's recording scared me to death. I was surprised you handled it so well. But I knew it wouldn't last. I figured it might trigger something—and apparently it did." She rubbed his arm gently.

"I'm so glad you stayed with me." Joseph brushed a few loose strands of hair from her face. She was so pretty, even first thing in the morning. And she was kind and intelligent and witty and caring and . . . he felt he could go on forever. No one had ever been this kind to him before. Why now? Why did she come into his life at this particular moment?

"Do you believe in fate, Joseph?"

Her question caught him off guard. He pulled back his hand. "Kind of. I believe things happen for a reason—that we can learn from everything we experience, even if it's hard to endure."

She smiled. The dimple appeared. Joseph softened.

"Me too," she said. "I believe *you* were meant to help me through my hardships back at McKinley, and *I* was meant to help you through yours now."

"Me too," Joseph said. "But . . ."

"What?"

He grimaced and took a deep breath. "I don't believe it's over. I know now what happened back then, when I was ten. I'm going to take it to Dr. Wilder this morning. But I can't help the feeling there's more one thing to do—that I won't be able to completely rest until I confirm the dream."

Determination filled her eyes. The confident lawyer took over. But she still radiated compassion, caring. "All right, then. We'll finish breakfast, get cleaned up, and go to St Luke's. Did you have an appointment with Dr. Wilder?"

"No. But he's given me an open invitation . . . just in case."

She glanced at a wall clock. "It's 7:50 now. You go next door and hop in the shower, and I'll wash your clothes while you clean up. When you're ready, we can go into town and bring this whole mess to a close."

"We?" He smiled.

"Yes, *we*." She stood up and put her fists on her hips. "You're still my client, Joseph Ramirez. I would be a lousy attorney if I didn't see this case to completion."

Joseph's eyes saddened. "Just my attorney?"

She reached out and ran her hand lightly across the scruff of his whiskers. "I hope not."

Joseph took her hand and pulled her to him. She bent without resistance and met his lips with hers. The kiss was tender—of caring, of friendship, and perhaps a little more. And it was exactly what Joseph needed.

CHAPTER 52

DR. WILDER READ THROUGH JOSEPH'S manuscript twice. He then compared it with the other dreams and dream segments Joseph had written and compared those to his notes from their hypnosis sessions. He made several notes and often cocked his head to one side, eyebrows raised, as if reading something that surprised him.

Joseph and Michelle sat quietly on the couch. Joseph insisted she be present. Dr. Wilder didn't argue. As the psychiatrist continued to read, the quiet became suffocating. After only a few minutes, Joseph moved to the recumbent bikes and began pedaling. The nervous energy flowing through him was on overload. He had to burn some of it off. It was a good twenty minutes before Dr. Wilder called him back to his desk. Joseph sat in one chair, and he waved Michelle over to the other chair.

"This is fascinating material, Joseph. It's stuff worthy of publication, if you wouldn't mind. The only downside is what you've had to endure."

"Had to? Are you sure it's over? Doc, last night I had the worst nightmare of my life. But what's going to happen tonight?" Joseph hated the pleading tone in his voice, but he couldn't contain it. "I don't know how much more of this I can take."

Dr. Wilder nodded. "I don't believe you'll have to. All your dreams up till now have recounted events from your childhood that you have consciously repressed. That's why you haven't had to deal with them until now." The psychiatrist's deep voice seemed to be filled with extra understanding this morning. Joseph wished it instilled greater confidence in him.

"But something this horrible . . . I mean, how do I know my dream wasn't a—what did you call it?—a confabulation of partial events woven into a convenient scenario?"

"I don't believe it was."

"But *twenty years* later? It doesn't make sense," he persisted.

"Sure it does. As a child, you had no way of dealing with the trauma of what you experienced on that little island. So you blocked it out."

Joseph slowly shook his head. It seemed too easy an explanation. Surely an event that shocking would have come out sometime sooner than now. Why twenty years later?

"I know it might not seem logical to you, but look at it from a different point of view.

"In one of your hypnosis sessions, you said that you forced your mind to another place during a terrible event. You said your father was beating your mother and you were forced to watch, but you really weren't watching because you put your mind elsewhere."

"I remember," Joseph said softly.

"Through one horrific experience after another, you taught yourself how to remove yourself from young José's brutal life, just so you could survive until the next day."

"So why am I just now learning about it?" Frustration dripped from Joseph's voice.

The psychiatrist ran his hand across his scalp as he did when in deep thought. "My guess is that your head trauma did something to trigger the memories. I'm sure there's a scientific explanation, but darned if I can come up with it. I believe that had you *not* had the accident, you may *never* have learned of the repression—it was so deeply hidden in your psyche. But I'm glad you did."

Joseph frowned at his comment.

"I know it's been painful, Joseph. But just think what could have happened if it had come out some other time? Sometime when you didn't have professional help to get through it." He looked at Michelle and added, "Sometime when you didn't have the emotional support necessary to get through it."

Michelle ducked her head and smiled.

"Okay, super. This is all well and good," Joseph said, his voice still marred with frustration, "but why do I get the feeling it's not over yet? Why do I sense there's something left to do?"

Dr. Wilder thought for a moment then moved to his large windows and looked out at the gray autumn sky. He was silent for a time, as if debating with himself.

"I went down to the bird refuge the other day," he said without turning around. "I walked around the areas you've mentioned in your dreams and made some notes. Those islands are quite small, the biggest not more than thirty feet in diameter. Did you know that the estuary is a nationally registered nature preserve?"

Joseph shrugged. "No."

"The lagoon and its islands are protected under a mountain of restrictions from state and federal government agencies, the EPA, and even the Audubon Society. That's why no one is allowed to go out there—not even researchers. I don't think even a court order could cut through the red tape to allow someone to set foot on one of those islands."

"Okay . . . ?" Joseph prompted, unsure of where the psychiatrist was heading.

"Kind of makes me wonder if anyone has *ever* been out there. And if they have, if there's any evidence of it."

Joseph's breath caught. Michelle grabbed his arm, apparently coming to the same conclusion.

Dr. Wilder turned and favored the couple with a knowing look. "It would certainly bring closure to your dilemma."

CHAPTER 53

JOSEPH AND MICHELLE DROVE TO the Santa Barbara bird refuge immediately after they left St. Luke's Hospital. Even though the sky was overcast, a handful of people milled about, feeding the ducks and other waterfowl in designated areas. Joseph was surprised at how much the place had changed from his memories. Foremost, it was now called the Andree Clark Bird Refuge. He was also surprised at the realization that he had never returned to the area since leaving for college. The bungalow had been replaced with a stucco and tile-roof building with a gift shop, a bird food vendor, and public restrooms. The little dock was gone, and the feeding area was now sectioned off. Even the parking lot had a steel pole that was lowered in place at closing time. Signs dotted the shoreline warning of restrictions on feeding and interacting with the birds. Others warned of trespassing on federal property and listed legal repercussions should one choose to ignore the law.

After reading the fine and jail time associated with each infraction, Joseph said, "Well, at least I'll be able to afford the fine now."

"Twenty-five years seems a little steep for getting a closer look at waterbirds," Michelle commented.

Joseph scanned the area and estimated the shortest distance from the shore to the big island in the center of the lagoon. It wouldn't take long. He could be there and back in less than twenty minutes. There was no question as to *if* he would do it. It *had* to be done—the sooner the better.

"So when are we going to do this?" Michelle asked.

"*We* are not going to. I am."

"No, I insist—"

"*I* insist. You could be disbarred for something like this," Joseph argued.

"And you could lose your teaching credentials," she countered. "But that's nothing compared to spending twenty-five years in jail. *We* are going to do this because *we* both have a stake in it. You need resolution to your nightmares so they won't come back, and I need to know I've helped the young man who did so much for me so long ago." Her tone was serious, her expression stern.

"But Michelle—"

"No buts. Case closed."

"Perhaps we should just tell Detective McRae and let him go out there."

Michelle shook her head. "These restrictions look pretty permanent. I agree with Dr. Wilder: it would take some pretty influential negotiation to get permission—and that could take months, perhaps longer. Do you want sleepless nights for another year?"

Joseph put his arm around her shoulder and turned her toward the car. "Man, you're good. Remind me never to argue with you again."

Michelle put her arm around his waist and fell in step. "Deal."

* * *

Joseph felt kind of silly at the Big-5 Sporting Goods store in the Five Points Shopping Center. His cart was loaded with two pairs of black, neoprene surfing suits, black ski masks, dark gloves, and black boots. He also got a gray, inflatable two-man raft (it didn't come in black), a foot pump, and a couple of waterproof flashlights.

When the young man rang up his purchases, he quipped, "You sure you don't want some ninja throwing stars too?"

Michelle then drove Joseph to his car, which was still parked at the school board offices.

Leaning against his car, Joseph pulled Michelle to him. "I need to do some things around my house. I'll call you for directions to your house around seven."

"You don't remember how to get there?" She grinned.

"I remember you were very kind to me," he said, brushing a hand against her cheek. "But that's about it. I was a bit . . . overwhelmed."

"Oh. I'm sorry. I should have thought of that."

"It's okay. We'll grab some dinner, then we'll go have our adventure."

He wished he could sound flippant. He wanted to come across a thousand times more confident than he felt. But he was nervous, and he accepted that he could do little about it.

Michelle rose on her toes and kissed him on the cheek. "It's a date."

She then turned and walked into the office building. Joseph thought he saw a bit of a lighthearted skip in her step. It made him smile.

Joseph got in his car, started the engine, then turned it off. His emotions were so jumbled he couldn't think straight. Knowing he needed help beyond his abilities, he bowed his head and offered a heartfelt prayer.

Tonight was going to be a definitive turning point in his life. Hopefully in a good way.

CHAPTER 54

"I KNOW WHAT HAPPENED TO Papa," Joseph told Emily from his home phone.

There was a hollow quiet on the other end. Joseph could hear troubled, anxious breathing.

"It's okay, Emily. I'm almost through this. My psychiatrist seems to think I'm all but cured."

"That's wonderful, Joseph. Let's just leave it at that," she said with emotion straining her voice.

"I can do that, Em, but only after I get a couple more answers. One you can help me with, the other I'll learn tonight. I promise not to say a thing about it ever again after this. Please, Em, will you help me?"

The pause wasn't as long this time. "Okay."

Joseph had decided to be straightforward and just plunge right in with his questions, but when it came to vocalizing them, his throat constricted with nervousness. He swallowed hard.

"Did Mama have an affair?"

"How did—?" She stopped short. "Never mind. You seem to know everything now. Yes, she had an affair. But it was a one-time thing. Papa was being so brutal and domineering that she finally had had enough. There was this old friend from high school she bumped into one day at the market. It was right after Papa had exploded with one of his binges. Mama was an emotional wreck. I know that's no excuse, but in her defense, and knowing what Papa was like, I might have done the same thing. She never forgave herself for it. She came home and told Papa, and he lit into her like never before. I thought he was going to kill her. They didn't speak for months, and I'm sure their marriage was held together by us kids and Mama's insistence that divorce was wrong. They stopped . . . being intimate. That's why four years passed before you were born. And when you were, Papa blamed it on Mama's affair."

"That's why he called me *el falla*."

Joseph heard a stifled sob on the line. "Yes, but you *were* his son. He said your green eyes proved you were a bastard. Somehow, Mama made him promise to never call you that. So he came up with *el falla*. But you weren't either of those. Papa's own father had green eyes, as do some of our cousins. But, being Papa, he *knew* he was right, and no amount of logic could change his mind."

Now it was Joseph's turn to be silent. He mulled over the information and was grateful to finally know the truth. "Thank you, Emily. You have no idea how much this means to me."

"I'm glad. I'm so sorry for keeping you in the dark so long, but because you seemed to have forgotten all about that horrible part of our past, Mama and I promised we'd never tell you. Please forgive me. It was for your own good."

Joseph's eyes burned, but the tears were not all bitter. The majority of his emotion was gratitude. "It's okay, Em. I love you very much. Thank you for telling me."

"I love you too, Joseph. And you're welcome. Now what's your second question?"

"It's one I have to answer on my own. But when I do, it might reveal what really happened to Papa."

"Just *might*?"

"Yeah. If I come up blank, then we may never know."

"I think I prefer it that way," she said with urgency. "Something strange happened the night he disappeared. We all thought you were involved, but we never found out."

"Strange? How?"

He heard her take a steadying breath. "Papa came home very drunk one night. He was angry and tried to take you away to punish you, but I confronted him, and he knocked me out. Mama and Xavier were at work. When I came to, you were both gone. When

Mama and Xavier got home, I told them what had happened. We searched everywhere for you but couldn't find you. It was getting very late. Then Xavier came back around three in the morning, and he was carrying you in his arms. He said he found you curled in Papa's car parked at the bird refuge. You were soaking wet, and your skin was blue with cold. When we asked what had happened, you just had this blank look on your face. In fact, you didn't speak to anyone for almost a week."

"I don't remember any of that," Joseph said in shock.

"I wouldn't think so. You were in a stupor, like a vegetable or something. Then one morning, you just snapped out of it. It was like nothing had ever been out of sorts. We were so happy, we never said anything more about it."

"You'd think I'd remember something like that. I guess maybe I just forced it from my mind. But here's the thing, Em: I have a chance to find out for sure. And if I find what I think I will, it'll prove whether or not Papa is dead."

The silence returned. Then, "You do what you have to, Joseph, but I don't want to know. Papa was an evil man, and if he is dead, then I am not sad about it."

"So you don't want to know what I find?"

"No. And I don't want you telling Mama either. She's been through enough already. Promise me you won't say a thing."

Joseph felt a tear course down his cheek. And that was okay. "I promise, Em."

CHAPTER 55

JOSEPH AND MICHELLE PARKED ON the access road that ran between the Andree Clark Bird Refuge and the Montecito Athletic Club. At one in the morning, the place was deserted. The sky was still overcast but not threatening. Too bad. Joseph almost wished for a heavy squall to mask their illegal movements. Fortunately, the moon was a mere sliver behind the cloud cover, so ambient light was very low. A fine mist rose from the water and condensed in the air a foot above the surface. It wasn't a thick fog, but once they were on the water, it would help conceal their actions.

Using the foot pump, Joseph quickly inflated the raft in a shadowy spot on the shoreline. Shoving off, Joseph sat in front, Michelle in the back. They paddled as silently as possible. Traffic from the nearby Cabrillo Boulevard was sparse, but it still sent nervous sparks up his spine each time headlights penetrated the mist.

Worse than the occasional car were the memories churning in Joseph's mind. He heard his father's drunken slur, the biting words, the accusations and insults. It knotted his stomach. How could anyone be so cruel? Papa was convinced Joseph was not his son, but that was still no excuse for the belittling and the beatings. Joseph narrowed his eyes to fixate on a point on the biggest island and paddled with strong, steady strokes. They covered the distance to the tree-choked island in eleven minutes. It had seemed so much longer when he was ten. Rounding the island, Joseph found a break in the roots and branches. Was it the same place Papa had brought him? He couldn't tell. But it felt right. There was a dark aura emanating from the hollow. Papa's voice sounded louder in his ears. Joseph felt a trickle of sweat run down his spine. The ski mask made his face itch.

Pulling the raft into the hollow, he was able to secure it to a root that protruded out of the mud. He paused a moment and fought to corral his nerves. His hands trembled violently. His throat was raw. Dizziness made each movement awkward and dangerous.

A whisper sounded behind him. "We can go back if you want."

No! He'd come this far. He'd never be able to live with himself if he turned back now. Worse, he'd never be able to sleep again without fear of reliving the horrific nightmares. He shook his head forcefully and pulled a flashlight from his fanny pack. He had purchased a red lens to filter the harshness of the LED beam. He clicked it on and scanned the narrow, muddy bank. He could see no footprints—but then he didn't expect to. Twenty years was a long time to maintain that kind of evidence. There were several kinds of bird tracks and a few tracks that looked like muskrat prints.

Joseph stepped from the raft and turned around. "Stay here," he whispered.

"Not likely," Michelle replied.

As she crawled out of the raft, Joseph began stepping over roots and under branches, working his way into the thick tangles of the tiny island. He wondered if any of it would look familiar but then scoffed at the idea. It had been dark and foggy. He was ten and fleeing for his life.

Joseph moved slowly, scanning his red beam back and forth, up and down, looking for anything that might be a clue. At one point he stood perfectly still, listening to the clicking of insects and wondering how much of this vegetation had overgrown where he had been twenty years earlier. Was this an errand of fools? What could he really expect to find after so long?

"Fifteen minutes," Michelle whispered, indicating their time in illegal territory.

Joseph moved forward, trying not to break branches or slip on muddy roots. It was a slip that had caused a death two decades ago and that had caused his life to change so dramatically. Or had it? In reality, it was Estefan who had caused the downward slide of Joseph's life. It wasn't until Joseph blocked his father from his mind that he started life anew—that he truly grew into the man he was today.

Just then his light passed over something foreign looking, a shape and colors that didn't belong. Joseph froze. The objects were smooth and white. *Bones?* Joseph slowly panned his light around the object. His heart thudded in his chest. He forced himself to kneel and inspect the strange items. There were several pieces, fragments from something larger. They were all similar in shape, the same off-white color. He reached in and swept away some dead leaves and twigs to reveal a bird's nest. Two half-shells sat in an abandoned nest. Bits of broken shell littered the large nest. Joseph had no idea what kind of bird built the nest, but he wasn't feeling scientific enough to investigate just now. He huffed a breath against the fragile shards. The fragments all quivered under the force of his breath—except three along the edge, partially buried under a matting of rotted debris.

Using a twig, Joseph nudged some of the matter aside and exposed two more off-white objects. Only, they didn't look like shell fragments anymore. He used the twig to push on them. They didn't move. He tapped them; they felt solid, hard, like they were attached to something larger. Taking a small rock, Joseph pushed away the mud just above the objects and found a mandible, the lower part of a jaw. What looked like bits of shell were teeth. Human teeth.

CHAPTER 56

IT TOOK NEARLY TEN WEEKS for the paperwork to go through. When it did, the media had a field day covering the environmentalists and special-interest groups protesting the "rape of indigenous wetlands," as they put it. In reality, the county coroner was sensitive enough to hire two wetland experts from UCSB to go to the island and extract the human remains with as little disturbance to flora and fauna as possible. They were able to get a nearly complete skeleton from the ever-decaying ground. No tissue remained.

Dental records were vague but confirmed within an 87.6 percent probability that it was indeed the skeleton of Estefan Ramirez. Cause of death was assumed alcohol intoxication and possible drowning. No other factors indicated any other possibility.

The fact that Joseph freely admitted to trespassing on the island was factored into his sentence. He was charged a lesser fine, but insisted on paying the maximum penalty—as a gift to the bird refuge, he said. He was also sentenced to a hundred hours of community service, which he gladly accepted. He insisted that he'd acted alone. Because the penalty was so light, Michelle's involvement was kept between them.

The day after the ruling came down, Detective McRae visited Michelle at her office on Santa Barbara Street. He nodded cordially and handed her a small manila envelope. "I have no more need for this."

She opened the envelope to find a small cassette tape. With eyes wide, she asked, "Are you sure about this?"

He nodded. "From what I learned about Estefan Ramirez, he was hardly what you could call a man. That's personal opinion, which I'm not usually allowed to use in an investigation, but this case is kind of different. Since no one actually filed charges, no one will be disappointed if it just goes away."

"But I thought you opened a case," Michelle said in lieu of a question.

"A 'missing persons' case, not a homicide investigation. The person's no longer missing." He shrugged. "Case closed."

Michelle stood and extended her hand. "Thank you, detective. You are a credit to your department."

The stocky man smiled. "I'll take that to the bank. Oh, and you might want to let your client know that his brother's death *was* confirmed gang-related. His psycho dad had nothing to do with it."

"Actually," Michelle said with regret, "Joseph thinks Antonio joined a gang expressly to help deal with their father. You know— maybe strong-arm him some to get him to lay off Joseph. So in a way, Estefan *was* responsible for Antonio's death."

McRae shook his head with a scowl. "What a waste." The lawman turned then hesitated.

"Is there something else, detective?"

He shrugged. "For what it's worth, your client *is* a good man. Again—just my opinion. But I'm a pretty good judge of character. You'd have to look pretty hard to find another guy like him."

Michelle blushed. "Thanks. *I'll* take that to the bank."

McRae tipped an imaginary hat and left.

* * *

That evening, Joseph sat on the floor in front of his couch, listening to the soft strains of Claude Debussy in the background. It was Michelle's CD, but he had immediately loved the gentle melodies of the classical French composer.

Sitting next to him, Michelle took another sip of sparkling cider. "I could probably get used to this stuff," she said. "I like the bubbles."

"If you stick with me, you'll have to get used to all sorts of weird things," he said with a smile.

"That's fine. I like a challenge."

"Hey!"

She bumped against him playfully. "Just teasing."

They had been sitting and talking for hours. It was a comfortable, easy conversation covering everything from the past to the present and even a bit of the future. The more Joseph learned about Michelle, the more he liked. What's more, he sensed the same reaction from her.

"So . . . how about your sleep issues?" she asked hesitantly.

"I'm sleeping safe and sound, all through the night," he said confidently. "Ever since we got confirmation on my father's remains, it's like this huge weight was lifted from me. It's strange." He shook his head and grimaced. "I never knew what I was carrying around in my head. I just figured I had had a fairly standard childhood that, for some reason, I couldn't remember. In a way, I'm glad I didn't know. And yet, now that it's out in the open and out of my soul, I feel so . . . light, so . . . free. Does that sound weird?"

"Not at all," she said, laying her head on his shoulder. "In a sense, it means you can start over."

"Exactly. And you know what's even better?"

"Hmm?"

He gently tilted her head up and stroked her hair back. "It might be somewhat presumptuous of me, but I'm hoping I won't have to do it alone."

Michelle smiled. "No objection here."

"Seriously?"

Cupping his cheek, she kissed him tenderly. "Case closed."

About the Author

Gregg Luke was born in Bakersfield, California, but spent the majority of his childhood and young adult life in Santa Barbara, California. He served an LDS mission to Wisconsin then pursued his education in biological sciences at SBCC, UCSB, BYU, and subsequently graduated from the University of Utah College of Pharmacy. His biggest loves are his family, reading, writing, music, science, and nature. You can visit Gregg at www.greggluke.com.